CW00520614

Lockdown at the Secondhand Bookworm

EMILY JANE BEVANS

LOCKDOWN AT THE SECONDHAND BOOKWORM

DEDICATION

This novel is dedicated to the memory of
Rupert Brooke, The Smuggler - RIP

LOCKDOWN AT THE SECONDHAND BOOKWORM

CONTENTS

LOCKDOWN AT THE SECONDHAND BOOKWORM

ACKNOWLEDGMENTS

Special thanks again to Anne Honiball

LOCKDOWN AT THE SECONDHAND BOOKWORM

1 LOCKDOWN

"We have to close The Secondhand Bookworm after today." Georgina Pickering said grimly at the end of the telephone line. "I expect Castletown will become a ghost town anyway with the locals self-isolating. And no one will want to be out and about buying books during the pandemic. You've only had three sales this morning as it is."

"But books are listed in the top three necessities of an apocalyptic survival guide." Nora Jolly pointed out.

Georgina laughed.

"Where did you read that?"

"Cara told me." Nora smiled slightly, referring to her colleague and sister-in-law who ran the other The Secondhand Bookworm in Seatown.

"Hmm. Why doesn't that surprise me?" Georgina mused. "Well, if I were you I'd get things organised now so you can leave the bookshop safe and sound for the unforeseeable future. Make some signs and notices for the door and windows to let people know we're closing in line with the British government guidelines, and

1

check that the fridge is empty of perishables. As it is, I'm always discovering something green and hairy growing on forgotten wedges of cheese or inside milk bottles there. I'll pick up the till float on my way through to keep it safely off the property. You might think about relocating yourself to the Duke's castle, just in case the Lockdown is enforced for a long time and no one can leave their houses for the next year or so."

"Oh that sounds lovely." Nora said wistfully. "How exciting."

"Nora!" Georgina rebuked. "We're in the midst of a global crisis."

"Sorry. Just trying to make the best out of it. I'll see what James thinks of it all." Nora amended, sheepishly.

"Well, I'm sure His Grace will be more than happy to have his girlfriend stay at the castle with him for who knows how long." Georgina deduced. "And it would be a shame for you to be stuck in your flat at the top of the hill all alone when you could be a guest of the Duke of Cole in those gorgeous quarters he's put aside for you."

James, the Duke of Cole, was Castletown's very own royal resident. He had recently come down from his estate on the Scottish borders and moved into his newly renovated castle behind the row of ancient old shops, which for centuries had given the historical town its name.

Nora had first encountered the Duke of Cole when she had opened up the bookshop for a day of trading a couple of Christmases ago during a particularly heavy snowfall. The Secondhand Bookworm had been the only place mad enough to open and the Duke had discovered it during his secret ramble about the deserted town.

As well as making the bookshop's acquaintance he had made Nora's acquaintance, and, after some interesting events and happenstances over the following months, he and Nora had become good friends. That friendship had turned to romance when Nora had amiably 'broken up' with Humphrey Pickering (Georgina's brother), and now she and the Duke of Cole were enjoying a relationship that to begin with only a few people knew about, but which had recently made the newspapers.

Nora had stayed in a guest bedroom at the castle over Christmas just past and a few times since. The thought of being in Lockdown with the Duke for the 'unforeseeable future' in his magnificent residence held a definite charm amidst the uncertainty and worries of the current global pandemic, as a particularly contagious, ancient virus that had lain dormant for millennia had reappeared in melted permafrost in the Arctic, crossed from an unsuspecting polar bear colony into a group of scientists and was now spreading like wildfire throughout the human population of the world.

Even though everyone was getting nervous, and Nora kept covering her mouth and nose with her jumper whenever a customer came into the bookshop (she did that a lot anyway because most of them were smelly), as Nora thought of James she grinned happily, and then felt guilty and cleared her throat.

"Can I take some books to keep me occupied?" Nora asked Georgina, looking around the front room of the bookshop.

The Secondhand Bookworm was a three floored shop packed to the brim with almost thirty thousand books for sale. They were organised into cases, lined upon shelves, stacked into piles upon the floor, crammed into nooks, crannies, above doorways, behind doors, and even on windowsills, all jam packed into the variety of rooms that branched off a creaky, winding staircase leading from the ground floor to the slanting attic.

Georgina Pickering owned the two branches of The Secondhand Bookworm, but she was currently planning to move to the USA with her American boyfriend and intended to sell the business to Nora and Cara.

"His Grace has at least three libraries at his castle!" Georgina pointed out in reply to Nora's question. "You don't need to take any with you from the shop."

"Fair point." Nora smiled.

She sighed wistfully at the subjects of books in the front room of The Secondhand Bookworm. There was an art section, which included books about sculpture too and a recent acquisition of eight books about Tiffany glass; a topography section opposite the front door, with lots of tomes about Castletown, including local fields where buildings had once stood, as well as detailed histories of outside toilets or ghosts that haunted roads or houses; a section for Folio Society books on the left hand side of the bay window, and a case of small white Observer books on the right hand side of the bay window.

In shelves under the front of the counter were runs of leather tomes, new ordnance survey maps, odd volumes of literature with pretty bindings, and Penguin book jacket mugs. A spinner containing Shire albums sat on top of the counter with a till, PDQ machine, cash book, business cards and selected volumes displayed amongst it all. A computer monitor stood to the side with a computer tower and printer located beneath.

Behind the counter were the rare, antiquarian and first editions, kept in neat rows in sturdy cases. A small private walkway led under the staircase where boxes of carrier bags and a stock of now out of print postcards sat, as well as bags of books people brought in for sale, paper carrier bags for postcards, coats, personal bags and a few odd items such as a broken kettle from the kitchen, some fancy free standing book shelves Georgina had snagged on a call and three cardboard boxes of cheap paperbacks to go outside. There were also some small cardboard boxes full of free maps which topped up a box with a plastic front that leaned against the outside bay window low wall for visitors to help themselves.

A public walkway led through to the first floor stairwell which had books about transportation in cases surrounding it. In the back room were topics such as history, royalty, nautical and war. A large door led into a tiny private kitchen that backed onto a small mossy yard surrounded by the tall buildings of other shops and flats, including the back of the Indian Restaurant which had caused many a sewage catastrophe by pouring cooking oil down its sinks and clogging up all the drains.

On the next floor there were two rooms and a stairwell. The room at the front contained topics such as gardening books, showbiz biographies, music books, tubs of sheet music and travel books and guides; the room at the back was solely for children's books, easily distinguished by the kiddies road map rug on the floor and posters of fairy tale characters Nora had tacked to the rare spaces of wall (her favourite was David Bowie as The Goblin King from the movie Labyrinth, even though it scared a few children, and one adult, who was her colleague, Roger).

A door was located down a tiny narrow corridor in the children's room which led to the staff toilet. It was mightily inconvenient being located one floor up, especially if Nora was running the shop by herself and had to remain in the front room to deal with customers and guard the till from robbers, but she had developed a skill for flying upstairs quickly during quiet moments. The outside loo in the yard was obsolete and just contained boxes of Christmas or Halloween shop decorations and hundreds of spiders.

In the second floor stairwell stood a case containing humour books as well as a display area and a large case for cookery books. Leading up to the next floor were shelves hugging the wall filled with brand new Wordsworth classic paperbacks which Cara ordered from a new book supplier, merging into a shelf of Doctor Who or Star Trek novels (they always seemed to have an excess of those) and crime novels.

In the front room on the top floor there were many different subjects housed in endless cases, such as science, religion, equestrian, crafts, occult, sports and astronomy and finally, a converted attic room with slanting ceilings stood up a flight of three stairs and overlooked the yard, especially designated as a paperback fiction room.

The building itself had an interesting history. It was centuries old and had been a barber shop and then a baker shop in the 17th century, which Humphrey believed was the origin behind Sweeney Todd. The character of Sweeney Todd had first appeared in The String of Pearls, a penny dreadful written by an unknown author that had been published in England in 1846–47. Humphrey insisted the story had its roots in macabre and dastardly human pie making that took place in what was now The Secondhand Bookworm. Although he only said it to tease Nora, Roy who ran the Castletown TV station had recently interviewed Humphrey about it and many tourists to the town lapped up his theory keenly. Nora often found people cutting their hair in the attic while taking selfies.

In later years, the building had been a family home where a mad woman had thrown her children down the stairs and a boy had been slung into a covered well (Nora still occasionally avoided the flagstone area by the door where the well was covered and the boy's ghost supposedly roamed). It had also been a tobacconist shop which had supplied pipe tobacco for the author of The Lord of the Rings trilogy J. R. R. Tolkien, and then a bookshop, owned by a Mr and Mrs Lodbrook who had specialized in Norse mythology.

Mr and Mrs Lodbrook had transformed the whole building with fitted shelves throughout but had kept the attic for storage. They had retired from the world of bookselling and now lived in a boathouse on the River Thames.

Georgina Pickering had purchased The Castletown Bookshop in a fit of enterprising ambition several years ago while she still ran her original bookshop in Piertown. That had since closed down but Georgina had employed Nora to run her new branch in Castletown and Nora had inherited several eccentric customers, including Mr Hill, a potty old man who had sold and bought back the same fifteen books for the past thirty years. At practically the same time, Georgina had also purchased a smaller bookshop in nearby Seatown from two hippies, which was managed by Cara Jolly, Nora's sister-in-law.

Now trading as The Secondhand Bookworm, the rambling old bookshop in historic Castletown sat in the shadow of the Duke of Cole's newly restored castle and had been enjoying a surge of commerce due to Nora's publicised relationship with His Grace, which had been revealed during the past Valentine's Week festival.

It was a fun place to work, even if Nora feared being crushed by over twenty-seven thousand books weighing upon the creaky and cracked ceilings above her and even though she found bookworms a very special breed that required exceptional patience.

She sighed, looking around the room and imagining locking up the shop for an indefinite time, thus depriving all the local and visiting bookworms of their books.

"Well, at least I'll have a break from my stalker." Nora decided optimistically, picking up a folded note from the desk.

Now a regular occurrence, a piece of paper was found on the mat by the front door on random mornings, having been posted anonymously overnight. It was always addressed to Nora Jolly and simply read:

Nora Jolly. You are being watched.

And the worrying thing was; Nora did feel as though she was being watched.

"Hmm. I had hoped that would have stopped after your ex-fiancé was arrested for murder on Valentine's Day." Georgina mused, grimly.

"Braxton was never my fiancé." Nora corrected for the umpteenth time.

"Oh yes. Sorry. But he did propose to you at least five times while you were dating."

"And I always said no." Nora reminded her. "And it was years and years ago."

"Be that as it may, do you think he could be orchestrating it even from behind bars?"

"I don't think so. I get the feeling that whoever is doing it is someone from the town."

"That's ghastly. We'll have to get the Duke onto the case as well as the police. And Humphrey has offered to be your bodyguard; you should take him up on the offer."

Nora snorted.

"That's not a good idea. Besides, he's spending most of his time in London at his old international business now. I've hardly seen him over the past four weeks."

"He's been helping with past clients of his but is heading back here this afternoon for the Lockdown." Georgina revealed, biting into something crunchy. "Fluffy! That's Chubby's toy." She rebuked her cat, defending the property of one of her Leonberger dogs.

Nora giggled.

"So he's setting up shop here at home with me and Troy." Georgina concluded.

"He's so crafty." Nora chuckled. "He knows you'll wait on him hand and foot during The Lockdown."

"I will." Georgina sighed regretfully. "I can't help spoiling my little brother."

"Who is almost thirty years old." Nora laughed.

The bookshop door opened and a customer stepped down into The Secondhand Bookworm, sporting a pale blue surgical mask to protect him from anyone carrying *Polar-Bear 9*, which was what people were calling the virus outbreak (Nora often wondered what the other eight Polar-Bear related viruses and diseases had been). Nora blinked and then grimaced. He looked very much like Johnny Depp so she couldn't help but think of Sweeney Todd.

"Blooming Humphrey." She muttered, watching the man turn to browse the topography section next to the door.

"What did you say?" Georgina sang in her ear.

"Oh, nothing. I have a customer so I'd better go."

"Okay. Well, I'll be here in Seatown with Cara and Amy organising the shop for Lockdown. Sort out some signs and remember to leave the till float for me to collect tonight. And pass on the information to Betty. I expect she's especially nervous about it all, being that she's well over seventy five."

"Don't let her hear you say that." Nora almost laughed.

Betty was one of Nora's bookshop colleagues, the oldest member of the staff, who worked part-time in The Secondhand Bookworms. She loved books, despised '*greyheads*' (as she disparagingly referred to her generation), was extremely sensitive about her age and provided Nora with often shocking entertainment whenever they worked together.

Presently, Betty was putting some Robert Galbraith Cormoran Strike series novels, which Nora had bought from a man earlier, on the crime fiction shelves. She had a walkie-talkie with her so Nora didn't have to yell up the three flights of stairs but Nora's kept picking up taxi chatter.

'Customer needs picking up from Market Street. Heads up, she's an old crone' a man's voice said loudly over the static as Nora and Georgina said their goodbyes and hung up.

Sweeney Todd turned slowly around with wide eyes. Nora smiled apologetically, holding up her walkie-talkie.

"Taxis. Sorry." She apologised.

Sweeney Todd just stared at her. Nora wasn't sure if he was smiling or grimacing behind his mask, so she cleared her throat and pressed a button on the device.

"Betty? When you've finished putting the books away up there I'll make us a cup of tea. Georgina just phoned and has some instructions for us to put The Secondhand Bookworm into Lockdown." She spoke into the walkie-talkie. "Over."

A moment later:

"Sorry, Nora, I did hear you but I couldn't work this blooming thing properly, that's me all over; you probably heard earlier that I had a conversation with one of the local taxi drivers who rudely told me to get off the channel so I gave him a piece of my mind, the old letch, and I hope he hears this, sorry Nora, thanks for listening." Betty's voice sailed out loudly, followed by crackling static and a beep. "Over, Nora. Sorry, thanks for listening. Blasted walkie-talkies. I'll be down in about five minutes."

Nora stifled a laugh.

"Roger that, Betty. Over." she concluded and popped the receiver back onto its cradle.

Sweeney Todd was still staring at her. Nora deduced he probably thought she was a bit mad so she smiled politely and set about making some signs on the computer to go up on the windows ready for Lockdown.

"You have a sock in your window."

Nora yelped, turning to find that Sweeney had glided silently up to the counter and was speaking to her in a muffled voice.

"Erm…yes?" Nora replied, assuming he had said *book* rather than sock.

There were a lot of books in the window display so Nora hoped he would be more specific.

"It's about toenails." He said.

Nora blinked.

"Toenails?" She frowned.

"BARN OWLS!" The man corrected in a louder, still-muffled voice.

"Oh! Yes, sorry."

"A cow is clutching it." Sweeney next said.

Nora stared at him and remained silent, deeming it wise not to repeat what she had heard, and concluding that this new mask fad was going to be trouble.

"I said, How MUCH is IT?" Sweeney repeated, loudly.

"Oh! I'll have a look for you." Nora said, feeling an urge to burst out laughing. She stood up.

"Keep your mitts off!" Sweeney then exclaimed.

"What?" Nora stood still.

He backed slowly away from her to the county of Cole books in the topography section by the door.

"I said, KEEP YOUR DISTANCE!" The man repeated. "I don't know if you're carrying *Polar-Bear 9* and I don't want to catch it. Hence the mask."

"I gathered that." Nora smiled politely. "Very wise."

"Hopefully it will become man and hippy." The man next said.

Nora deduced he had said *mandatory* so nodded, edging along the art section to make her way to the window and fetch the book at a safe distance.

"I say! Do you Moomin Valley?" He next asked, backing even further away.

"What now?" Nora smiled politely. "Do we stock Moomin books?"

"What the what?" The man gawped.

Nora growled, silently.

"Ahem. Sorry, I'm having trouble understanding you because of your mask." She explained.

Sweeney Todd shook his head.

"I said, DO YOU FUMIGATE?"

"Erm…no, we haven't fumigated our books..."

"Well then, magnetic! I don't show him your hook, line and sinker!" He decided, turned around and made a run for it, up the step, out the bookshop doorway and off along the street.

For a long moment Nora stood in the middle of the room trying to work out what Sweeney Todd had said and decided upon 'Well then, forget it! I don't know if your books are infected!' She shook her head, turned back to the counter and jumped as her iPhone buzzed in the back pocket of her jeans, alerting her to a text message.

The message was from James, Duke of Cole, so Nora smiled, sat down in the swivel chair and read it.

'Hi, how's your day going? Xx'

Nora wasn't sure how to relay her morning so far so simply typed back:

'Hi, not too bad, thanks. Yours? Xx'

A moment later:

'I'm heading down to the town hall for an emergency council meeting where we'll decide upon procedures for Castletown during the pandemic. When I'm done I'll come to the bookshop to see you xxx'

Nora arched an eyebrow at the thought of emergency meetings being called.

'Okay. Stay safe xxx.' She sent back. And then: *'You can let the councillors and the mayor know that Georgina has decided to put the bookshop on Lockdown from tonight xx'*

'Thank you, Nora, I will do, and that's very wise. You keep safe, too. See you later xxx' The Duke replied.

'Customer needs picking up from The Black Hart pub opposite the bookshop in town. That's one for you, Mike. Watch out for that old bat in the bookshop that keeps interfering with our radios' a man's voice hollered out of the walkie-talkie.

Nora almost dropped her iPhone. She held still and grimaced. Sure enough, a moment later:

'Yes you had bloody well better watch out you old sod; I may sound like I'm a decrepit old bat but this old bat has an exceptional aim with a book from the top floor, you horrid pig! Watch yourself, MIKE! Sorry Nora, thanks for listening. Over.' Betty retorted loudly.

Nora's shoulders shook with laughter.

"Perhaps I'd better put the kettle on." She told herself wisely and set off quickly for the kitchen.

That morning at The Secondhand Bookworm passed slowly due to a stark lack of customers. Usually, Mondays at the end of March at the bookshop were busy, with large parts of the Duke of Cole's castle preparing to open to the public for exploration of the endless magnificent newly built rooms, heirlooms, gardens, towers and the ancient Keep, and with additional events happening about the historic town, thus drawing tourists to the rows of shops surrounding the cobbled square and into The Secondhand Bookworm for postcards and books.

But, due to James deciding to postpone opening his castle to the public until he was certain what was happening in the wake of *Polar-Bear 9*, and due to many people deciding to self-isolate already, so far Nora and Betty had only had to deal with the man selling his Robert Galbraith novels, Sweeney Todd, a married couple looking for books about self-sufficiency, a man asking where he could buy toilet rolls and another customer wearing a face mask, who presently stepped down into The Secondhand Bookworm.

"Do you have a copy of The Last Man by Mary Shelley? I'd like some tips." The woman asked clearly from behind her mask.

"I can have a look on our shelves for you." Betty offered with a glamorous smile.

"Can't you check your computer? Or don't you know how to use it?" Mask-Lady asked Betty, insensitively.

Betty stared and then took a long, offended breath.

Nora stepped in, hastily.

"We don't list our books on our computer, I'm afraid." She apologised.

Mask-Lady tittered behind her mask.

"Really? How odd. How do you find a book in here then?"

"I hobble about checking the shelves, squinting through my thick glasses in the hope I can still read!" Betty replied sarcastically.

Mask-Lady stared at her.

"I'd be happy to check our shelves for you." Nora offered. "They're organised into sections, with fiction in alphabetical order of author, so they're easy to find. I can run up now."

"No, no, I can do that. I wouldn't want to put you and your dear old grandmother to any trouble." Mask-Lady refused. "Where do I go?"

Betty was glaring at the woman like a Gorgon. For a moment, Nora thought the lady might turn to stone.

"Up to the attic room." Nora indicated.

"Oh, it snows lots and lots," she noticed and set off. Nora interpreted that she had actually said, 'it *goes* up and up'.

When Mask-Lady was out of earshot, Betty gave Nora a look.

"Okay, Nora, I won't say a word." She promised witheringly. "Thanks for listening."

Fortunately, Nora's signs had finished printing so she was able to distract Betty from any vengeful plotting by setting the both of them to the task of tacking them on the glass of the bay windows and the shop door.

"I hope you're going to relocate up to the castle, Nora." Betty said as she stuck her poster on the door window beneath the OPEN sign. "It would be a shame for you and His Grace to be apart during this Lockdown they're all talking about, being that you've only just become a couple."

"Well, James is coming down to the bookshop later so we'll talk about what we're going to do." Nora said, kneeling up in the bay window awkwardly.

"It could be up to you and His Grace to repopulate the earth. Think of the magnificent legs your babies will have." Betty mused.

Nora almost fell out of the window.

"What?" She choked on a laugh.

Betty cackled, mischievously. She had a bit of an obsession with the Duke of Cole's legs.

"Oh to be young and agile again. Danny and I will probably just sit doing crosswords and arguing about which channel to turn Freeview to," she predicted, referring to her boyfriend, Danny, whom she had met at a Book Club Nora had hosted at The Secondhand Bookworm over Christmas and the New Year.

"Well, hopefully the Lockdown won't last too long," Nora mused. "And you and Danny are happy together, so that's good."

"Oh Nora, my daughters all still hate him. They keep trying to set me up with my son-in-law's recently widowed dad, but he is such a greyhead, and a wicked old letch, Nora. Just because we engaged in a lot of snogging at my grandson's birthday the other week, they all got it into their heads that I'm on the meat market again, so I had to make them promise not to tell Danny about it. He was staying with his daughter for the weekend you see and I let it slip to my son that I was fed up with Danny, oh aren't I a wicked old cheater? So I said, I'm fed up not hard up. Thanks for listening."

Nora was trying hard not to laugh.

"Oh dear. Well, perhaps spending the Lockdown together will rekindle your relationship with Danny again." Nora suggested with a small grimace.

"Hmm. I've put aside some saucy paperbacks to buy at the end of the day so that might help." Betty added outrageously.

Nora snorted, stepping down from the bay window as one of their regular customers paused from walking past the bookshop, read the signs on the window and headed for the door.

"Greetings." Spencer Brown said, standing on the doorstep.

Spencer Brown lived at the top of the hill in a gothic house with a tower. He was an avid collector of occult books, had white shoulder-length hair, piercing blue eyes and often sported a coat that looked like a cape. Presently, he was convinced the Duke of Cole was a vampire and allowed a coven of vampires to live on his estate. He had been a member of Nora's recent Book Club.

"Good morning, Mr Brown." Nora smiled cheerfully.

"So you're closing up, then." He gestured his head towards the notices.

"As of today." Nora nodded.

"Hmm. You know it's all a ploy of course, to keep people in their houses for a *first wave* trial run, to see if people will be obedient to the government." Spencer told her with a cautious glance over his shoulder.

Nora smiled politely, used to Spencer's conspiracy theories.

"Well, it looks like we at The Secondhand Bookworm are *sheeple* then." She said good-humouredly, walking around to stand behind the counter.

Spencer stepped down into the shop.

"The second wave will be permanent." He told her, nodding wisely.

"Oh dear." Nora humoured. "Is it an alien takeover?"

"No." Spencer assured her solemnly. "It's because a thousand asteroids are on route for earth. NASA knew about it forty years ago, they saw it through their telescopes. Now the asteroids are arriving. This is why everyone is trying to get to Mars with all these rockets and space programs. They want to leave for a brave new world."

Betty rolled her eyes and pulled a face behind Spencer.

"So you don't think the *Polar-Bear 9* virus is real?" Nora asked him, sitting down in the swivel chair.

"It could be a weapon." Spencer allowed. "But DON'T have any vaccines they will offer as some form of cure or protection. It will change you, rewrite your genetic code into an animal-hybrid, you won't be human anymore, you'll sprout wings and antlers. It's all because of the Nephalim that live in the hollow earth. With Godzilla."

Nora listened patiently as Spencer jabbered on about secret elite plots and the coming of our reptilian overlords from hidden caves in Transylvania while Betty continued to roll her eyes, move both her index fingers beside her temples in slow circles while going cross-eyed and then pretend to strangle him, all behind his back. When she noticed the last one, Nora choked back a disapproving laugh.

"Well, let's hope it doesn't all come to that." Nora told Spencer cheerfully, rummaging under the counter where the reserved books were kept.

"Seeing as we're going to be self-isolating, or forced into hiding, I thought I'd check out your occult section so Astrid and I will have enough to read. Any books put aside for me from Georgina?" He asked, picking up a tome from the counter about making romantic-themed cakes, left over from the bookshop's Valentine's Week window display.

"Nothing down here." Nora assured him in a strained voice.

"I'll check the shelves upstairs just in case. Publishers often change the covers of books, you see, so I sometimes have repeats or overlook titles. Astrid and I are working on a new book about Aleister Crowley so we'd like as much material about him as possible. Will you be staying up at the castle with His Grace then, Nora?"

"Oh, I haven't made any plans yet." Nora replied.

"Make sure you go down into the basements at night and look for any coffins. I expect His Grace sleeps in a grand one down there somewhere." Spencer said, heading towards the walkway.

"I can assure you he's not a vampire." Nora insisted.

"Just take some garlic with you. And some stakes." Spencer warned, winked and set off for the occult section on the top floor, front room.

Betty sighed.

"Ridiculous man." She muttered, rudely.

"Hmm. James was eating one of those delicious pastry hors d'oeuvres which contained garlic at the Valentine's Ball and showed Spencer, but he said James had some temporary immunity from it." Nora whispered with a small giggle.

"I'd like some temporary immunity from *Spencer*." Betty decided frostily. "He was telling me about the orgies he holds in that tower of his and when I hinted about coming along he cut me off with a look of horror. Would I really look that revolting naked, Nora?"

Nora had taken a sip of water and sprayed it everywhere as she choked.

Betty's eyes twinkled.

"Sorry, Nora. Terrible aren't I." She apologised.

"I don't know why I'm so shocked about what you say anymore." Nora almost laughed, thumping her chest as she coughed and gradually recovered.

They spent the next five minutes using tissues to blot the water spray from the cash book, desk, computer monitor and several copies of local books by an author called David Bone, and when they had finished Nora suggested Betty go for lunch.

"Thank you Nora, I do need some food to keep my old withered body going." She said with a playful wink, picking up her bag from under the stairs. "Are you sure you'll be alright on your own?"

"Yes. I don't think we'll have any customers. The town is so quiet and I've noticed less car traffic about. I'll be fine." Nora assured her.

"Alright, well, I'm going to go and buy some toilet rolls from the Co-Op over the bridge. At my age you can never have too many and I don't want to be caught short if people start panic buying." Betty announced, heading for the door.

"Good idea." Nora nodded, amused, waved her goodbye and once Betty was strolling off away from The Secondhand Bookworm, Nora set about preparing the bookshop for the impending Lockdown, deciding she quite needed a rest from bookworms!

Spencer had left empty handed and Betty had only been back from her lunchbreak for five minutes and was tidying up the topography section by the door when James arrived at The Secondhand Bookworm. Nora spotted the Duke of Cole walking past the bay window, his brow furrowed seriously. He had worn a baseball cap when he and Nora had first started dating so as to remain inconspicuous, but now he walked around as himself, easily recognised by the locals, with his dark hair tousled from the fresh March breeze, sporting a collared shirt beneath a navy wool sweater and casual but smart navy chinos. He carried a small white paper bag.

"Good afternoon, Your Grace!" Betty gushed, fluttering her eyelashes and sinking into a curtsey when the Duke stepped down into the bookshop.

"Good afternoon, Bethany." James smiled, using Betty's favourite name for when she wanted to pretend she was younger.

Betty gazed at him with grateful adoration and indicated to the counter where Nora sat.

James scanned the interior for Nora, who stood up from her chair.

"Hello!" Nora greeted.

"Hi." James smiled warmly and held up the bag. "I brought hot sausage rolls. I thought you'd probably be busy getting ready to close for the Lockdown and would like to just snatch a break here?"

"An excellent plan." Nora approved.

Betty was impressed with the Duke's consideration and ushered them away to the kitchen.

"I'll man the fort here, Nora. Any problems and I'll fetch you."

"Okay, Betty." Nora grinned as James took hold of her hand.

The Duke and Nora walked through to the back of the shop, past the many bulging bookshelves, and into the tiny kitchen. It had a plastic roof and was perpetually cold, with only enough room for one person to sit and eat lunch, and two people to make tea. Nora and James easily squashed inside and once he had greeted her properly with a royal kiss ('I think kissing your girlfriend is still allowed', the Duke had chuckled 'and we all wore face masks at our meeting') they stood and made tea, chatting and eating their rolls.

"I'm heading back up to the town hall again after here." James explained, passing Nora two mugs from the cupboard.

"It sounds serious." Nora mused.

"Yes, I believe it is. At the instructions of the government we're going to ask all non-essential businesses to close, with the bank and post office having reduced hours. People will be asked to practice social distancing and make sure there are only one or two people at a time in the grocery shops." He explained.

Nora listened as James shared all the decisions the council had made so far to keep Castletown safe during the pandemic, which was spreading now throughout the county of Cole.

"There haven't been a large amount of cases, yet. We hope to curb it as quickly as possible here." James said, taking a bite of sausage roll as Nora poured hot water into their mugs. "And the residents of Cole are quite sensible."

"I hope we're not on Lockdown for long." Nora said, adding milk and sugar.

"Me too." James nodded. "But keeping people safe is priority."

Nora glanced at him, fondly.

"Shall we go outside into the yard? After the bargain book yard we had out there last November for Black Friday, Humphrey has kept it scrubbed clean and weed free. It's a little bit mossy because of the shade, but he even added Georgina's old white iron table and chairs."

"Lead the way." James agreed.

They took up their tea, Nora grabbed some anti-bacterial wipes and handtowels (The Secondhand Bookworm always had a large store of anti-bacterial wipes), and she used the keys to unlock the back door. It was fresh and cool in the small yard, with pigeons sitting cooing on the roofs high above and a solitary bird foraging by the black wooden gate that led to the bins. Subtle scents of Indian food came from the restaurant at the far wall. Fortunately the estate agents weren't using their very loud air conditioning unit that day which backed into the yard.

James pulled a chair out for Nora and they sat together at the table.

"I'm pleased Georgina is closing the bookshop." James confessed. "I can rest easy knowing you won't be among the public."

Nora smiled.

"Bookworms do carry a lot of bugs." She agreed.

He laughed.

"How would you feel about coming and staying at the castle in your guest rooms there?" James asked her, sipping his tea.

Nora tossed a small flake of pastry for the bird.

"I'd like it." She nodded, happily.

James grinned.

"Me too. Will you relocate there tonight, Nora? I can help bring anything you need from your flat after you've finished here. We can use the door from your garden leading onto the estate to bring anything easily through to Jeeves."

Jeeves was James' valet. Upon first learning his name, Nora had been inspired to give the Duke a first edition copy of The Inimitable Jeeves by P G Wodehouse, published in 1923, and thus started James collecting the series. So far, Nora had found him first editions of the first five in the series, with The Code of the Woosters being one of her Valentine's Day presents to him last month.

"Perfect." Nora concurred.

"I'm glad, Nora. There's plenty we can do together to help people get through this while we're at the castle. And there's no one else I'd rather be in Lockdown with."

Nora was touched.

"I agree." She told him warmly. "Will the churches be closing in the town, too?" Nora then wondered.

"Canon Gerry will be at this afternoon's meeting." James explained. "The Cardinal of England is meeting with the Prime Minister later today and then the Bishop will make an announcement for our Diocese. Meanwhile, people have been popping in to our church to pray, nervous about what's going on."

The Duke of Cole was one of England's rare Catholic Royals, with an Elizabethan ancestor of his enshrined in a special tomb in the local Catholic church up the hill, an Earl who had died for the ancient Faith of England during the Protestant Reformation and who had been canonised a Saint and Martyr of the Catholic Church.

James attended weekly Sunday Mass at the church and had his own pew on the right hand side at the front, cordoned off with blue ropes. Recently, Nora had been attending the same Mass with him, so the effect of the pandemic upon their place of worship was of interest and concern to them both.

The sound of a window creaking open drew their attention.

"I thought I heard voices." A familiar voice joined in. "Nora. Your Grace. Can I interest you in some onion bhajis?"

Nora and James turned.

"Hello, Max." Nora waved, no longer frosty towards the owner of the Indian Restaurant since their recent re-acquaintance.

Max had purchased the Indian Restaurant a couple of years ago and had promised Nora that he wouldn't follow in the previous proprietor's footsteps by allowing his chefs to pour cooking oil down the sinks. In the past, the oil had solidified and built up in the drainage pipes, ending by causing horrendous blockages of the sewers that inevitably backed up into the bookshop yard and made it like a crime scene.

Nora still had the occasional memory about having discovered several grotesque situations that had required professional drain unblocking companies to come out and save the day. Georgina had always had to foot the bill.

However, despite his promises, Max had shortly thereafter placed an uncle of his in charge of the Castletown Indian Restaurant while he relocated to London to open another branch. The sewers had blocked again and Max's uncle had been rude and irrational, blaming The Secondhand Bookworm for flushing their books down the toilet and causing the blockages instead.

It was discovered that the chefs had indeed continued pouring oil down the sinks and they were to blame, so Georgina had taken Max to court. Max had sent his uncle, who had played the fool up on the stand by sharing his book flushing theory and lost the case to Georgina's niece who was a lawyer. Max had had to pay all the past *Dynorod* bills and stayed away in shame.

He had finally returned during Valentine's Week to apologise and make amends (with bottles of Prosecco from the new Prosecco shop due to open in April which had had a stall on the cobbles during the said festivities) and to introduce Nora to his cousin Reynash who was now running the restaurant and who had assured Nora he would never allow his chefs to pour oil down the drains. It was a classic The Secondhand Bookworm escapade.

"Ooh, they look nice." Nora said, glancing at James who looked keen. She stood up, crossed the small stone floor and watched as Max placed the plate of freshly cooked bhajis from their lunchtime menu on the window ledge before stepping back.

"I'm already practising social distancing." Max told the Duke. "And my chefs are wearing plastic face visors as they cook."

"Good idea." James approved.

"Thank you." Nora appreciated, picking up the plate.

"And apparently the virus doesn't pass through cooked food." Max assured them. "Despite that, hardly anyone has come for lunch today. We're planning on closing for the Lockdown anyway." Max revealed with a grim sigh.

"The Secondhand Bookworm is closing after today, too." Nora revealed.

"The cooks have Castletown TV on in the kitchen here." Max gestured behind him as wafts of cooking scents sailed out of the open window. "They've been talking about the meetings taking place in the town hall today and that announcements will be made soon."

"Paul from the Chamber of Commerce will give an interview and announcement on the channel this evening." James explained. "You will probably be able to do home deliveries for a time, but you won't be able to allow people to sit in your restaurant."

"I'll head off to London when I'm finished here so I don't get stuck in Castletown for the Lockdown." Max decided.

James told Max it was more likely that London would have more cases of *Polar-Bear 9* and that he should stay in Castletown on the south coast, but Max said he had a new house in London with two hot tubs so would prefer to be in Lockdown there.

Max then left them to finish their lunch and once the bhajis had been devoured (five each!), Nora placed the empty plate on the windowsill and they returned to the bookshop kitchen. Nora made a round of tea for her and Betty, then she locked the outside door and she and James joined Betty in the front room of The Secondhand Bookworm.

"There's a request from Cara on the Skype chat, Nora." Betty revealed.

"Ah, okay, I'll take a look." Nora smiled.

She and James said their goodbyes and the Duke set off back to the town hall for the afternoon, leaving Betty polishing the till and Nora reading Cara's message.

'Request for any books about isolation for a local customer. Georgina said she would pick any up and drop them in to the man if you do. Any ideas? Cara xxx' Nora's sister-in-law had written.

"Hmm." Nora pondered the query for a while.

'Robinson Crusoe would be the most obvious that comes to mind xx' She sent back.

A moment later, Nora watched the orange pen start moving and then a reply came through.

'Yes, found that one for him. Also, any movie suggestions too? Xx'

'Who is this man?!' Nora wondered, thinking it was rather grim.

'The bogeyman lol xx' Cara sent back.

Nora smirked.

'Contagion, Outbreak, The Andromeda Strain, World War Z....'

'Zombies!!!! Yay.' Cara replied and Nora laughed.

Nora left Betty cleaning so as to browse the fiction shelves upstairs and came down five minutes later with a copy of 'Where the Crawdads Sing', which had themes of loneliness throughout, and a copy of 'Into the Wild' by Jon Krakauer, with its theme of leaving civilization behind and seeking enlightenment through solitude and contact with nature.

She Skyped the titles through to the Seatown branch and a little later Cara asked if she could put them in the transfer box for Georgina to pick up that evening.

'Will do x' Nora concluded.

The telephone started to ring.

Nora answered.

"Good afternoon, The Secondhand..." He voice trailed off when she recognised the sound of wheezy, heavy breathing.

Nora grimaced.

"Hello? Hello?" Mr Hill called down the line, followed by coughing and more spluttering wheezes.

"Hello, Mr Hill." Nora greeted politely.

Betty heard and pulled a face from where she was taking the expensive books out of the front of the window display to protect their jackets from prolonged time in the sun during Lockdown.

"Who's that?" Mr Hill asked Nora.

"It's Nora, Mr Hill." Nora sang.

"Clara?"

"Nora!" Nora corrected tightly.

"Oh, Nora! Nora, in the back room, on the left, five shelves up, do you have a copy of 'Military Uniforms of Britain and the Empire', volume four? It's red cloth."

"I know the one." Nora pointed out bluntly, having located it and put it aside for him a thousand times.

Mr Hill coughed and spluttered.

"Do you have it?" He insisted.

"I'll have a look." Nora sighed and set off into the back room carrying the phone.

It only took her a moment to locate the familiar greasy-spined book.

"Yes, I have it here."

"Oh! Oh you do? You have it there do you, Clara?"

"Nora."

"And how much is it?"

Nora leaned the book against the shelving to open it.

"It's priced at seven pounds fifty." Nora read. "As usual." She added under her breath.

"Seven pounds fifty. I'll take it. Could you put it by for me?"

Nora was examining the page of rubbed out pricing and pound signs that had almost eaten away the entire page.

"Yes, but we will be closing after today for the Lockdown." Nora explained.

Mr Hill coughed and wheezed. Nora heard him break wind.

"Yes, Georgina told me that, but could you still put it aside for me. Thank you. B-bye!" He said and hung up.

Nora growled like a Chihuahua.

She carried the book into the front room and was about to tell Betty when the phone rang again. Nora knew who it would be.

"Good afternoon, The Secondhand Bookworm." She answered cheerfully.

"Hello, It's Mr Hill. Who's that?" Mr Hill asked.

"Hello Mr Hill, it's Nora." Nora replied tightly.

Betty made a rude hand gesture about him so Nora turned away so as not to laugh.

"Nora? Hello, lad!" He greeted enthusiastically. "You have a book put by for me."

"Yes, the 'Military Uniforms of Britain and the Empire' volume four." Nora confirmed patiently.

"And how much is it again?"

"Grr. It's seven pounds fifty, Mr Hill."

"Seven pounds fifty is it? Grand. I'll have it. In your back room, in the history section, on the left, five shelves up, do you have a copy of 'Military Uniforms of Britain and the Empire', volume three? It's red cloth."

"I know the one." Nora sang as she walked off to fetch it.

Mr Hill's breathing turned rapid and heavier. Nora grimaced and held the phone slightly away from her ear.

"It's red cloth." He repeated.

"Found it!" Nora announced.

Mr Hill breathed loudly.

"Oh! You have. And how much is it, Nora?"

"Seven pounds fifty, Mr Hill." Nora said without even having to check. She had priced it just last week when Mr Hill had sold it to her again.

"Seven pounds fifty is it? Hmm. Okay, I'll have it!"

"We're closing today due to the Lockdown, Mr Hill." Nora pointed out.

Loud, heavy breathing. A splutter. Three hiccups.

"So, if you could put it by for me, I'd be very grateful. Thanks, lad. B-bye." He gasped and hung up.

Nora returned to the front room, wondering if she sounded like a bloke.

"Mr Hill is putting all his books aside but I can't see how he's going to catch his usual bus to come over and buy them back," she told Betty, adding the smelly old book to the greasy old book on the counter top.

"Maybe he hasn't heard the news yet?" Betty proposed.

"Hmm, it's possible, but…" Nora was interrupted by the phone ringing again. "Argh! I know that's Mr Hill."

"Oh shall I deal with the old book grub, Nora?" Betty asked, flexing her muscles.

"No, don't worry. Hello, Mr Hill." Nora answered.

There was silence and then loud spluttering and raucous breathing.

"Hello? Hello? Hello?"

Nora knew she had thrown him by revealing she knew who he was and felt guilty.

"The Secondhand Bookworm." She indulged.

"Hello, is that the bookshop?"

"Yes! It's Nora at the bookshop, Mr Hill!" Nora almost exclaimed.

"It's Mr Hill!" Mr Hill said.

"Yes!"

"Is that Nora?"

"Yeeeees!" Nora said between her clenched teeth.

"Nora, you have two books put aside for me. Can you tell me the prices of them again, please?"

"Seven pounds fifty each." Nora relayed, slapping her forehead.

"Seven pounds fifty each, you say?"

"That's correct."

"I'll have them!" He said, pleased. "Also, Laura..."

"Nora."

"Laura. Could you also check your shelves for a copy of an historical biography? It's black cloth and it's called 'King Charles II' by Antonia Fraser. Back room, left hand side, in the historical biography section."

Nora marched off to locate it.

"I have it here." She told him, wondering if she had stepped into The Twilight Zone again.

"Oh! Oh you have it there, do you? And how much is it?"

"Seven pounds fifty." Nora replied, having priced his books at a standard amount for the past four years.

"Seven pounds fifty, is it? I'll take it!"

"Okay, I'll put it by for you, but…Mr Hill, The Secondhand Bookworm is…"

"Thank you, Laura! B-bye!" Mr Hill said loudly and the line went dead.

Nora stared ahead for a long moment before repeatedly pressing the end call button and stomping back into the front of the shop. She added the volume to the pile and prayed they didn't have any more of Mr Hill's books in stock. He was a famously annoying regular customer whom Georgina had indulged for the past thirty years by buying from him the same set of books and selling them back to him almost every week. She had inherited him from when her mother had opened the original bookshop in Piertown, which had since closed. Usually the two remaining shops divided Mr Hill's grubby, smelly books between the two branches to keep him entertained and Nora presently recalled she had meanly sent most of his books to the Seatown branch the last time he had sold them to her.

She waited tentatively, expecting another phone call from him, but when ten minutes had passed happily by in silence, Nora relaxed and set about helping Betty clear the window and put interesting yet inexpensive books on display for the duration of the Lockdown.

Betty had just made a final round of tea when the bookshop telephone started to ring. Nora was watching Alice and Phil, who ran the delicatessen on the corner next to the butcher shop, sweep out their shelves and baskets while putting up signs saying they would be closing temporarily due to *Polar-Bear 9*. She headed towards the telephone with a grimace.

"Shall I get it, Nora?" Betty offered.

"No, don't worry. I'll deal with him." She smiled and pressed answer.

"The Secondhand Bookworm." Nora greeted, cheerfully.

"Hello, Nora it's me again." Georgina's sing-song voice greeted.

"Hello!" Nora replied in relief.

"Now…Mr Hill's books."

"Hmm!"

"I know, he's a blooming nuisance, but he's lonely and worried about not having them to read during Lockdown."

"Then why does he sell them to us every other week then?!" Nora was exasperated.

"We never ask that question." Georgina replied.

Nora shook her head.

"Okay, well I've put them all in a bag for him so I'll leave it with the till float for you to collect." She said.

"Lovely. How's it going over there?" Georgina asked.

"Deserted." Nora said, looking out into the empty town and expecting to see tumbleweed roll past. "I think all the residents, except for Spencer, are deciding to self-isolate. Erk! I spoke too soon!"

Nora had spotted another local jogging across the cobbles, his eyes fixed on The Secondhand Bookworm.

"Who is it?" Georgina asked with a trace of amusement in her voice.

"The Terminator." Nora groaned.

Georgina laughed.

"I'll leave you to it then. You may as well close up early, Nora, if it still remains dead there. I think everyone is self-isolating now. The Prime Minister has just made announcements on a special edition of Prime Minister's Question Time that has declared the closing of the schools at the end of the week. So close up the smelly old bookshop. Everyone's staying home."

"Okay, that's probably a good idea." Nora agreed, watching The Terminator, whose real name was Harry, jog up to the window.

"Speak to you soon!" Georgina sang.

Betty was sipping her tea while admiring the theme-less window display and noticed Harry, who was standing flexing his biceps at Nora. Betty choked and then stood ogling him. As well as being a regular at the bookshop, Harry didn't hide the fact that he was romantically interested in Nora. When she had first met him he had strolled into The Secondhand Bookworm looking like Arnold Schwarzenegger in *The Terminator* with his crew cut, black t-shirt, black jeans and had even uttered the famous phrase *'I'll be back'*. He collected Beano and Dandy annuals for his nephew.

When he spotted Nora through the bay window Harry waved, lifted his eyebrows a couple of times and headed inside.

"Hello, Harry." Nora greeted, warningly.

"Hi, Nora. So, you're closing down then." Harry said, jogging into the shop and running on the spot before the counter.

"Only for the duration of the Lockdown." Nora assured him.

She watched as he dropped to the floor and started counting press-ups using just one hand. Betty was delighted and stood fanning her face with a book. Nora tried not to smile.

"Sure, sure. So, are you going to be self-isolating with the Duke of Cole or in your flat by yourself? If it's the latter would you like me to join you?"

"No!"

"Fair enough." Harry said and leapt up. "I shall be staying with Corrine," he revealed, referring to his girlfriend who ran the new cake shop in town.

"Then why did you ask to join me?" Nora shook her head.

"Thought I'd give it a try." He winked.

"Bye, Harry."

"I just wondered if you had any Beano or Dandy annuals in stock for my nephew. If he has to isolate next week he'll need something new to read." Harry explained, flexing his biceps.

"If we had we would have called you as you're on our database." Nora reminded him.

"Ah, yes. Fair enough. Nora, can I ask you a question?"

"No." Nora walked around the counter to usher him out.

Harry looked down at her, grinning.

"Have you ever considered being a contestant on Love Island?" He asked her anyway.

Nora was baffled.

"What do you think?"

"If you and the Duke of Cole are going to be living in isolation from the outside world during Lockdown we could fit video surveillance throughout the castle; it would make for fascinating viewing, and I could be one of your guests…"

"You're quite mad, Harry." Nora decided, opening the door and gesturing for him to leave.

He winked at her.

"Mad for you." Betty mumbled from behind them.

"It's probably a good thing you haven't been on Love Island." Harry decided thoughtfully. "Several people linked to the show have died by suicide. But have you ever considered letting people watch you in the bookshop like on a reality show? I have boxes of surveillance cameras."

"That's very sad about the suicides, and no, I've never considered being on a reality TV show or creating my own! I'm not even going to ask about the cameras. See you after Lockdown, Harry."

"Bye, Nora. I'll be back." Harry saluted and set off, jogging down the street and glancing back at the bookshop as Nora closed the door.

Betty was highly amused.

"Oooh if I was fifty years younger, Nora." She said, terribly.

Nora shook her head, beginning to think Lockdown at The Secondhand Bookworm was a good idea!

2 THE STAY HOME PLAN

Nora sat staring up at the ceiling corners in the front room of The Secondhand Bookworm not long after Harry's visit, toying with the idea that Harry could be her 'note' stalker, since he had made a comment about having a boxful of surveillance cameras and her almost-daily note said 'you are being watched'. Sometimes she had the feeling she was being observed and wondered if there were pinhole cameras about the room, or, as Cara had suggested, tiny cameras fixed to houseflies or resident spiders…But after careful consideration she shook her head and decided it wasn't something Harry would do because he was so blunt and forward about his annoying fixation on her and would probably show her his boxes of video tapes he would have acquired from watching her!

It was still quiet in the bookshop so Betty was upstairs sweeping the floors and tidying the shelves while Nora busied about with paperwork and organising the counter, aware of strange things happening outside.

Several locals were now running frantically about loaded with carrier bags of groceries and armfuls of toilet rolls. As she watched them, the door opened and a said local entered The Secondhand Bookworm.

"Hello, Gina." Crossword-Lady greeted.

"Hello, Mrs Booth." Nora politely replied.

Mrs Booth was nicknamed Crossword-Lady because she usually popped in daily to ask Nora the literary question in her newspaper crossword. Crossword-Lady always called Nora Gina because she was convinced Nora was actually the British actress Gina McKee, working at The Secondhand Bookworm to research various television or film roles and nothing Nora could say would convince her otherwise. She was obsessed with donkeys and had been a member of Nora's recent Book Club.

"I see you will be closing The Secondhand Bookworm for the Lockdown." Crossword Lady noticed, rustling her newspaper as she stepped up to the counter and placing several packs of toilet paper at her feet.

"We are I'm afraid."

"Hmm, that is a shame. What will I do about the literary questions in my crossword?" She asked, spreading it open on top of the counter.

"Oh, erm…" Nora felt sorry for her. Mrs Booth lived alone in a small house in Castletown and lived in perpetual fear of rapists. "Well, I could give you my email address and you could ask me the question each day by email." She proposed, hoping she wouldn't regret it.

"That would be really helpful, Gina. Thank you. I have a new laptop and shall be using it to petition the government during the Lockdown about the care of donkeys. We shall be doing minimal shifts at the donkey sanctuary so as to maintain social distancing but the children won't be able to visit and pet them or give them carrots and they won't have as much company as they're used to. Perhaps it's something your husband, the Duke, would consider helping us with? Maybe he could have the donkeys on his estate during Lockdown?"

"Well, the Duke isn't actually my husband." Nora corrected patiently.

"Isn't he, Gina? Are you sure?"

"I would know if he was so, yes I'm sure." Nora assured her with a bemused smile.

"Hmm, that's strange. Then whose royal wedding did I attend over Christmas?" She mused.

Nora thought Crossword Lady might need some sanctuary as well as her donkeys.

"Perhaps you saw one on television in a soap opera?" Nora prompted.

Crossword-Lady looked blank.

"Ahem." Nora cleared her throat. "With regards to the donkeys, I could certainly ask His Grace about them. I'm sure he'd be more than happy to have them relocated to the castle grounds during Lockdown," Nora added, secretly meaning that she would like all the donkeys in the castle grounds during Lockdown.

"That would be wonderful, Gina." Crossword Lady nodded. "Jonathon, who runs the sanctuary, thinks he came into contact with *Polar-Bear 9* at the weekend so he is self-isolating already and isn't allowed to leave his house for fourteen days. I haven't seen him anyway so I'm certain to be clear and his local GP thinks his snotty nose is just the March flu, but they won't let me take over the running of the sanctuary in his place. It's down to Hermione who is very unreliable and Kenny, who is convinced we can catch the virus through all animals so is frightened of the donkeys."

"Well, we'd be more than happy to help out if we can," Nora promised.

"That's good news, Gina. When you've asked your…His Grace, let me know as soon as possible."

"I have your telephone number so I'll give you a call later on," Nora nodded.

"Thank you, Gina." Crossword-Lady said, pleased, and rustled her paper loudly. "Now. Today's literary question."

Nora inwardly sighed.

"Go ahead."

"The Island of Doctor *blank* by H. G. Wells."

"Moreau." Nora answered and spelt it out.

Crossword-Lady counted out the squares.

"Yes, that fits, thank you, Gina."

"You're welcome."

Crossword-Lady wrote it in and then put her paper away.

"I have to go to the care home up by the church now to take some excess boxes of hand sanitisers we use when caring for the donkeys."

"Is that what all the loo rolls are for, too?" Nora asked, curiously.

"Oh no, I just bought these for me. People were stripping the shelves like madmen so I thought I'd better join in and make sure I don't go short during the quarantine." Crossword-Lady explained, gathering all the toilet rolls.

Nora looked blank.

"Your email address, Gina?" Crossword Lady then prompted.

"Ah, of course."

She took a pen from a broken green Penguin book jacket mug that was kept on the desk and used as a pen pot, carefully wrote down her email address on a bright pink Post-It and handed it to Crossword Lady.

"I have an iPhone so I get an alert if I receive an email." Nora promised.

"Thank you, Gina. And let me know about the Duke's estate for the donkeys over the Lockdown as soon as possible."

"I will!" Nora nodded, keenly.

As soon as Crossword-lady left Nora sent a text message to James whom she assumed would still be in his meetings.

'How would you feel about playing host to twelve donkeys from the donkey sanctuary over the Lockdown? Xx' She wrote and pressed send.

The door opened and a man wearing a bright red Santa hat, left over from Christmas, stuck his head in the bookshop.

"You have a book in your window about tree felling." He said.

"I'll take your word for it." Nora nodded, standing up.

"I plan to use the Lockdown to fell some trees in my neighbourhood. I thought the book might be useful." He explained, remaining on the step. "I think the fewer trees we have the better so I'm keen to get chopping."

Nora hid her look of disapproval. She reached into the window shelving and retrieved the said book.

"It's priced at eight pounds." She told him after checking.

"Alright, well I'll take it." The man nodded, digging out his wallet. "I want to make sure I do it right. I expect it will tell you how to hold a chainsaw. I don't want to accidently lob my wife's head off."

Nora gawped.

"Yes, it does say *'Modern Lumberjacking: Felling Trees, Using the Right Tools, and Observing Vital Safety Techniques'* as its subheading." She assured him.

"Great. Here's a tenner. Keep the change."

"Oh, that's kind of you but I can get you your two pounds."

"No, don't worry about it. I can see you're closing for the Lockdown so I expect you'll need the extra cash." He smiled, taking the book Nora passed him from a distance.

She took his ten pound note in the tips of her fingers and kept it at arm's length.

"Thanks," she said appreciatively.

"No worries. Bye."

When he had left, Nora popped the ten pound note in the till, rubbed her hands with an anti-bacterial wipe and then wrote down the sale.

Betty came down the stairs.

"All done, Nora." She said, pleased, and emptied the dustpan contents into the bin. "I can go into the kitchen next and clear out the fridge and empty all the bins if you don't need me out here?"

"That'd be great, are you sure?" Nora nodded, pleased.

"Yes. I'm not decaying yet." Betty said with a small smile.

The door opened.

"Where can I buy some toilet rolls?" A man called in. "I'm passing through to Port Town and am stopping at every town on my way through. People are suddenly panic-buying them."

Nora and Betty stared.

"Oh Nora, I'm so pleased I bought some extra ones while on my lunch break!" Betty exclaimed.

"You have some? I'll give you two quid a roll!" The man offered, keenly.

Betty thought about that.

"It's tempting but I'll need them, I'm sure of it. Who knows how long we'll be…"

"Yeah, yeah, fine, I don't want your life story!" The man snarled rudely.

Nora's eyes popped.

"The only place for toilet rolls would be the Co-Op."
Nora told him aloofly.

Betty was grinding her false teeth and glowering.

"Yeah, but they're all gone, so you'll have to settle
on using your sleeve." Betty told him with sadistic glee.

The man looked thunderous.

"If greedy old grabbers like you left enough for
everyone then I wouldn't be on the lookout myself!" He
yelled and left, slamming the door behind him, hard.

Nora was astounded.

"Flippin' pig!" Betty hissed.

Nora watched him stalk up the road and then stop and
speak to a local woman who had several packets. They
stood talking for a moment, the woman then hugged the
toilet rolls close to her chest, gave a yelp, and ran away
from him quickly.

"This is a bizarre and unexpected development."
Nora gawped.

Betty was reading a Skype message from Cara.

"You might want to think about buying some toilet
rolls on your way home, Betty. Georgina said people are
panic-buying them all over the County of Cole – Cara
xx." Betty read aloud.

She looked up and clenched her jaw.

"I obviously look like an incontinent old lady then."
She said, bitterly.

"Not at all." Nora assured her, although she had to
control her trembling lips because of the ridiculous
situation.

"Lucky for me I have plenty of toilet paper to wipe
my crinkly old bottom during Lockdown. And if I get
desperate I shall use Danny's clothes."

Nora burst out laughing, meanwhile the door opened
again.

"Do you sell toilet rolls?" A woman asked.

Nora's smile faded and she clutched her head, amazed.

"This really is like the Twilight Zone" she decided and left Betty dealing with her, heading to the kitchen to make some tea!

James replied to Nora's text message saying he would be more than pleased to give the donkeys from the sanctuary a home during the Lockdown and that there was plenty of room in the old stables that used to be part of a training stables, once managed by a Derby winning trainer who had ran them until a few years ago. The stables were part of the Duke's estate and had been closed due to the trainer's passing before the Duke moved in.

Nora had the feeling the Duke was just as excited as she was about the thought of having twelve donkey companions during Lockdown.

'Jeeves used to help at the stables with the horses at James Hall; he'll know how to care for them xx.' James had added. And then: *'It will give him a good focus during quarantine xx.'*

'That's good news. I'll let Mrs Booth know xx'

Nora telephoned Crossword-Lady who was delighted. She in turn telephoned Jonathon who telephoned Nora and they made arrangements. Jonathon knew Jeeves already and revealed to Nora that the Duke's valet was a bi-weekly visitor to the donkey sanctuary. He said the donkeys could be herded to the former training stables that evening and the sanctuary benefactors would be pleased they would be in good hands.

"We have twenty four hour live streaming on the donkeys for schools and locals. You might think about setting it up at the training stables so the local children can tune in and watch them during Lockdown."

Jonathon proposed while sniffing and coughing and sounding like he had the bubonic plague.

"I'm sure His Grace would be more than happy to accommodate that." Nora decided, screwing up her nose and glad he was quarantining. "Hope you get better soon!"

Betty came through from the kitchen as Nora hung up.

"I'll make us some hot chocolate, Nora, to use up this milk." She proposed.

"Lovely." Nora agreed.

While Nora was spraying anti-bacterial solutions about the shelves, door handles, ledges, edges, counter top, computer monitor and cases, wiping them clean and opening the door to let in fresh air, another local entered The Secondhand Bookworm.

She was a small, plump woman in her early thirties with very bushy brown hair, wide brown eyes and her customary flowery skirt, tight brown t-shirt that clung to her ample curves and large bosom, and she was carrying an enormous carpet bag.

Nora inwardly sighed.

"Hello, Nora." Dora Magic greeted loudly.

Dora Magic was a self-published author who wrote profusely and who was obsessed with The Secondhand Bookworm and Nora. She consistently showered Nora with affirmations, was passionate to the point of madness that Nora should own The Secondhand Bookworm rather than work for Georgina, and hoped that one day The Secondhand Bookworm would stock her self-published books.

"Hello, Dora." Nora greeted in reply.

Dora giggled.

"Isn't it always a source of wonder and delight that our names rhyme?"

"Er…yes, quite." Nora humoured.

EMILY JANE BEVANS

"I see The Secondhand Bookworm will be closing over The Lockdown." Dora pointed to each poster with a repetitive jab of a finger.

"It will be." Nora confirmed and watched Dora place her huge carpet bag on the floor at her feet.

"And you will be self-isolating with His Grace at the castle?" Dora asked, looking as if she already knew that to be true.

Nora always felt uncomfortable about the amount of personal information Dora had on her, but thought it best to keep her sweet because she seemed to be a bit of a mad woman.

"Yes, I shall be staying in a guest room at the Duke's castle until the Lockdown is lifted."

"Wink, wink!" Dora said and sighed wistfully. "Ah, you and His Grace are becoming a source of intense fantasizing for me, and that always means the makings of a new series of novels."

"What kind of novels?" Nora asked, alarmed.

Dora Magic wrote a large spectrum of genres including steampunk, romance, crime and erotica. Nora prayed it wasn't the latter.

"Romance of course!" Dora said and giggled.

"Hmm, I'm not sure if I'm happy about that."

"Nonsense, Miss Jolly. You are important, many adore and observe you, you are wonderful, you will come to see you are admired and magnificent, Nora Jolly, you will." Dora gushed.

Nora kept her polite smile but it was beginning to hurt her cheeks.

"Er…thanks." She finally responded.

Dora beamed.

"I anticipated the Lockdown of course, being a very insightful writer, so I prepared for this situation with you in mind!" Dora then exclaimed and stuck her head and shoulders into her carpet bag, rummaging loudly around inside it.

Nora always expected her to produce a lit lamp, like Mary Poppins.

"I have them in here somewhere, among the toilet rolls." Her muffled voice said.

Nora suddenly felt like laughing and had to control her trembling lips when Dora emerged, her hair standing on end like she had had an electric shock.

"I had these published at the weekend for you to enjoy during the Lockdown, Miss Jolly." Dora announced and produced a very large pile of bright paperbacks tied together with a yellow ribbon. "They arrived this morning by special delivery. I'm sure you'll enjoy them thoroughly and one day, who knows, they will be stocked at The Secondhand Bookworm and I shall sign author copies for many fans. I have ten boxes of each novel in storage at home but these are for you and I signed them."

Dora plopped the books onto the cash book. Nora stared at them with arched eyebrows.

"You just wrote them?"

"Yes, over the past three weeks. As you know, I'm a fast and prolific author."

Nora had once decided that Dora Magic suffered from Graphomania, also known as scribomania, which was an obsessive impulse to write.

"It's a delicious series of wartime novels centred round a family of vampires who refuse to drink the blood of humans but eat caterpillars instead." Dora explained. "They make an exception when female Nazis invade their town. It's a cross between horror and romance and war. One of the vampires is called Nora and she falls desperately in love with a caterpillar farmer called Humphrey. It's dystopian and set five hundred years in the future."

Nora was both baffled and delighted.

"A caterpillar farmer called Humphrey?" She repeated, drawing them towards her.

"Yes, in the future the caterpillars are the size of Chihuahuas."

Nora was trying her best not to laugh.

"How many did you write?"

"There are ten in the series so it should keep you well occupied during the Lockdown." Dora Magic said and clapped her hands, excitedly.

"Thank you. I believe it will." Nora agreed, already drawn with bemused fascination to the top book which was a bright green, fat paperback with a thin man on the front, sporting a Tom Selleck Chevron Moustache, a long black cape, red bowtie and black suit while holding a silver platter above his head with a huge yellow caterpillar in the middle with a fork sticking out its plump body. It looked like an Edward Gorey drawing. The title of the book was in a large yellow font and read 'The beginning of the Caterpillar Wars, a tale of Vampire-Farmer love at the time of War' by Dora Nora Magic.

Nora frowned when she saw her name.

"I hope you don't mind but I've taken your name as my middle name in this series." Dora simpered, closing up her carpet bag.

"Erm…" Nora thought it best not to argue so laughed politely.

"I know you are now dating the Duke of Cole, but I was smitten with your relationship with Humphrey Pickering, Georgina's handsome brother, and I still have lots of writing juices left to squeeze out of that." Dora said.

Nora thought that was a gross way of putting it but continued to smile politely, after all, it really was only Nora who read the crazy woman's books. And she did read them. They were so terrible and preposterous that Nora found them highly amusing and enjoyable. Amy, who also worked at The Secondhand Bookworm, was Dora's only other fan.

"Well, thank you. I shall certainly read them during the Lockdown," she promised.

"Wonderful, Nora. And I shall miss not seeing you every day." Dora sighed, gazing at Nora intently.

"Well, I'm just up the hill." Nora smiled.

"Hmm, yes, maybe I can come up with a way of seeing you in the castle." Dora mused and looked suddenly quite sinister with an odd plotting face. "But it would take some stealth."

"Er…" Nora stared.

Dora then broke into a smile and shrugged.

"We'll see one another soon, Miss Jolly. Soon enough, I'm sure. Now, I'll leave you to your cleaning and sorting and preparation for your Lockdown. Stay safe and happy reading. God bless you!" Dora said, and drew an enormous air heart with both arms after dropping her carpet bag to the floor with a huge thud.

Nora wondered if she kept a body in there.

"Stay safe." Nora smiled.

"Stay safe!" Dora smiled back.

They stared at one another for a long moment until Dora bent down, picked up her bag, blew Nora a kiss and set off.

"You are appreciated, Miss Jolly. And one day The Secondhand Bookworm will be yours. Mark my words! You are a star! A star attraction. Goodbye, goodbye, goodbye…" Dora sang and closed the door behind her on her way out.

Nora stared blankly for a long moment and then decided she needed a shot of brandy in her tea, but that she had better not suggest it to Betty because Betty would agree!

*

Betty did a fantastic job with the kitchen, leaving it sparkling clean with the fridge switched off, door open and interior empty and the handles and surfaces disinfected and smelling fresh.

They sat and had another hot chocolate, admiring the extremely neat bookshop, which was a rare thing since it was rummaged through daily, when the telephone rang.

"I hope that's not Mr Hill again." Nora grimaced.

"Oh Nora, I hope not, too." Betty scowled.

"Good afternoon, The Secondhand Bookworm." Nora answered cheerfully.

"Hello." A high, sweet voice responded. "This is Miss Raven."

Nora was about to take a sip of hot chocolate but held the mug still so that it steamed up her glasses.

"Hello, Miss Raven." Nora responded, surprised.

Betty's scowl became a withering look.

Miss Raven was the daughter of Mrs Raven, making up a duo of bookshop customers who collected children's books, carried mountains of carrier bags and black sacks, argued in whispers, demanded discounts and had both made the recent Book Club a memorable affair. Miss Raven had shown a keen interest in Danny at the beginning of the club, when Danny was fresh meat to the older ladies of the book group, and Betty and Miss Raven had almost fought over him, so Betty considered Miss Raven a rival.

"I just spoke to Georgina in the Seatown branch." Miss Raven said, sounding high pitched and passive-aggressive, as usual.

"Oh yes." Nora replied, amiably.

"I would like all the Disney books you have in stock put by for me and mother. Georgina said she will collect them on her way through tonight and drop them in to us once she has disinfected them all. We require more reading material for this frightening Lockdown," she explained.

"Okay." Nora agreed, warily.

"And could you do our usual discount on them. IT WOULD MEAN A LOT!" Miss Raven demanded shrilly.

Nora decided Miss Raven was freaked out because of the pandemic.

"Of course, that's no problem." She assured her, kindly.

"Please bag them up for us. We would require no more than five books in each bag!"

"But Disney books are light and we won't have many…"

"IT WOULD MEAN A LOT!" Miss Raven shrieked.

Nora pursed her lips.

"Very well. I'll make sure we only bag up five in each."

"Thank you. Be certain to get every single Disney book you have. Last time I was in there I noticed several Classics Storytime Collections with titles such as Tangled, The Lion King, Moana and Frozen."

"Yes, I expect we still have them."

"If you could do it now before anyone snaps them up."

"We haven't had many customers so I wouldn't worry about…"

"IF YOU WOULD BE SO KIND!!" Miss Raven screeched.

Nora decided the Ravens needed some form of sedative to get through the Lockdown. She heard Mrs Raven in the background, wheezing and whispering loudly:

"Ask her if…ask her if…ask her if she'll do our discount…"

"I HAVE POPPET!" Miss Raven screamed.

Nora winced and cleared her throat.

"Ahem. I'll get onto it right away."

"Thank you, Nora. Goodbye." Miss Raven said breathlessly and hung up.

Betty was peering at Nora grimly over the top of her spectacles.

"Is the old bat having a meltdown?"

"It sounds like it." Nora nodded, standing up.

Betty stood up too.

"I'll go and get them. I couldn't help but hear she wants all the Disney books and I sorted them out earlier so it won't take me long to find them." She offered.

"Thanks." Nora nodded, sitting back down.

A Skype message arrived from Georgina in Seatown confirming Miss Raven's demands and Georgina's new chauffeuring books business. Nora had just replied when another local popped in. She turned and saw Imogene who ran the organic greengrocer shop located over the bridge.

"Oh. Hello, Imogene." Nora greeted, still a little chilly towards her.

Over Valentine's Week, Imogene had teamed up with Braxton Parker-Hodge, Nora's ex-boyfriend from over ten years ago, the one who had kept proposing to Nora and considered himself her fiancé despite Nora's rejections.

He had run The Otter Shop, located down Market Street across the cobbled square, which had backed onto the old salt factories. The shop had been dedicated to the conservation of otters, which Braxton had worked with at local nature reservations. The shop had contained items with an otter theme, such as otter earrings, otter shaped chocolates, beach towels with the faces of otters on and ladies lingerie.

Because Imogene had a crush on Humphrey, she had agreed upon a plan with Braxton to try and drive Nora away from Castletown by making crank calls to the bookshop and then to eventually kidnap Nora and Humphrey at the old salt factories in an insane plan that saw Braxton propose to Nora again and then confess to murdering his former girlfriend Claire and burying her, along with all the otters who had ever bitten him, in the salt factories.

Braxton was now in prison awaiting his trial for murder and Ottercide while Imogene had apologised profusely for her part in the scheme (she hadn't known about the murder part and had ended up helping Humphrey and Nora to escape) and hoped they could all go back to being co-workers and friends. It had been the talk of Valentine's Week, more so than the news that Nora and the Duke of Cole were now a romantic item.

"Hi Nora." Imogene greeted.

"All ready for the Lockdown?" Nora asked her conversationally.

"Yes. How's it been here? All my shelves are stripped bare and the Co-op is out of loo rolls."

"There's a strange thing going on with loo rolls."

"I saw it on Twitter." Imogene said. "Everyone's panic-buying them. Apparently people are fighting in the supermarkets over them as well as over anti-bacterial hand gels and wipes."

Nora looked blank.

"Well, I guess people are planning to stockpile, but there should be plenty to go around." Nora supposed.

"Yes, I expect all the old people don't want to go out again during Lockdown so are supplying bunkers."

Nora thought that was almost amusing.

Imogene then cleared her throat.

"Ahem. I hope you don't mind me doing this Nora, and I apologise in advance, but I told him I would just this once."

"Who and what?" Nora asked, noticing that Imogene was carrying something.

"Ahem. This is a letter to you. From Braxton."

Nora's lip curled.

"Braxton isn't allowed to contact me."

"I know. He said it would just be the one letter, he doesn't expect you to write back, and he understands we're going to testify against him at his trial, but he wrote to me apologising that he got me involved, it was quite sweet really, and asked if I would pass this on."

Nora sighed.

"Fine." She nodded and took the letter.

"So, is Humphrey still with Amy?" Imogene asked, keenly.

Nora arched an eyebrow.

"After what you did with Braxton, tying Humphrey to a chair and helping to kidnap me, I very much doubt you have a chance with Humphrey, Imogene." Nora told her practically.

Imogene sighed.

"Yes, I guess you're right. He's so much like Harvey Specter from Suits though, don't you think? You can't blame me for having a crush on him."

"I suppose so." Nora smiled.

"Well, good luck with the Lockdown. I expect you'll be up at the castle with the Duke?"

"Yes." Nora nodded.

"And what is Humphrey doing?"

"He's coming down from London this afternoon and will be staying with his sister." Nora replied.

Humphrey had moved down to the County of Cole from London a couple of years ago after having run a highly successful international business company for eight years. He had found the pace of his life too fast and needed a change so was currently living with Georgina and Georgina's American boyfriend, Troy. His sister often had him doing maintenance work for her about the house or the bookshops, something Humphrey enjoyed. She also cooked for him and cleaned his clothes so he was having a lovely time.

Nora had met Humphrey when she had first made Georgina's acquaintance and on several occasions over the following years whenever he had popped down from London. When he had retired from his business and moved down to Cole he had started to help out at The Secondhand Bookworm and he and Nora had become firm friends. They had dated for several months and, although Humphrey had been keen on Nora, he had agreed to return to being just friends before Christmas to leave Nora free to start dating James, the Duke of Cole. After a rocky start to the new arrangement they were now the best of friends again. Nora thought of him as another brother (she already had three of those).

Since the New Year, in addition to the maintenance business he had set up in Cole, Humphrey had been working occasionally back at his London enterprise with his former business partners to help them out with specific deals, so he often arrived at The Secondhand Bookworm looking like he worked at the London Stock Exchange or was a debt-collector for a crime lord.

"Okay, well, see you when this is all over!" Imogene sighed and set off.

A man replaced her.

"Any books about Pyrography?" He asked, remaining on the doorstep.

Nora blinked, thinking for a moment that he had said 'pornography'!

"Ah, Pyrography, as in pokerwork or artistic burning on wood." Nora understood.

"That's right." The man nodded.

"We have a craft section upstairs in the front room on the top floor with a couple of shelves of woodworking.

"Forget that. You could be infected." The man decided, turned around and hurried off.

Betty appeared at last with more hot chocolate as Nora shook her head.

"Sorry I was so long, Nora. Flippin' microwave plug fuse blew. I had to hunt out a spare one and a screwdriver in the kitchen drawers."

"Did we have any of those things?" Nora was incredulous.

"We did! And I managed to change it so it works again, although I did think I'd blown myself up at one point, I heard a terrible sound, turns out it was just me. My lentil and avocado roll didn't agree with me."

Nora snorted.

"Oh dear."

A woman loaded with toilet rolls stuck her head in the doorway.

"Any books about Vintage Hand Lettering? I thought I'd work on my penmanship during Lockdown." She hollered.

"We have a calligraphy section here." Nora said, standing up and walking over to the art section.

The woman waited patiently in the doorway. Suddenly, she dropped several packets of toilet rolls about her feet and then screamed when the man from Port Town, who was still lingering, grabbed one and ran off up the street shouting 'Zoinks!'

"Oh my." Nora breathed, watching the scene.

Betty was enjoying it immensely while sipping her hot chocolate, smiling.

"Forget the book! I'm going to the police station to report that wicked man!" The woman exclaimed and marched off.

"Oh Nora. I think it's a good idea to go into Lockdown. Society has gone mad." Betty decided.
Nora agreed.

While Betty was showing a woman the transportation section around the stairwell behind the front room, and having a discussion about face masks, Nora tentatively opened Braxton's letter to her.

"Why am I doing this?" She asked herself and drew out the missive with a frown. She opened it up, arching an eyebrow to see a sticker beside the letter heading, which was of two cartoon otters hugging one another with the words *'We Otter Get Married'*, floating amidst hearts. Nora growled.

'My darling Nora,' the letter began.

"Grrrr!" Nora repeated.

'I hope this letter finds you well and full of good thoughts and warm fuzzy feelings towards me, as I have towards you. Always, my love! I know you now understand why it was I kidnapped you and attempted to strangle Humphrey Pickering in the salt factories behind The Otter Shop during Valentine's Week. MY HEART BEATS FOR YOU ALONE and I longed for us to be together forever in Dartmoor. But let us not fret that this plan has been foiled. I am pleading guilty at my trial and understand you will be testifying against me, but only because you will be under duress from Pickering, who still has you in his clutches. The one thing that keeps me sane is that the prison I will go to for life will allow conjugal visits and when we are finally married, we will be able to be together again. Nora Jolly, will you marry me?...'

Nora screwed up the letter before finishing it, threw it over her shoulder and shook her head.

"Why am I not surprised." She mused aloud, turning to read a new message on Skype chat from Cara instead.

'Georgina says to close up as soon as you're done getting ready for Lockdown there. We'll be shutting up shop here in about half an hour. Seatown is deserted! xx' Cara had written.

'It's empty here too, but bizarre things are taking place. Seems like the locals of Castletown have got wind of the toilet roll panic buying, pardon the pun xx' Nora sent back.

Cara replied with a row of hysterically laughing emoji's.

"I won't be wearing a mask even if the government makes it mandatory. I am not a Muslim woman and I won't be told what to do." The woman with Betty was saying as they returned to the front room, laden with books.

"Oh I've already had my boyfriend and lover order a couple of packs from Amazon this afternoon. Blue surgical masks." Betty explained cheerfully.

Nora smirked at Betty including the word 'lover' in her reply.

"You have a lover?!" The woman exclaimed.

"Yes! I'm not in the ground yet and some men like shrivelled bodies!" Betty shot back and gave Nora a look. "We'll be wearing our masks if we go out for supplies, we're living together you see. I've always wanted an excuse to cover up my witch-like face when out in public."

Nora was trying not to laugh so her eyes started watering. The woman just gawped at Betty mutely.

"Shall I take those for you?" Nora offered, blinking back her tears.

The woman threw her pile of books on the counter top with a loud crash.

"Yes, but keep your distance and please wear gloves while touching them." She requested.

Nora and Betty looked at one another.

"I'll do it, Nora." Betty said, already wearing the yellow marigold gloves from the kitchen (apparently the woman had insisted while Betty showed her the transportation section).

"Okay." Nora nodded and stepped out of the way.

While Betty carefully ran the prices of the books through the till and bagged them up, making endless mistakes on the till buttons because of her fat rubber fingers so that it beeped loudly, Nora noticed Humphrey arrive. He was strolling past the bookshop, looking very much like a version of Harvey Specter from season one of the TV show Suits, as Imogene often said.

Humphrey waited outside when he noticed Betty serving her customer, and stood back for the woman to pass him when she left, laden with her books and having spent eighty pounds.

"Cheeky old mare." Betty grumbled as she wrote the sale down in the cash book.

"Hello, having fun?" Humphrey greeted, stepping down into The Secondhand Bookworm.

Betty looked up and pursed her lips.

"Hi, Humphrey." Nora welcomed, warmly.

"I hope you're going to behave, Mr Pickering." Betty warned, gesturing to Nora.

Humphrey flashed a dashing smile.

"Me? Behave?" He winked. "Unlikely."

Betty smiled but gave Nora a look that told her she was there to throw Humphrey out if he crossed any boundaries of friendship. At the first Book Club meeting Humphrey had stood up and loudly declared that he was still in love with Nora. Although they were now the best of friends, it was no secret that he still held a candle for her and Betty often offered to throw herself at Humphrey as a distraction. James had appointed Humphrey Nora's bodyguard over Valentine's Week so as to focus Humphrey's attention on Nora as someone to watch over instead of dream over, and that had worked out quite well.

The telephone rang so Betty answered it and headed off to the back room with the customer on the end of the line, who was requesting grim War Biographies to keep him occupied during the Lockdown.

"I thought I'd come and say hello and goodbye seeing as we probably won't see one another for a while." Humphrey explained, standing by the bay window to keep a good social distance.

"Georgina said you'll be staying with her." Nora nodded.

"She has a whole pantry of food to last a lifetime." He grinned. "I might pick up some loo rolls, though."

"You had better get in quick. I think Castletown is now out of them." Nora said.

"How bizarre. Will you be alright in your flat during the Lockdown? You can always come and stay at Georgina's."

"I'll be heading to the castle after work." Nora replied, tentatively.

Humphrey smiled brightly.

"Good idea. There's plenty of room there." He nodded.

"I have my own guest rooms." She assured him. "And I shall be working with James to help the townspeople during Lockdown."

Humphrey kicked moodily at a box of cheap books that usually stood on the pavement outside, but smiled and nodded good-naturedly.

"Great. So you have your Stay at Home plan prepared, too. Be sure to keep in touch." He said, meeting Nora's eyes.

"I will." She promised.

"Have you been busy today?"

"Well, I did feel like I was in The Twilight Zone with Mr Hill," she admitted. "And after a visit from Dora Magic, who has written a series of novels with you as a futuristic caterpillar farmer and me as a vampire I concluded I was in The Twilight Zone."

Humphrey looked blank.

"I wonder if I'll miss the bookworms during Lockdown." Nora laughed.

"*Witness Mr. Henry Bemis, a charter member in the fraternity of dreamers. A bookish little man whose passion is the printed page, but who is conspired against by a bank president and a wife and a world full of tongue-cluckers and the unrelenting hands of a clock. But in just a moment, Mr. Bemis will enter a world without bank presidents or wives or clocks or anything else. He'll have a world all to himself... without anyone.*" Humphrey said in a slow, spooky voice.

Nora stared at him.

"It's from The Twilight Zone." Humphrey hinted. "The episode called 'Time Enough at Last'? It's the opening narration. Didn't we watch that one when we were dating?"

Nora thought hard.

"It doesn't sound familiar."

"Remember I put on some of the first episodes of The Twilight Zone? We went back to Georgina's house after dinner one evening."

Nora laughed.

"Oh yes. We'd been talking about the movie 'Ace Ventura: When nature Calls'."

"*There's someone on the wing. Some...thing.*" Humphrey quoted with a grin.

"I do remember. You showed me the original Twilight Zone episode that the quote had come from starring William Shatner. But I don't remember the bookish little man episode."

"I'm surprised I didn't show it to you being that it's book related." Humphrey mused.

"It's funny that you're obsessed with The Twilight Zone series." Nora chuckled.

"It's great. Well, in Time Enough at Last, Henry Bemis is a man who loves books but who is surrounded by people who prevent him from reading them. The episode follows Bemis through a post-apocalyptic world and has thought provoking messages about the dangers of reliance upon technology and the difference between solitude and loneliness."

"Hmm. That's interesting."

"At the end of the episode, Bemis sees the ruins of the public library. When he goes there to investigate, he finds the books are all still intact; all the books he could ever hope for are his now to read, and he has time to read them without interruption."

"What a lovely idea." Nora mused.

"However…"

"I don't like the sound of that." Nora knew that tone.

"Bemis happily sorts the books he looks forward to reading for years to come. But, just as he bends down to pick up the first book, he stumbles, and his glasses fall off and shatter into pieces. In shock, Bevis picks up the broken remains of his pair of glasses without which he is virtually blind. He bursts into tears, surrounded by books he knows he now can never read."

"You have a sadist streak, Humphrey." Nora pointed out, although her lips twitched with amusement.

"It will be like the locals here. A bookshop in the town, loaded with all the books they could ever read during the Lockdown. But the shop is closed. And they can't get to them." Humphrey said.

"I will certainly feel sorry for them." Nora mused.

Humphrey smiled and checked his watch.

"I'll drop the DVD box set of The Twilight Zone up to the castle gates tonight. You can binge watch it during Lockdown." Humphrey proposed. "I bought the sixtieth anniversary edition on Blu-ray – it's a Limited Edition Box Set of five thousand numbered copies only."

"They're spooky episodes and I shall be staying in an enormous old castle with a lot of history and several ghosts." Nora was reluctant.

"I'm sure James will enjoy them. I could always come and stay with you both instead of Georgina and Troy, and then you can enjoy my commentary." He suggested, blue eyes twinkling.

"As fun as that would be, I don't think James will be too keen."

"I just hope this Lockdown doesn't last for long." Humphrey decided. "I shall be like Sargent Mike Ferris, thinking I'm visiting The Secondhand Bookworm or visiting you up at the castle, when in fact I've been in isolation at Georgina's house for months, all alone and slowly going mad. *The barrier of loneliness: The palpable, desperate need of the human animal to be with his fellow man. Up there, up there in the vastness of space, in the void that is sky, up there is an enemy known as isolation. It sits there in the stars waiting, waiting with the patience of eons, forever waiting...in The Twilight Zone*." Humphrey quoted. "The closing narration from the first episode of The Twilight Zone titled *Where is everybody?*"

Nora found that most amusing.

Betty came back having hung up on her caller.

"Oh Nora, the man was a real misogynist. He kept asking if there were any men to look for his books. He seemed to think I was incapable of checking the shelves for any because I'm a woman. I should have hung up on the scum mid-sentence." She wailed.

Humphrey snorted.

"Thanks for listening." Betty said.

"Well, I think we can close up The Secondhand Bookworm." Nora decided, watching Tim and Sam locking up their butcher shop. "We've organised our Stay Home Plan and everything is ready for Georgina."

"Okay, Nora. I'll go upstairs and make sure all the windows are closed and I'll turn off the lights." Betty agreed.

Humphrey watched her go and as she was creaking up the stairs a man peered into the bookshop.

"Do you have any books about carving geometric patterns in wood?" He asked.

"We're about to close up now." Nora told him.

"Your loss." The man said and stormed off.

"Where are your business books?" Another man asked as Nora picked up her keys to hastily lock up.

"They're on the top floor but we're closing now because of the Lockdown." Nora explained.

"What bunkum." The man hissed.

Humphrey grinned, helping Nora bring in the postcard spinners from outside.

"I do enjoy visiting The Secondhand Bookworm." He said.

"Do you have any poetry books by Pam Ayres?! She always cheers me up!" A man with a bright green wig called loudly from the middle of the cobbles.

Humphrey did his best to cover up his laughter.

"We probably do but we're closing now!" Nora called back.

"Fair enough." The man with the green hair shrugged.

Nora assumed he had been to The Wig Emporium, a new wig shop that had appeared in Market Street in place of a restaurant Amy had once run.

Nora picked up the free maps and passed them to Humphrey as a man wearing a black mask over his mouth stopped and peered inside the shop.

"Got any Guinness Book of Records books? I'm going to see if I can beat some during Quarantine." He asked in a muffled voice.

"I'm afraid not." Nora shook her head and closed the door quickly.

"I know you're going to miss working at The Secondhand Bookworm during Lockdown." Humphrey said knowingly.

"Don't count on it." Nora said with a wry smile and locked the door. "I shall be quite happy self-isolating with my Stay Home plan!"

And with that, Lockdown at The Secondhand Bookworm had well and truly begun.

3 THE QUARANTINI CASTLE

Betty paid for her pile of saucy paperbacks much to Humphrey's amusement. Afterwards, he left Nora and Betty cashing up the till, waved them goodbye and set off to where his car was parked on the cobbles in the middle of the deserted town. Nora wondered when she would ever see him again.

"Oh I expect this Lockdown will be over soon." Betty tried to comfort. "And you have the Duke of Cole to keep you occupied."

"Plus this entire collection of dystopian novels which were written especially for me by Miss Dora Nora Magic." Nora pointed out, placing them in her bag.

Betty just stared.

They were then distracted when through the bay window they saw a large man with three chins, angrily waving a fistful of toilet rolls at Humphrey for parking on the cobbles. Humphrey dove into his sports car and screeched off, leaving Three-Chins surrounded by smoke. Three-Chins had arrived in Castletown last year and had designated himself the local traffic warden. Nora knew Humphrey would have departed in a flash of satisfaction at leaving the pesky man in a fog of exhaust fumes.

Chuckling to herself, Nora placed the money float into a bag and all the money from the takings and the safe with it, popping it on the counter with Mr Hill's books, Mrs and Miss Raven's books and the books for the Seatown customer interested in isolation themes. The Secondhand Bookworm was now ready for Quarantine.

"I shall miss you, Nora." Betty pouted as they turned off the lights, set the alarm, scrambled around the counter and out of the front door.

"I shall miss you, too." Nora replied, turning her key to lock up.

"I won't give you a hug and a kiss goodbye, in case we get arrested." Betty said. "And not just because we make a beautiful couple."

Nora was still chuckling about that as she walked up the deserted hill to her flat above The Fudge Pantry. It was eerily quiet, with most shops closed and displaying signs in their windows saying they would be shut until further notice because of *Polar-Bear 9*.

Oliver, who ran The Fudge Pantry, had left a box of treats on Nora's doorstep; full no doubt with sweets and fudges. Nora scooped it up eagerly and was standing examining the contents when James arrived.

The Duke of Cole looked weary. He had a habit of stroking his straight dark brown eyebrows with the index finger and thumb of his right hand when he was deep in thought and was doing so as he approached the flat, almost as if massaging away a headache.

"Hello!" Nora greeted him warmly.

"Hello." James smiled, leaned in and kissed her cheek. He noticed the box. "Fudge?"

"Enough to keep us well supplied during the Quarantine." Nora nodded.

James smiled.

"Oliver knows you so well."

"That he does." Nora agreed. "How did the meeting go?" She asked as James took the box, leaving Nora free to open her front door.

"Intense." He sighed. "But fruitful. We have everything organised and underway for the people of Castletown."

"Good." Nora nodded, leading the way inside. "Well done. I'll make you a nice strong cup of your favourite tea and you can sit and relax while I gather some things."

James smiled at that.

"Thank you." He said with appreciation.

They kicked off their shoes and climbed the staircase, James carrying the box of sweets.

"How was the afternoon in The Secondhand Bookworm?" He asked.

"Well," Nora stepped into her bright lounge through the door to the right at the top of the stairs. "The Secondhand Bookworm is now truly locked down."

"Hmm, that it is."

"Humphrey dropped by. He's going to lend us his entire collection of The Twilight Zone on Blu-ray for the Quarantine."

James looked interested.

"He likes that too?"

Nora glanced over her shoulder as she headed for the kettle in her neat kitchenette.

"Too? Are you a fan?" She asked the Duke dubiously.

He flashed a grin.

"I am. We could also watch my collection of Alfred Hitchcock movies?" He proposed, hopefully, placing the box of fudge on the coffee table.

Nora bit back a smile.

"Alright, but only if we can counterbalance them by watching this Firefly DVD boxset. It's the only way I'll get you to watch an American Space Western drama television series."

James laughed.

"Deal." He agreed.

Nora grinned.

They turned on the radio to listen to the news announcements as Nora busied about making James a hot cup of Earl Grey and then ordering him to sit on her sofa to drink it and try and relax. She knew he would be drained after a day of council meetings. Usually after attending a general meeting that lasted an hour or two he had a headache, so he was probably about to have a full on migraine after a day of it all.

It took Nora half an hour to pack for an undetermined stay at the Duke of Cole's castle. Once her bags were in the lounge, she made sure her windows were all secure, turned off any electrical items and she and James set off down the stairs laden with holdalls and the box of fudge. They stepped into their shoes, Nora made sure her front door was locked and then led the way down a short, narrow corridor.

At the end of the corridor was a door that led into a secluded garden. It was surrounded on two sides by ancient stone walls that connected to the Duke's vast estate; the end wall and the wall on the left. The wall to the right belonged to the unused gardens at the back of an antique shop next door while the wall and back windows from the kitchen and bathroom of The Fudge Pantry overlooked the little garden from behind. Oliver Braithwaite, who owned The Fudge Pantry, had never even peeped out for a nosey and kept the frosted windows of his shop's little used bathroom and kitchen covered with net curtains. He was only interested in his fudge business. The garden was Nora's.

As soon as she had moved in and discovered the garden was part of her lease, Nora had set up a rustic iron table and chairs in the centre on the moss covered flagstones, added a bird table, planted some flowers in the beds, nailed up some garden mosaics on the ivy covered walls and discovered a door with an ancient looking lock behind a heavy curtain of passion flower vines.

James had soon informed her that he held a key to the door and had then met her for lunch in the garden over Halloween Week a year or so before and entered said garden by unlocking it. He shared with Nora that he had discovered in a journal in his library in his home in Norfolk that a great, great, great aunt of his would stay with the last Duke who lived in Castletown, before the fire that burned down the former castle, over one hundred and eighty years ago. She wrote of a romance the Duke had with a young lady who was a tenant of the property Nora now leased from James. It was often the subject of Nora's whimsical daydreams and she thought it wonderful that she and the current Duke were repeating the tale.

James had the key with him so unlocked the door, they stepped through and came practically face to face with Jeeves on the other side. At least, Nora supposed it was Jeeves; he currently wore a blue surgical mask and was waiting on the neat rise of grass several feet away to assist the Duke and Nora with her belongings.

"Hello, Jeeves!" Nora almost laughed.

Jeeves bobbed his head.

"Miss Jolly! Your Grace." He replied in the now customary mask-wearing muffled voice. "I'm so pleased we are able to have you come and stay at the castle, Miss Jolly. His Grace plans to keep you safe and sound during these strange and troubling times."

"Thank you." Nora replied with appreciation and gave James a fond look.

He returned it with warmth and reassurance in his deep, intense gaze. Nora knew she was incredibly fortunate to be spending Lockdown in the attentive company of the Duke of Cole.

At James' instruction, Nora placed two of her holdalls on the grass and stepped away. Jeeves then approached and picked them up, observing the advice now trending through the County of Cole for social distancing.

A refurbished four seater black golf buggy stood not far from the secret door into Nora's garden, with the Duke's crest emblazoned on its sides and black canopy. The little vehicle was perfect for travelling around the Duke's vast grounds.

Jeeves loaded up the back while Nora and James climbed in. Jeeves then took the wheel. They set off along a neat gravel path, heading further into the estate, past sloping lawns and a chapel. The grounds were vast and beautiful. To the left was the Norman Keep while further walls and towers surrounded the land beyond the moat that was never open to the public because it was part of the Duke's private estate. Most of the castle and grounds were open to the public for six months of the year.

It was easy to reach the rest of the restored castle interior from the Duke's private quarters, but he had three libraries, two parlours, two sitting rooms, three dining rooms, vast cellars, twelve bedrooms, a big kitchen, and three galleries of his own so there was no need to use the rest of the stately castle.

Usually, the Duke was attended upon by several maids and footmen, with cleaners, a housekeeper, his valet, cooks and secretaries to keep everything in order. James had sent them all home that very day, with promised continued pay, until Lockdown was over and, after checking that all the public rooms were well protected with dustsheets and the windows and doors secure, the staff had reluctantly said their goodbyes.

ʹJeeves lived at the gatehouse at the top of the hill by the private entrance and would stay on with the Duke. But James explained to Nora that it would literally be just the two of them in the entire sprawling estate for the duration of the Lockdown. Secretly, Nora was delighted. She had never really had him completely to herself before.

Most of the Duke's private quarters had been additionally prepared with dustsheets and locked up, leaving a network of several rooms that James and Nora would use.

Jeeves stopped the golf buggy to unlock and open a door set in the high stone walls over the drawbridge, hopped back into the buggy and drove them through to the quadrangle. It was stunning, with an oval lawn in the centre, fountains and topiary trees standing amongst the grass and brand new four storey high gothic buildings surrounding it on the north, east and south sides, tall and immense. To the west was the high hill leading to the Keep with high walls and towers enclosing the quadrangle. Tennis courts and gardens for the Duke's private use were to the north. An Audi was parked close to one of the many doors on the left, one of James's four cars.

Once they disembarked the buggy, James insisted that Jeeves return to his own home.

"I'll take it from here." The Duke nodded, already unpacking Nora's holdalls.

"Your Grace…" Jeeves' muffled voice protested.

"Go home, Jeeves." James smiled. "By Royal Order."

Nora grinned and Jeeves sighed, bowed and reluctantly hopped back in the buggy to drive himself back to the gatehouse.

Nora and James waved him off and once Jeeves had locked the enormous gate, securing them inside the quadrangle and the Duke's private dwellings, James put down the holdalls and boxes and wrapped Nora in a very tight embrace.

"I've always wanted to do this." He confessed, spinning her around and then kissing her thoroughly.

"Well...I...I can see why!" Nora laughed, fanning her face.

"I often wondered what it would be like to kiss you in the quadrangle." James chuckled, pressing his lips to hers once more. "But there's always someone passing a window or waiting on me in the shadows so I've never been able to see."

"I can't help being glad you've had the chance to try it out." Nora smiled, pleased, kissing him back so that he closed his eyes. "And now we're alone."

A familiar bark disagreed.

James and Nora looked down at their feet where the Duke's miniature schnauzer, Marlow, sat looking up at them.

Nora laughed and she and James crouched down to fuss over him.

"Not quite." James flashed a teasing, rueful grin.

They gathered Nora's things and, accompanied by Marlow, walked across the quadrangle to a heavy arched doorway and entered the Duke of Cole's castle. They made their way through the silent, grand wing, passing the halls and parlours which were closed up for Lockdown, climbing stone stairs and walking long corridors, to where Nora's guest chambers were located. It all smelt of anti-bacterial spray and wipes. Nora didn't think a single germ or speck of dust was present!

"I'll leave you to freshen up as I go and start dinner." James said, placing the last of Nora's holdalls inside the room.

"Your Grace, are you going to cook me dinner?" Nora turned to look at him, delighted.

"Absolutely." He lingered to press kisses once more on her lips, her cheeks and the knuckles of both her hands, looking reluctant to leave her alone even for a moment. "I'm pleased to have you here with me, Nora." He confessed, tenderly.

"Thank you for having me, Your Grace." She returned.

He kissed her once more before reluctantly heading to the doorway.

"See you there in half an hour?"

"Where?" Nora laughed.

"The kitchens."

"Of course." Nora grinned and, after he had taken his leave, she leaned out the doorway, watched him head off down the long corridor.

Thoroughly chuffed at being the sole guest of the Duke of Cole during Lockdown, Nora turned around to unpack.

When Nora reached the Duke's kitchens, she sniffed the air keenly, realising she was famished after a day at The Secondhand Bookworm preparing for Lockdown.

A pot of sauce was bubbling on the stove and James was grating cheese, his shirt sleeves rolled up, wearing a blue apron. Marlow was asleep in a basket by the door.

"Lasagne." The Duke explained, laying out sheets of pasta.

"Delicious!" Nora approved and sat down at the kitchen table to watch him.

"You might find those interesting." James nodded to a large heavy dresser set against one of the walls.

Once she had spotted the collection of books, Nora headed quickly over. Marlow jumped out his basket to join her, so Nora tickled behind his ears for a moment until the little dog was satisfied and returned to his bed.

"Whose were these?" Nora asked, impressed by the book collection.

"My late mother's."

"The Duchess cooked?"

"She insisted. And she was very good at it. She taught me to cook too, saying a man should be able to cook for his wife…or…or girlfriend." James added, hastily.

Nora looked away from the rows of cookery books, smiling at the Duke who looked endearingly handsome when he was flustered, the tips of his cheeks reddening slightly. He cleared his throat and picked up a tomato, smiling at her.

"She sounds like she was a very wise woman." Nora approved, smiling back.

She turned back to the books and was soon lost in their culinary depths. Not only were there useful cookery books for everyday use, but there were some very rare and unusual tomes. Nora carefully picked up a First American Edition of *The Compleat Housewife*, printed in Williamsburg in 1742, a very rare book. With it was *The Frugal Housewife*, published by Boston and re-printed and sold by Edes and Gill, printed in 1772.

Both books were bound in leather and were the first two cookery books published in America. There were two engraved plates in The Frugal Housewife. There was also a later edition published in the 19th century of the same book which had additional recipes adapted to the American mode of cooking. Nora flicked through them and saw recipes for buckwheat cakes, pumpkin pie, maple molasses and maple beer.

The late Duchess must have been a serious book collector as well as an accomplished cook. She had a delicious variety of books about food and drinks. Nora picked out a very early copy of *The Savoy Cocktail Book* by Harry Craddock.

"The Savoy Cocktail Book. Being in the main a complete compendium of the cocktails, Rickeys, Daisies, Slings, Shrubs, Smashes, Fizzes, Juleps, Cobblers, Fixes, and other drinks, known and vastly appreciated in this year of grace 1930, with sundry notes of amusement and interest concerning them, together with subtle observations upon wines and their special occasions." Nora read to James. "Being in the particular an elucidation of the Manners and Customs of people of quality in a period of some equality. This is a lovely book and it's an early edition."

James was listening attentively to her while pouring his homemade sauce over the pasta.

"A lot of them are quite rare." He nodded.

"This particular one would be worth a couple of thousand pounds at least." Nora said, gently stroking the cover. "Maybe we should mix some of these cocktails over Quarantine. I like the sound of the Brainstorm Cocktail. Most handy for crosswords and puzzles."

James grinned.

Additionally, during her browsing and reading, Nora discovered a very rare copy of '*Delightes for Ladies, to adorne their Persons, Tables, Closets and Distillatories. With Beauties, Banquets, Perfumes and Waters.*' It was by Sir Hugh Platt, with woodcut decorations and borders, bound in calf leather and published in 1615. She also plucked out a copy of a scarce oblong octavo book called '*Eight Cocktail Napkins, Hand Blocked, with Recipes and the Histories of Eight Famous Drinks*' published in 1925. All of the napkins were present and in excellent condition. It contained a history and recipes for the following cocktails: Manhattan, Blue Blazer, Deadwood Duck, Rip Van Winkle Sleeper, Belmont Park, Alabama, Barbary Coast and New Orleans Drip. Nora told James it was a stunning and rare piece of Prohibition Americana. Nora thought an interesting cocktail theme was presenting itself to her.

She was happily admiring a first edition copy, complete with dust wrapper, of *'1700 Cocktails For The Man Behind The Bar'* published in 1934 with an illustration of a mixer who looked just like Jeeves shaking a cocktail, when James announced that dinner was ready.

"Already?" Nora closed the book and placed it carefully back on the shelf.

While Nora had been lost in the world of literary culinary, James had dished up the lasagne onto two round blue plates and served it with a rocket salad and green olives.

"This looks delicious!" Nora admired.

James was pleased. He picked up both plates.

"I prepared a table in the south dining room."

"When?" Nora asked, popping an olive between her teeth.

"While you were reading." James laughed.

Nora grimaced.

"I didn't even notice you leave."

"I know you didn't," he said, pouting playfully and led the way.

Marlow jumped up to join them.

Nora followed, savouring the silence of the Duke's quarters in the enormous castle. They took their places at the far end of a long table, next to one another, James led a simple prayer before the meal, and then they tucked in, talking over their day, the new rules in place for the Lockdown, and concerns they had for the townspeople.

EMILY JANE BEVANS

"Perhaps Roy, the Castletown TV host, and Paul from the Chamber of Commerce will let you give an encouraging message every day via Castletown TV to the locals." Nora mused, dipping bread into the dressing James had mixed for their salad.

"Like the King's Christmas speech?" James teased, pronging a forkful of lasagne.

"Exactly like the King's Christmas speech. Isn't he your fourth cousin twice removed, Your Grace?"

"Where did you hear that?"

"I read about it in The Castletown Times. They also declared you to be the fourth richest Duke in England and that your family, the Ravenstones, are the eldest noble family in the land, with the earldom you also hold created in 1138 for the Norman baron Stephen d'Aubigny."

James smiled.

"I'm pleased you're so interested in me." He told Nora warmly.

Nora blushed slightly.

"Well, of course I am." She assured him.

"Glad to hear it." The Duke of Cole winked. "And I expect that's all true."

"Hmm." Nora stabbed an olive, pondering him with fascination.

After dinner, James and Nora washed and dried up and then settled down in the south sitting room to watch Castletown News with Marlow. Usually, when Nora was a guest of the Duke's, they spent their time in the library, but James wanted to be aware of the latest announcements so he sat with Marlow next to him, stroking the content schnauzer, before a large television with Roy interviewing a very snotty Jonathon about the donkey sanctuary, before Jonathon had run home to impose self-quarantine upon himself (it was unlikely to be *Polar-Bear 9* because the virus had quite different symptoms but everyone was happy he was in isolation anyway). Nora was interested in mixing cocktails so occupied herself at the long white and well-stocked bar and mixed a drink to start their Lockdown.

"I think I'll call this The Mad March Quarantini." Nora decided, sitting next to James on the sofa and passing him a glass.

The Duke moved Marlow onto the floor and took the drink. He looked impressed.

"What's in it?" He asked, inhaling the scents.

"Cointreau, Cranberry Juice, Castletown Gin, Apple Juice, a slosh of Cole Brew and a dash of Champagne with hawthorn berry juice in each. I was hoping to add a strange March nutty taste from Hawthorn leaves but the berry juice should have a nice tangy taste." Nora explained.

James watched her take a sip.

"Well?" He didn't wait for her to reply before he took a sip too.

"I like it." Nora confessed.

"So do I." The Duke agreed and sipped some more.

Jeeves knocked on the door, having arrived wearing his blue surgical mask and carrying the Blu-ray box set of the Twilight Zone Humphrey had promised. As he did, Nora received a text message which she assumed would be from Humphrey.

"Hello, Jeeves." James stood up to greet the valet.

"Your Grace. From Humphrey Pickering." Jeeves placed the box set on a side table. "I have wiped it thoroughly with antibacterial wipes just to be on the safe side, but Mr Pickering assured me he's quite clean."

"I'm sure he is." James smiled.

Nora read her text message.

'Jeeves has the box set. I get the feeling he thought I might be Typhoid Mary, but he took it for you in the end. Enjoy! Xx'

Nora grinned and replied.

'He's just brought it in. Thanks. James is looking forward to it xx'

'Excellent. Take care, speak soon xx'

'You too xx'

"The donkeys have arrived." Jeeves also announced to them.

Nora could see the valet was pleased about that.

"That's good." James was reading the back of the DVD box set with keen interest.

"A Mrs Booth from The Donkey Sanctuary and I have settled them into the stables, fed them and she will return tomorrow to help manage them. We were both wearing face masks, Your Grace," Jeeves assured the Duke. "And seeing as she has no family or acquaintances of her own we have deemed it wise to include one another in a strict social bubble, thus we will be quite safe caring for the donkeys together during the Lockdown."

Nora thought that was very romantic.

"My brother Wilbur is happy to come over tomorrow and set up video surveillance for live streaming." Nora told Jeeves, referring to a conversation she had had with her elder brother after dinner. "Would that be okay?"

"That would be perfect, Miss Jolly." Jeeves nodded. "I expect it will be the last day any outsiders will be permitted to interact before the strict government Lockdown measures are in place; and as long as your brother wears a mask and practises social distances I will permit it." He gave a protective glance at the Duke and then at Nora. Nora thought it was lovely the valet included her in his protective mission. "The local school children will enjoy watching the donkeys over the Lockdown. The animals already seem happy."

"How sweet," Nora enthused. "Do you know their names?"

"Yes, Miss Jolly." Jeeves said against his surgical mask. "Tapestry, Bailey, Pineapple, Sebastien, Buttons, Curly, Jewel, Lemon, Needle, Merlin, Berry and Pablo."

Nora thought they were wonderful names for donkeys.

"I think it calls for some drinks." James decided, standing up and heading for the bar.

"Quarantinis?" Nora grinned.

The Duke laughed.

"Perfect. I expect that will quickly become a household trend during Lockdown."

Nora helped the Duke blend The Mad March quarantini and they toasted the arrival of the donkeys. As they did so, a special report came on Castletown TV about toilet roll shortages in the town as well as throughout the country. Footage showed people running through Castletown with armfuls of toilet rolls, stripping shelves, bashing into one another and concluded with a panoramic of the empty shelves in the local Co-Op with Imogen standing in front of them with a look of dismay.

"Oh dear." Nora grimaced.

"That's not good." James said, shaking his head, slightly bemused.

"We have a room full of toilet rolls, Your Grace."

"Perhaps we can sort some out for people in the town who don't have any. The castle has about twenty bidets."

"Twenty bidets!?" Nora repeated, amazed.

James choked on a laugh but nodded.

"Another thing my late mother insisted upon. Have you ever used a bidet?"

"Yes. This isn't a conversation I ever imagined having with the Duke of Cole." Nora confessed.

Jeeves snorted.

"Well, if you're happy to use a bidet, then we can give away half our supply of toilet rolls." James proposed.

Nora tried to stop her lips from trembling.

"I think that's a very noble gesture, Your Grace." She approved.

"I'll have Jeremy make an announcement on social media." James decided with a smile. "People can collect any from the gatehouse if they need them."

"Who's Jeremy?" Nora enquired.

"He runs my new official Facebook, Twitter and Instagram accounts." James replied.

"Ah, yes, of course." Nora nodded.

"The official office of the Duke of Cole proposed I have social media accounts. Jeremy suggested I send him regular photos during Lockdown so he can keep the accounts updated."

"That's a great idea." Nora agreed.

"I shall take care of supplies for you both, Your Grace." Jeeves announced. "I think that you'll give a good example to the locals about staying inside during the Lockdown by self-isolating at the castle. The older and vulnerable scared people will feel safe as they will be led by example."

James nodded.

"Yes, we decided that at the town meeting." He smiled. "Thank you, Jeeves. We'll sort the toilet rolls out in the morning."

"Very good, Your Grace." James bowed, winked at Nora and set off.

Nora and James returned to the sofa, joined by Marlow, for another round of The Mad March Quarantini. While Nora sipped hers, she smiled at the Duke who was still examining The Twilight Zone DVD box set.

"Would you like to watch one?" She asked.

"Would you mind?" James grimaced.

"No. We're only in an enormous empty castle, with parts that are almost a thousand years old, and with several ghosts, during a global Lockdown. I'll be fine." Nora assured him.

James chuckled.

"You're with me." He encouraged, standing up to put in the first disc. "I'll keep you safe, Nora. Always."

Nora smiled up at him, warmly.

"I know you will, James" She said, happily. "I wonder if there are any episodes about bidets." She then mused.

James thought that was highly amusing and was still chuckling about it when they parted company to retire to sleep in the early hours of the morning.

4 A BOOKSHOP ZOOM PARTY

The following day Nora awoke to an eerie silence. Commercial plane travel had officially been suspended so the usual sounds of airplanes from the main airports sixty miles away, many of which had their flightpaths over Castletown, had ceased.

Nora showered, dressed, and made her way through the soundless castle to the kitchens, trying not to think of the four The Twilight Zone episodes they had watched last night, and finding James engaged in a conversation via Skype with Paul from the Castletown Chamber of Commerce. He smiled a warm hello to Nora and gestured to the breakfast bar where a jug of cool fresh orange and clean glasses stood.

After greeting Marlow, she poured herself a glassful of juice, examined the ingredients laid out for pancakes and set about making them a stack each while James concluded his conversation.

"Have you been up all night?" Nora asked.

The Duke looked tired, although he was fresh and clean and wore his casual Duke's clothes; crisp white chinos and a navy shirt.

"No, I've had a few hours' sleep. I was down here at five." He stood up to help her with the pancakes.

"I've got it." Nora insisted. "You sit down."

"You're my guest." James objected.

"And so I'm making myself useful." Nora waved the heavy frying pan at him to sit back at the table. With a huff of a laugh, James did as he was told. "Any updates?" Nora asked, busying about making and serving the blueberry and coconut pancakes.

"The county is now in strict Lockdown. No one in Castletown is allowed to leave their house except to get emergency groceries. Fines are in place if the police catch anyone not making a specific and extremely necessary trip. They hope to be able to allow people to leave their houses for one session of exercise outside within a few weeks but now everything in the town and the county is closed; public parks, pubs, barbers and hairdressers, schools, most work places, and you can only converse with and see members of your immediate household."

"It sounds ominous." Nora frowned. "What can we do to help?"

"Encourage people to stay home to stop the spread of the virus." The Duke said. "Paul and the Castletown Council and my official team have expressed their desire that I remain in the castle as a good example. But they'll keep me involved and informed with what they're doing for the townspeople, and they'd like for me to give social media messages and updates throughout. I've passed that onto Jeremy so will just send him information to do updates. The priority is to make sure the elderly are okay. I have a Zoom meeting with the council at two o'clock today to discuss specific measures."

"*Zoom* meeting?" Nora looked bemused.

"It's like *Facetime* I think, but for conferences. I'm currently downloading the App. It appears that several computers can log in at once and have conference calls."

"Aren't you clever." Nora praised, filling a white whistling kettle with water for tea.

James grinned.

"So, it will just be you and I trapped in the castle alone for the unforeseeable future. With Marlow of course."

Marlow gave a concurring yap.

"Perhaps I should relocate to the tower, like Rapunzel." Nora teased. "Oh, we're forgetting that we have Jeeves and twelve donkeys, too."

"And thousands of books."

"Then we'll be fine." Nora smiled.

James agreed.

After breakfast and clearing away, Nora and the Duke climbed up to the Keep to get some fresh air and look down over the town. It was deserted. The roads that led from Seatown and Piertown and across the rolling hills were completely empty. The air was silent except of course for birds, including the Duke's noisy resident rooks and Eurasian jackdaws. Two curious jackdaws hopped close along the walls and stared at Nora and James expectantly, wanting food treats.

"Oh look, there's Crossword-Lady with Jeeves." Nora pointed out.

They saw below them and in the distance, the Duke's valet walking along the paths leading to the stables with Crossword-Lady at least twenty feet before him. Both of them wore face masks and were having a shouting conversation across the distance between them. Nora thought that was very amusing.

"She's going to email me her crossword literary question every day." Nora told James.

"Really?" He quirked an eyebrow.

"I know. No peace for the wicked." Nora chuckled. "I'll take a look and see…oh…."

Her iPhone started to ring as she drew it from the back pocket of her jeans.

"Who's that?" James asked, trying to entice a jackdaw nearer.

"Georgina." Nora smiled and swiped her screen. "Good morning!"

"Halllllooooooo!" Georgina sang cheerfully on the end of the line. "How is it going in Castletown?"

"It's deserted." Nora replied. "Everyone is self-isolating."

"It's the same here in Piertown."

"Isn't it spooky!"

"It really is. It looks like businesses will be closed for a long time."

"Oh dear."

"So I'm going to organise a Zoom meeting for all the members of staff of The Secondhand Bookworm. Have you heard of Zoom?"

"As a matter of fact I have. James downloaded the App on his laptop this morning."

"Wonderful. Well, that's all done-did for you then. Will he let you use it for a meeting with us all on Thursday evening? It'll take me that long to organise everyone, especially those members of the bookshop who are in the November of their lives."

Nora snorted.

"Betty is quite savvy with her laptop." Nora assured her. "But yes, I expect that'll be alright. I can always download the App onto my own laptop anyway. I have it with me."

"That's excellent! I can explain to everyone what I intend to do about wages during the Lockdown."

Nora grimaced.

"Now, I know no one is allowed out from after today, but if you could somehow keep an eye on The Secondhand Bookworm, I'd really appreciate it." Georgina said.

"Of course. James and I could always go down after dark in hazmat suits to make sure everything is hunky-dory." She laughed.

"Don't put yourself at risk. It's not that important. They're only stinky old books. But I do worry about vandals and local yobbos."

"I'm sure Paul from the Chamber of Commerce will keep a very close eye on it. He's promised to do the rounds of all the businesses about Castletown twice a day to keep people's minds at ease."

"Of course, many shop proprietors don't even actually live in the town." Georgina realised.

"I can also pop down to the Co-Op for some essentials at some point and take the opportunity to check on the bookshop, too." Nora proposed.

"A good idea." Georgina approved.

Once that was settled, they rang off and Nora shared with James Georgina's plans. She then read Crossword-Lady's email out load:

"*Gina. I was worried about rapists in the town, but Jeeves the Valet has promised to watch out for me. I can see his gatehouse residence from my bedroom window so I feel safer already. Also, I shall be visiting the donkeys in the company of Jeeves every day during Lockdown. Since we have already been socialising we are a safe bubble of two and we will wear face masks and keep a far social distance.*"

Nora looked at James.

"Hmm. A possible Lockdown romance?"

James grinned.

"*And so, today's literary crossword question, Gina.*" Nora continued to read. She tightened her jaw at being persistently called Gina. James was amused. *"The Little white **blank**, by Elizabeth Goudge."*

"Horse!" James exclaimed.

Nora looked up.

"Yes. Well done."

"I know it's one of your favourite books. Because of the film, The Secret of Moonacre." He smiled warmly.

"You are correct." Nora grinned and typed her answer back to Crossword Lady.

They waited up in the Keep, chatting and observing the strange silence of the town, until they watched Jeeves escort Crossword-Lady back to the gatehouse while keeping their distance and continuing their shouting conversation, which made Nora giggle again. James and Nora then made their way down to the stables to meet the donkeys, holding hands and pausing to steal kisses along the way as the Duke savoured being able to shower affection on Nora wherever he wished thanks to the absence of his staff.

As they walked the neat paths across the sprawling estate, Nora received a text message from her older brother Wilbur, telling Nora that he and Milton were on their way to set up the live streaming feed in the stables. They had received conditional permission from Jeeves that they wear masks and gloves and would arrive looking like brain surgeons.

James telephoned Jeeves to inform the valet that they were on the way, who said he would wait at the gates and drive the two brothers to the stables in one of the Duke's refurbished golf buggies.

"I expect this will be the last time I see my brothers for a while." Nora pondered as they approached the paddocks. "And they'll have to keep a distance while they are here setting up."

"You can keep in touch with them all using Zoom." James proposed.

Nora liked that idea.

The Duke of Cole's stables were a rustic delight. Once run as a racing horse stables by a famous former Derby winning trainer before the Duke had restored the castle on the grounds, they had been kept in exceptional condition and still remained so today. There was a paddock surrounded by smart, clean buildings and a clock tower. The complex had been considered recently as a location by the son of a legendary Derby winner, a distant living relative of the Duke of Cole's, and an expert in racing horses. Nora had googled him and had been shocked at how he and James were alike, almost like identical twins! However, unlike the horse racing expert, who had the sport in his blood, the Duke of Cole was anything but a horseman.

"After breaking my arms four times, an ankle twice and a wrist once and after dislocating my shoulders at least three times, my father decided horse riding wasn't for me." James confessed with a small smile as they entered the compound.

"Poor Duke." Nora sympathised, taking hold of one of his hands and rubbing his fingers consolingly. "It's because you're a nerd, like I am." Nora consoled him.

James grinned, lifted their hands and pressed a kiss to her knuckles.

To Nora's surprise, when they reached the stables, Wilbur and Milton were already there.

"That was quick!" Nora greeted her brothers, who indeed looked like surgeons and who were up ladders fitting special cameras to the exterior walls. There were wires, cables and equipment everywhere. Jeeves was lending a hand.

"Hey Nora. Hello, Your Grace!" Wilbur greeted cheerfully.

"Hey sis! Hi James." Milton saluted.

"Hello. Thank you for doing this." James appreciated, examining the cameras with interest.

"Just out of curiosity," Nora mused, distracted from the donkeys momentarily as she too, pondered the technical set up, "these cameras will be strictly located in the stable and not the castle?"

Wilber laughed behind his mask.

"Do you think I work for MI5 and that the Duke of Cole is under surveillance?" He teased. "Of course they'll be strictly centred on the paddock and the stables inside. That's all."

James gave Nora a curious look.

"It was just something Harry said." Nora explained.

"Do tell."

Nora told James about Harry as they made their way over to the paddock, where the twelve donkeys were having a wonderful time. The donkey named Tapestry was on his back rolling about braying, while Buttons and Curley were playing with a big brightly coloured ball. The others came to greet Nora and James, seeking treats.

The video surveillance was up and livestreaming within a couple of hours. Wilbur sent the link to the live feed to Paul and also to Roy at Castletown TV. The site quickly went viral among the school children and locals who were keen to see the newly located sanctuary and catch glimpses of the Duke of Cole.

At Paul and Roy's urging over a telephone call, James agreed to introduce the new set up. He stood before the cameras fixed outside the paddock and explained to the audience how the donkeys were staying at the castle, how they would be cared for, and he introduced Nora as his guest, explaining that she was staying at the castle during Lockdown in special guest quarters.

Afterwards, Roy asked if the Duke and Nora would give a tour of the castle, including Nora's guest quarters (apparently people were phoning in, wanting to be nosey and see them) and so it was arranged that James and Nora would do a live stream event each evening from the Castle via Nora's iPhone to keep people informed and amused.

Finally, Wilbur and Milton packed away and the two brothers said their goodbyes to Nora and James once the golf buggy was loaded up. Nora stood at a sensible distance from her brothers to bid them goodbye before they set off in the buggy with their equipment.

"I'll certainly be watching your livestreams." Wilbur promised Nora and James as he got ready to leave.

"And I shall be making regular TikTok videos to keep everyone amused." Milton announced. "I'm planning on taking it over."

"TikTok? Like that little tubby robot character in the movie 'Return to Oz'?" Nora stared.

"No." Milton laughed. "It's an App for making and sharing short-form mobile videos. I shall be lip-syncing to popular songs and sharing my days during Lockdown."

"How thrilling." Nora teased him.

"You'll definitely be thinking that." Milton decided confidently. He then quickly led Nora out of range of the cameras and gave her a tight hug. "To see you through Lockdown." He grinned.

Nora ruffled his hair.

"I'll miss you."

"Just tune in to my TikTok videos and it will be like I'm with you all the time." He told his sister.

Nora giggled. Her youngest brother was already a hit on Instagram so she expected his TikTok videos would be quite interesting.

Once Nora and James had waved off the Duke's golf buggy, they returned to the castle, pleased the donkeys were settled and planning their livestream content. That evening, while James checked in on members of his family who were located about the country and on the borders of Scotland, and who comprised of several old aunts, a younger brother and a younger sister, all of whom Nora had met when she had stayed at James Hall over the New Year, Nora continued inventing Quarantinis and decided to open a bar room in The Secondhand Bookworm when Lockdown was over.

"This one is called The Fever Reliever." Nora told James, sinking into the seat next to him and passing him a glass.

James eagerly took it.

"Now there's an idea for a livestream." He decided, took a sip and grinned.

Over the next few days, Nora settled into a routine that looked set to define her Lockdown stay at The Duke of Cole's estate. She and James spoke regularly with Paul and other members of the council, presented their livestream videos about the castle and estate, which lasted for an hour in the evening and which attracted a lot of viewers, spent time in the library reading books, cleaning books and reorganising books on bookshelves, corresponding with Georgina, Cara and other members of The Secondhand Bookworm leading up to Georgina's special Bookshop Zoom conference, and working with Jeeves to organise the distribution of toilet rolls.

It was quickly evident that Nora and James would have to embark on a cleaning schedule for the castle quarters they were using, despite Jeeves insisting that he do the honours. James cooked most of the meals and he and Nora donned aprons and gloves and enjoyed polishing, dusting, hoovering and mopping the rooms that were in use. This was a subject of one Livestream which Cara said was her favourite episode so far. Nora quickly became proficient at filming using her iPhone and even made videos to send to Jeremy for the Duke of Cole's social media.

The new way of life for the residents of Castletown, the County of Cole and indeed the whole country and world, now incorporated connecting with one another through the internet. Actors, talk show hosts and singers opened up their homes to their own Livestreams and shows and the Duke of Cole's evening 'episodes' extended to curious and delighted viewers beyond the County of Cole. Nora grimaced as she realised Harry was getting his wish after he left approving and blunt comments about her beneath the videos each evening. When she pointed them out to James he was alarmed.

Despite being on Lockdown for less than a week, Cara had already become a professional at origami and Nora had finished book one of Dora Magic's new dystopian series of novels. She was looking forward to starting book two which was called 'The Vampire and the Caterpillar Farmer'. James found it highly amusing.

After their Livestream video on Thursday evening, Nora set up her laptop in the Duke of Cole's main library, on a coffee table, ready for the promised Bookshop Zoom Meeting which was to begin at eight-thirty. She had made a round of Quarantinis and took a sip of 'The Social Distancer' (which included a hint of garlic), joined by James on the comfy sofa, who was looking forward to witnessing what would probably be a typical Bookworm escapade.

Georgina was the host of the Zoom meeting and had set it up with a scheduled time for everyone who had been invited to join, so Nora clicked the button and was the first one to 'arrive'. She was given a view of Troy walking past Georgina's laptop in pink flannelette pyjamas as Georgina poured herself a large glass of Prosecco and sat down in front of her screen.

James paused in mid sip of 'The Social Distancer' and stared.

Nora decided this was *definitely* going to be a typical Bookworm escapade!

"Hiiiiiiii, Nora!" Georgina mouthed.

It was quickly discovered that Georgina had her setting on mute so both she and Nora made sure the mute button was unticked and everyone could be heard.

"This is great!" Nora decided once the sound was working.

"So lovely to see you, Nora! Good evening, Your Grace. We're enjoying your livestreaming shows from the castle." Georgina gushed.

"Thank you. Good to see you, Georgina." James smiled, tapping the sofa seat beside him for Marlow. The little schnauzer jumped up and got comfortable beside the Duke, ready for the Zoom meeting, too.

Another box appeared. Roger was shown sitting at a kitchen table, his face extremely close to the screen so that Nora and James jumped back.

"IS THIS WORKING?" Roger shouted.

"YES!!!!" Georgina glowered. "Sit back a bit, Roger!"

"Humph!" Roger grumbled, edging his kitchen chair away from the screen and revealing a jumper with a Christmas pudding knitted on the front. "Well, here I am on schedule. I can only see you, Georgina and, hello Nora. Hello, Your Grace."

Nora waved, hiding her smile of amusement about his very large face that had filled the screen. James saluted with his Quarantini.

"Glad you can join us." Georgina sang while shuffling reams of paper.

Amy suddenly appeared. She was wearing earphones while behind her a young man was painting a picture on a canvas at an easel, his back to them all, wearing white dungarees and no top. Nora and Georgina leaned in closer, gawping.

"Hello!" Amy greeted cheerfully.

"Who's *that*?" Georgina ogled.

"Oh, that's my new housemate, Finn. He moved in last week, just in time for Lockdown." Amy gushed and winked broadly.

Nora choked on an amused giggle.

The said Finn turned around and gave a wave with his paint pallet. He looked to be about thirty years old and was very nice looking with golden muscled arms.

"Where are the ladies?" Georgina asked, referring to Amy's daughters Henrietta and Charlotte.

"With their father. *Luckily*." Amy smiled. "Hello, Roger."

Roger was behind a newspaper. It rustled briefly in response.

Georgina rolled her eyes.

Humphrey was suddenly behind Georgina, using weights to do arm curls. Nora blinked.

"What the what?" She asked.

"Hi!" Humphrey leaned in, looking sweaty and grinning broadly.

"Get that out of my face." Georgina moaned, slapping at the weight as though it was a fly.

"Back in a minute." Humphrey said and disappeared.

"What was that about?" Nora laughed, glancing at James who had picked up his bowl of popcorn and was settling down as if this was a movie.

"Oh, Humphrey ordered an entire gym and has taken over the spare room upstairs. He's lifting weights and running on a treadmill." Georgina grumbled.

"Apparently a lot of people are getting into exercise over Lockdown already."

"I heard the Prime Minister warn that this Lockdown could be for at least two months." Amy joined in, pouring herself a glass of wine.

"Oh that would be ghastly but I heard it too." Georgina agreed, distracted by Finn behind Amy who was bending over mixing paint.

Cara suddenly joined. Her hair was bright blue and she was eating a cupcake.

"Hallllooooo! It works!" She exclaimed with a grin. "I am a Smurf!"

Everyone greeted Cara and a long conversation followed about her hair colour. Cara often experimented with hair colours and styles and being on Lockdown now presented her with the perfect opportunity to be more outrageous. Her childhood heroine was Jem from the same named 1980's American cartoon. Cara was, like Jem: Truly Outrageous.

"Could you tell me if it's true that Russia unleashed five hundred lions onto its streets to enforce lockdown?" Roger asked, folding his newspaper.

Amy coughed and sprayed her wine everywhere. Cara looked delighted.

"Whaaaaaaat?" The latter giggled.

"I heard it was eight hundred lions and hyenas." Lucy joined in. She had suddenly appeared in her box.

"Hello, Lucy." Everyone chorused.

Lucy was the newest member of staff at The Secondhand Bookworm. She had worked for fifteen years in a clothes shop and was still in the habit of asking people if they wanted to try on a different sized book. She was married to Lee who looked like a sleepy koala bear.

"Is that true about the lions and hyenas?" Georgina asked, blankly.

"No, it's a hoax. There are tons of hoaxes and conspiracies about *Polar-Bear 9* floating around the internet so don't believe anything." Lee joined in.

He was leaning over Lucy's shoulder and looked exactly like a koala bear, with his round brown eyes, wide, flat nose, small smiling mouth and silvery-dark hair, moustache and beard.

"Betty!" Nora greeted.

Betty had suddenly appeared on screen. Everyone did a double take but then relaxed, relieved. For a moment it looked as though Betty was sitting in the nude, but she was wearing a skin-toned tight-fitting sweater and the lighting of her lounge had given her a decidedly naked look.

"Oh hello everyone, how wonderful you look, so flattering and professional. I look like a naked old witch, but that's me all over. Thanks for listening." Betty said.

Danny walked past her wearing a very small towel wrapped around his waist.

Everyone stared.

Fleur then suddenly arrived, followed by Peaches, two college-aged girls who worked Saturdays. They were the last members of staff (Paperback Pam was a part-timer but she was employed *ad hoc* to mainly sort out the paperback rooms and Georgina had dealt with her separately. Pam wasn't planning on working at either bookshop any time soon!) so, after a round of helloes and some squeals and giggles when they spotted the Duke of Cole, the meeting was ready to begin.

Humphrey returned and pulled up a chair beside Georgina, eating an ice-cream.

"I know I'm not a member of the bookshop but I wanted to be a part of this meeting." He grinned.

"So did James." Nora grinned back.

"Have you watched any more episodes of the Twilight Zone?"

"We're on season two."

"You'll enjoy The Obsolete Man from Season two, Episode twenty-nine. *'You walk into this room at your own risk, because it leads to the future, not a future that will be but one that might be. This is not a new world; it is simply an extension of what began in the old one. It has patterned itself after every dictator who has ever planted the ripping imprint of a boot on the pages of history since the beginning of time. It has refinements, technological advances, and a more sophisticated approach to the destruction of human freedom. But like every one of the super-states that preceded it, it has one iron rule: logic is an enemy and truth is a menace. This is Mr. Romney Wordsworth, in his last forty-eight hours on Earth. He's a citizen of the State but will soon have to be eliminated, because he's built out of flesh and because he has a mind. Mr. Romney Wordsworth, who will draw his last breaths in The Twilight Zone'.*" Humphrey relayed dramatically and then licked his ice-cream. He had a talent of remembering word for word the opening narration of every episode of The Twilight Zone and hypnotising everyone when he repeated them.

Fleur and Peaches squealed.

"Oh that was so atmospheric!" Fleur gasped.

"You should be an actor." Peaches gushed.

"Nora, we've been watching Milton's TikTok videos, oooh he's amazing!"

"And so talented."

"Excuse me! This meeting is for bookshop matters not a personal chinwag!! Georgina rebuked.

James was hiding his quiet laughter behind his glass of quarantini.

"Thank you!" Roger agreed, his frowning face filling the whole screen once more.

Amy yelped.

Georgina banged her table like a judge trying to resume order in her court and her laptop lid shut, sending her box black.

Everyone disconnected and it took ten minutes to resume connection again.

Cara was wiping tears of laughter from her eyes when she re-joined as the last member.

"Ahem. Let's get straight down to business shall we and get this meeting done-did before anything else goes wrong." Georgina ordered grimly.

Humphrey was now nowhere to be seen. Nora assumed he had become bored waiting to reconnect, or run away from Georgina's moodiness, but he was soon back, this time eating tacos.

"In light of the Lockdown and both branches of The Secondhand Bookworm being closed for the unforeseeable future, I have had to decide upon some changes and difficult resolutions." Georgina announced.

Everyone looked worried.

"I shall start with the Saturday staff. Fleur and Peaches. As you already know I had to let Penelope go because of cutbacks on my Saturday employees. I will be unable to pay you any money during this Lockdown but you will still have jobs when we are finally able to reopen, whenever that will be."

Peaches burst into tears and logged off.

"Oh dear, the poor thing." Betty sympathised and glared upwards at Georgina's box with a rebuking look.

"Er…oh, oh dear…oh well, it can't be helped." Georgina grimaced.

"I understand." Fleur said bravely. "I'd best go into Peaches' room and see how she is."

Loud sobbing could be heard in the distance.

"Are you two staying together during the Lockdown?" Georgina blinked.

"Yes. We're flat sharing with six others from college. It's all we could afford. I share a bedroom with two people and Peaches with two others. Bye, all. Stay safe." Fleur replied and thought she had logged off. Instead, she picked up her iPad and carried it with her so that everyone felt as though they had been shrunk and put in Fleur's pocket.

"Er…" Nora pointed.

"Ooops." Cara grimaced.

"Doesn't she realise she's left it on?" Betty asked.

Everyone looked at one another's boxes awkwardly so that eyes were moving in all directions. Nora found this most comical. James was mesmerised.

There was a snoring sound. Roger had fallen asleep with his newspaper open again and over his face.

"How are we going to wake him up?" Amy wondered.

"Someone phone his mobile." Cara suggested.

Georgina tutted and scowled and dug out her phone to call Roger. Meanwhile, Fleur had carried them all into a corridor and was knocking on Peaches' door. Peaches wailed and sobbed for a good five minutes. Several college-aged boys arrived to see what was happening. A fight erupted and Fleur was covered in fizzy orange. She carried everyone into the kitchen to wipe herself off and then Fleur took her iPad into the bathroom announcing she needed 'a tinkle'.

Everyone screamed.

"Oh no!" Amy exclaimed.

Humphrey covered his eyes and James turned away.

"Hello?" Roger answered his phone.

"You fell asleep. And now Fleur has taken us into her toilet." Georgina told him loudly.

Fortunately, Fleur heard everyone shouting her name.

"I am so sorry! Georgina! Please accept my resignation!" The young woman exclaimed, flushing bright red, and promptly hung up, too.

Nora and Cara were trying their hardest to control their laughter. In the end, James made Nora a cup of black oolong tea and Seymour appeared in the screen to sober up his wife by reciting Shakespeare in a very boring monotone to Cara. Betty enjoyed the entire jaunt.

Once everyone had settled back down, Georgina continued, although everyone was now watching her as though she was Donald Trump in The Apprentice.

"I shall be giving full pay to Nora and Cara as you are my full-time employees, but as Roger, Amy, Lucy and Betty are contracted part-time, I shall have to pay you at a reduced rate." Georgina said, looking nervous.

"Bah!" Roger grumbled.

"Understandable." Amy nodded.

"Thank you, Georgina." Lucy said.

"Oh Georgina, that's so kind of you, thank you." Betty said appreciatively. "You never know, the government might consider a furlough scheme if this Lockdown is prolonged."

"Hmm." Georgina pursed her lips, looking sceptical.

The rest of the meeting was spent discussing how everyone could earn the money Georgina was forking out for them during the Lockdown. It was decided that Cara would work on the accounts from home and log into Skype every day with Georgina to discuss the accounts and banking. Nora would go down to The Secondhand Bookworm in Castletown to check in on it and do some sorting and stock-checking as part of her once a day permitted excursion. Lucy was to do online blogs and social media advertising to keep people updated about The Secondhand Bookworms during the Lockdown and to draw more people into awareness of it and hopefully drum up future business; while Amy was to pop into the Seatown branch and do the same as Nora. Betty and Roger would be expected to telephone all the regular customers each week to check in on them. That included Mr Hill. Roger grumbled about all his wages being swallowed up with that strategy.

Once Georgina had concluded the meeting and said she would organise with everyone a follow up meeting in a week or two, Betty suggested that they should hold a Zoom Book Club and asked if Nora would organise it, seeing as the recent Book Club held at The Secondhand Bookworm had been such a success.

"I think that's a great idea!" Nora agreed.

"Oh wonderful, Nora." Betty was delighted.

"Shall we invite the former members of our last club?" Cara asked. "I expect they are all lonely and isolated?"

Humphrey looked intrigued.

"Do you mean your mad bookworms? Please do." He grinned.

"I think that's a wonderful idea!" Amy enthused.

"I'll contact Mrs Booth." Betty offered. "She and I have been having a chat about relationships every day this week."

Nora blinked several times.

"I can call Miss Raven and Spencer for you if you like." Georgina proposed. "I need to speak with both of them about books they owe me money for."

"Nice." Humphrey smirked.

"Roger. Are you in?" Nora asked.

"It could stop my brain from rotting." He mused gloomily.

Cara clapped her hands, excited.

Gradually, everyone logged off and the first Bookshop Zoom Meeting was officially over.

Nora flopped back in her chair next to James, who put his arm around her shoulders and kissed her cheek.

"Thank you." He chuckled against her hair. "That was most enjoyable."

"Interesting word choice." Nora laughed and set about planning a Zoom Book Club for Lockdown at The Secondhand Bookworm!

5 THE GREAT TOILET ROLL ROBBERY

By the end of March, Castletown, and in fact, the County of Cole, had quickly lost its brief spell of peaceful tranquillity with the arrival of what Nora referred to as, *British Hell's Angels*; a stream throughout the day and night of speeding motorcyclists. The local police attempted to take the opportunity during Lockdown to crack down on speeders and noise-polluters, but the Captain of Castletown Police Station told Roy in an interview that although they were confiscating many motorbikes and scramblers, most of the bikers didn't even have licenses, were drunk, failed to turn up in court for their charges, and simply acquired other bikes and continued making the whole of Castletown and Cole and its areas sound like Monte Carlo.

Alongside the bikers polluting the soundwaves, the residents of Castletown started to pollute the air with bonfires galore. From her guest bedroom window, Nora watched plumes of smoke rising up in various places as though the locals were sending one another smoke signals to communicate. The air was laced with pungent scents of burning plastics and paper. People were also having frantic clear outs of their garages and lofts and because the charity shops were closed they were leaving odd items outside their houses, from bookcases and sofas to small boxes of books and items of clothing, with giant handmade signs that read 'FREE'. Nora was quite glad when the rainy weather arrived on the first day of April.

A new social movement called *Clap for Our Carers*, also known as *Clap for Carers*, *Clap for the NHS* or *Clap for Key Workers*, popped up around the country. Every Thursday evening at 8pm, people were invited to come out of their houses or lean out of their windows and clap, or bang pots and pans, to show their appreciation to the NHS who were saving lives and helping many people during the *Polar-Bear 9* pandemic.

On the first Thursday of April, James and Nora climbed to the top of the Keep and listened to the bizarre sounds of clapping and tin being pummelled which echoed up from the town.

"I think it's a great idea." Nora said and '*ooooohed*' when someone let off a firework.

James agreed and took a sip of Nora's latest Quarantini, *The SOS*.

"Perhaps we should film us clapping and banging some pots for a Livestream video next week." Nora proposed.

"I'm sure it will be of interest." James was bemused. It seemed like people were keen to devour watching anything and everything from their homes and even found the Duke of Cole and Nora interesting.

"I feel so sorry for the people in tiny flats or with noisy neighbours or horrible relatives." Nora frowned, pondering the town as the clapping and pot banging petered out, so it was just one enthusiastic resident bashing a tin dustbin lid.

"As do I." James nodded.

"I should feel guilty about having you all to myself in this magnificent castle and estate. With our twelve donkeys. But I don't." Nora grinned, contritely.

James kissed her cheek.

"Tell me that in another few months." He proposed.

Nora chuckled.

As it stood, Castletown, Cole and indeed the country, were still in a state of Lockdown, with three weeks having already passed.

People were expected to:

1)   Stay at home
2)   Only leave their homes to shop for essentials
3)   Only leave their homes to perform one form of exercise per day, if necessary (No three-legged races allowed)
4)   Travel to and from work *only* if necessary (many people were working from home)
5)   Not meet up with family members or friends

Nora and James had only seen Jeeves and Crossword-Lady *in the flesh*, so to speak, at a distance, and to wave to the rare resident they met when visiting The Secondhand Bookworm.

Nora had taken to spending four hours in The Secondhand Bookworm every morning with James. Together they were mending books, polishing books, tidying shelves, pulling off tatty tomes, stock checking, counting the stock and having a general sort. James was midway through painting the winding stair banisters a brilliant white. He had also fixed several windows and patched up some of the dodgy-looking ceiling cracks.

Nora had to confess she thoroughly enjoyed basking in the books of The Secondhand Bookworm without any customers!

April's arrival had brought sunshine, rain and gentle breezes. The churches and places of worship throughout the United Kingdom had all closed in line with the British Government guidelines so Nora and James tuned in to Canon Gerry's Mass broadcast live on Castletown TV every Sunday morning. They were also enjoying following the Pope's livestream events which included a solemn blessing for the whole world given in the doorway of Saint Peter's basilica in Rome on a very rainy evening. It was quite spectacular and both Nora and the Duke felt spiritually bolstered afterwards.

At last, after a lot of difficulties and arranging, Nora's Zoom Book Club was organised and was set to start on the Wednesday evening of the second week of April with the same people attending as before but now with the addition of Georgina and Troy, Amy's flat mate (and suspected lover) Finn, Lucy and Lee, Nora's sister Heather and their brother Milton.

The members of the Zoom Book Club were:

Nora and James
Georgina and Troy
Humphrey
Amy and Finn
Cara and Seymour
Miss Raven
Spencer
Crossword-Lady
Roger
Nora's cousin Felix, who had worked at The Secondhand Bookworm but who now ran a charity bookshop in Seatown
Lucy and Lee
Betty and Danny

Heather and Milton (who still lived in their parents' house)

Nora was going to host the meeting so had scheduled it on Zoom and sent around the invites. Everyone would log in at the set time and date.

"I do hope everyone's managed to get hold of copies of the book and finish them in time." Nora told James one evening as she snuggled up on the sofa beside him in his library to continue reading her copy aloud for the both of them.

"The Man in the Iron Mask is easy to come by." James nodded, passing Nora her glass of Quarantini, another *'The SOS'*. "And you and Cara spent the past three weeks organising a system."

"Yes, that was actually quite tricky. But at least Amazon is now doing deliveries. Although, that Amazon lorry overturned between Castletown and Seatown last week and Felix is convinced that his copy was one of the packages to roll out and get squashed."

James choked on a laugh.

It had been Cara who had chosen the first book for their Zoom Book Club to read because it had the word 'Mask' in the title. It was now a common look among the population, who sported simple blue surgical masks if they ventured out of their house, or flowery, comical and sometimes scary masks. Cara had also thought it would be good for them all to read a classic.

Nora had managed to retrieve three copies from the new Wordsworth Classic Paperback section in The Secondhand Bookworm and had posted one copy to Heather and Milton, left another copy inside a blue The Secondhand Bookworm bag on Spencer's grand doorstep and the last one with Jeeves for Crossword-Lady. James, of course, had a beautifully bound rare edition in his library so they were using that.

Cara had snagged three copies from the Seatown branch of The Secondhand Bookworm and posted one to Miss Raven, one to Amy and kept one for herself and Seymour.

Georgina already had a copy of her own, so Felix ordered one from Amazon because he wasn't allowed to open his charity shop and see if he had a copy. He didn't think he did, anyway. Roger likewise ordered a copy (there was a two week delivery delay hence the long-time setting up the Zoom Book Club meeting), Humphrey was listening to the audio version as he lifted weights and ran on his treadmill; Lucy and Lee had ordered their own, as had Betty and Danny.

For some reason, Betty's copy was coming from China, so there were ten days until the Zoom Book Club. Nora liked that she had plenty of time to read the old fashioned tome, so turned the page and set about doing so in the company of the Duke, holding her quarantini.

Despite the heavy rain the following morning, pattering the windows of Nora's guest chamber, the sound of racing motorbikes could be heard in the far distance, like annoying angry bees.

"Grr." Nora grumbled, throwing off her bedspread.

It was a boring Tuesday and by now everyone was getting used to a repetitive routine. Nora showered, dressed, stripped her bed and added her washing to James' down in the laundry room. Once the machines were on, she found him in the kitchen speaking with a colleague from one of the overseas charities the Duke of Cole patronised.

Quietly, Nora organised breakfast, noting that James hair was getting quite long and that he hadn't shaved.

"We're all becoming caveman and cavewomen." She mused with a small smile as she cracked eggs into a bowl.

As she grilled toast and fried bacon, Nora read her emails on her iPhone.

One was from Georgina. It said:

Morning Nora! I shall be organising a Zoom bookshop meeting for next week so we can all catch up. I have some revisions to the work force to share.
Georgina xxx

Nora thought that sounded a little ominous.

There was an email from Humphrey, too. It read:

Do this with James! I'm sending them around to the bookshop people. It's an emoji book quiz from my old colleagues in London. You have to name twenty four book titles based on a series of emojis. Some of the emoji sequences 'spell out' the words in the title but others serve as cryptic clues. The books represent a range of genres so you need to be a book buff to score full marks but I'm betting you'll get them all, Nora! No cheating!
Enjoy xxx

Nora stared with delight at the colourful emojis.

The customary email from Crossword-Lady was there, so Nora sent back the answer as a text arrived from Milton complaining that all copies of Animal Crossing, a game for the Nintendo Switch, had sold out. He had ordered a turquoise *Nintendo Switch Lite* console for Nora to be delivered to the castle with the game once it was available again (he had convinced their mother to buy them all one each and she had agreed). Apparently you built up a virtual desert island with ten animal villagers and then you could visit one another's islands via the internet. Milton said he liked the idea that they could hang out in the virtual world together without any Lockdown Rules. Nora was amused.

There were also several cheerful texts from Cara, continuing several conversations they were having, which Nora replied to.

The kitchen table was covered in items such as bottles, bowls, whisks and containers. Nora had been making hand sanitiser to give to the townspeople and had now mastered the simple recipe. It contained:

1 part aloe vera gel or 1 part glycerine (she made two types)

2 part isopropyl alcohol (rubbing alcohol) with a concentration of 91%

Lavender essential oil for scent

Everything was whisked up and placed in little air tight containers. Nora had even managed to order flowery jam jar labels from Hobbycraft and was able to write the ingredients on the labels and stick them to each container. She had a stamp with the Duke of Cole's crest and some royal red ink so added this to the labels as a finishing touch.

The hand sanitisers were a great hit. Jeeves took them to the castle gates and Karl, a spindly local man who offered a service about the town in his brightly coloured Tuk-Tuk, picked them up and chugged about delivering them for free to people who needed them. Roy was interviewing Nora about it that night and she had to give a tour of her ingredients and methods.

Nora's laptop stood on the kitchen counter, so while her eggs and bacon cooked, she wiggled the mouse and the livestream of the donkeys down at the stables popped up, just as James finished his call. He stood up, stretched and joined her, leaning his elbows on the counter after kissing her good morning.

"Everything alright?" Nora asked.

"Kelly, the head of the global charity missions wants me to get a video out there making everyone aware of how people in underdeveloped countries are being affected by *Polar-Bear 9*. A woman named Asal just lost her husband to the virus and he was the sole provider to her family, leaving behind four children."

"That's terrible."

"The missions are really helping our global family who don't have clean water, food or access to the health care they need to fight the virus."

"I love how you call everyone our global family."

James smiled.

"They are."

"We can make a video later if you like."

"That would be great." The Duke nodded, pondering the donkeys with a concerned frown as he contemplated the global crisis and suffering.

Nora watched Jeeves and Crossword-Lady feeding the animals. Tapestry was so excited that he rolled onto his back and moved his legs as though he was riding a bike. Nora giggled.

"Don't you think Jeeves and Crossword-Lady are getting nice and friendly?" She asked James.

He winked.

"They make a nice couple."

Nora dished up breakfast which she and James carried into a grand parlour to eat. It was still early and they had just finished and were examining a bookcase when Paul called the Duke's iPhone.

"Good morning, Paul. Yes. Yes, she is. I'll pass you over." James said and handed the phone to Nora.

"Hello?" Nora greeted, curious.

"Nora! I called your mobile but there was no answer. I assumed you would be with His Grace."

"Oh I must have left it in the kitchen." Nora realised. "Is everything alright?"

"I've just done my early morning rounds of the shops down here and it appears that The Secondhand Bookworm was broken into."

Nora's eyes widened.

"What?!"

"The window pane in the door is smashed, the door is slightly ajar and I'm standing outside looking at the debris and the building."

"Didn't the alarm go off?" Nora blanched, hoping she hadn't forgotten to set it.

"One of the locals, a little lady who says she is your most popular and regular customer and a famous author…"

"Dora Magic?"

"That's the one. She told me she heard the alarm for a moment an hour and forty five minutes ago, while it was still dark."

"They broke in only an hour and three quarters ago?"

"Yes. She said she was on the toilet at the time and heard it for ten seconds. And she didn't think anything of it. She assumed you had come down to do some sorting earlier than usual and hadn't reached the alarm in time from the front door. Apparently you did that once before."

Nora shook her head at Dora's nosiness.

"She said she was then distracted with self-publishing her books, which she said she had been up all night doing, and then finally turned her attention to The Secondhand Bookworm and realised that you weren't there and it wasn't open. She then claims that she noticed three men carry out armfuls of toilet rolls." Paul relayed in great detail.

Nora blinked.

"Toilet rolls?"

James arched an eyebrow.

"Not books?" Nora asked.

"Apparently not, but we haven't been inside and I sent Miss Magic back to her flat. She was very keen to assist but I've called PC Plod down from the station and he'll be here shortly."

"PC Plod?" Nora was momentarily distracted.

Paul did a small snort.

"I know." He muttered and stifled a choking laugh. "From the Noddy books. Pfffffft hehehe."

"Well that's good to know." Nora said, her lips trembling slightly. "PC Plod is a forthright police officer who never lets Toyland's crooks, especially Sly and Gobbo, the two goblins, escape from the long arm of the law."

James gave Nora a blank look.

Paul snorted and sniggered down the telephone line before forcing himself to sober up.

Nora's face straightened too.

"We don't have a state-of-the-art alarm at The Secondhand Bookworm; one of the burglars must have known how to override it. I'll come straight down, now." She said.

"I'll wait here for you, Nora."

"Thank you, Paul. See you in a bit."

Nora rang off and she and James looked at one another. Nora's lips trembled slightly with more unexpected mirth.

"A toilet roll robbery at The Secondhand Bookworm." She said.

The Duke of Cole looked so baffled about it all that Nora found it most amusing.

"Don't worry. Mr Plod from Toyland is on the case though." She giggled and bent over laughing.

James decided the shock had made Nora finally crack.

While James fetched their coats and shoes, Nora telephoned Georgina to make her aware of the situation.

"Rats!" Georgina exclaimed. "Are you sure it's just toilet rolls?"

"According to a witness." Nora said dubiously. "James and I are heading down there now."

"I'm not surprised about the alarm. I've been meaning to upgrade it. Apparently they're ridiculously easy to override. Rats, rats, rats. Fluffy. Don't eat carpet." She rebuked her Forest cat.

"James can patch up the door and make it all secure again. We'll assess the damage and check the bookshelves and the safe. It must have been someone local, surely. They had to have known about the first floor toilet and our stash of toilet rolls." Nora mused, stepping into her shoes after James had positioned them before her feet.

"I was meaning to come over and pilfer them for myself, but the panicky-buying has calmed down due to toilet roll rationing so we haven't been short."

"Panicky-buying?" Nora giggled.

"Oh that's what I call it. Troy laughed at me the other day about that. I said to our milkman, so you're not short of the milk then after all this panicky-buying? Troy heard and almost fell over laughing."

Nora thought it was a highly amusing phrase, too.

"We'll let you know the situation in The Secondhand Bookworm when we've checked it out." Nora assured her.

"Thank you, Nora. I'll come over after you've finished there, with Troy and Humphrey. Humphrey can check out the alarm and hopefully reset it. He's good at that. Perhaps make some signs for the windows saying 'NO TOILET ROLLS ARE KEPT ON THESE PREMISES'." Georgina suggested seriously.

Nora thought that was hilarious.

Once Nora and James had their shoes on and had shrugged into their coats, they set off from the castle for The Secondhand Bookworm. The air was damp, the skies cloudy, and motorbikes could be heard in the distance, but it wasn't raining, so they walked through the grand estate and reached the gatehouse.

James had his own key so unlocked the heavy doors that led into Jeeves' house and through a short corridor to the side door leading onto the street at the top of the hill beside the private castle gates.

The town was deserted.

"This is so strange." Nora said, gazing around as she and James slipped on their face masks. "Ooooh! Look!"

Rainbows had been freshly chalked over the drying pavements and pathways along with slogans thanking the NHS. The rainbow had been chosen by a nurse who wanted to create "a sign of hope" for patients and staff in hospitals across the country during the *Polar-Bear 9* pandemic and it had transformed Castletown into an array of striking colours. Although at first it looked as though Castletown was at the height of a Pride Festival, the NHS support messages and posters claimed the rainbow slogan as its own for the current crisis, many of which had been painted or drawn by children.

Nora also noticed that several windows had teddy bears, stuffed toys or works of art in them for children to count, spot and enjoy as a fun and safe activity while walking around their neighbourhood with parents for exercise.

Two enormous teddies, standing at six feet tall, had been placed in someone's front garden. Apparently the resident changed their position every day to show them watering the flowers, or cooking on a barbeque, or cleaning the car, for the townspeople's amusements. James thought it was fantastic.

"Morning, Nora!" Albert stood on the doorstep leading to his Print Shop opposite Nora's flat. He lived above his shop and currently sported a bright blue mask.

"Hello, Albert! How are you?"

"Ah, safe and bored." Albert nodded a greeting to James. "Everything okay at the castle? We've been tuning in to the livestreams."

"Yes, we're fine up there." Nora assured him.

"Popping down to The Secondhand Bookworm for the morning?" He asked, nosily.

Nora wondered if he was working for Phil, a local who doubled as a postman and a waiter at the Duke's Pie, a rambling but popular restaurant at the top of the hill. Phil had reimagined himself as a notorious gossip and even had his own blog and newsletter and currently his own livestream gossip videos.

"Yes, bye Albert." Nora waved evasively and she and James continued on.

Harry and Corrine were suddenly jogging towards them, wearing masks.

"Hiiiiiii!" Harry greeted, flexing his muscles.

"Hello, Harry. Hello Corrine." Nora smiled politely.

Corrine's eyes narrowed. Nora supposed she was snarling jealously at her behind her mask. It was no secret to her that Harry was obsessed with Nora.

"Are you coming down to join in the merriment tonight?"

"What?" Nora asked, staring at Harry who jogged on the spot in front of them.

"Every evening we've all been serenading one another from our windows." He explained in a muffled voice behind his mask. "Tommy from the antique shop has been playing a banjo and singing, I've been playing my conch shell down Market Street, and a group of old people from the care home have been dancing the conga through all the streets wearing masks with animal mouth designs. Apparently they're selling them on their Etsy shop after hand making them up at the home."

Nora laughed.

"How delightful! I'll hunt them out online and buy some."

Harry dropped to do some push-ups. James stared.

"So, if you're not busy, you can come and join in Nora, if you like?" Harry said.

"Nope. I'm busy." Nora assured him, giving Corrine an apologetic look.

She hissed.

"Okay then, nice to see you, keep safe, bye Harry. Bye Corrine." Nora concluded hastily, took hold of James' hand and hurried them away as Harry leapt up and offered Nora one last look at his leg muscles.

James was laughing.

"Oh I love this town." He decided.

Paul was standing outside The Secondhand Bookworm waiting for them. The square was empty with all shops closed in the immediate vicinity. A ball of tumbleweed rolled past. Nora did a double take but had to turn away as she met Paul at a safe distance just as PC Plod arrived.

PC Plod was a large, hulking policeman with a round face and a bushy beard.

"Oh dear." Nora grimaced from behind her mask as she took in the smashed glass on the pavement and the opened door. "How odd."

"What's odd?" Paul asked from behind his mask.

"Look." Nora pointed at the glass. "Correct me if I'm mistaken, PC Plod, but doesn't it look as though the glass has been smashed from the inside out, PC Plod?"

James nudged Nora's arm, knowing she just wanted to keep saying PC Plod's name.

"Indeed, indeed, indeed." PC Plod mused, rubbing the bits of beard poking out from his mask. "Hmm. How curious."

The sound of pattering feet approached them from behind.

Nora turned to see Dora Magic running towards her in a flurry of hair and fabric, sporting a pink, flowery face mask.

"That's far enough, madam!" PC Plod said, holding up his hand.

Dora Magic skidded to a stop a few meters from them all.

"Hello, Nora. How wonderful you look today, you are appreciated, you are wonderful…" Dora began to gush.

"Hello, Dora!" Nora interrupted quickly. "Did you see what happened here?"

"As a matter of fact I just…er…remembered, yes, remembered…that's it, I just *remembered* some additional details of my eye-witness account to this dastardly robbery of The Secondhand Bookworm." She announced, loudly.

James, Paul, PC Plod and Nora all stared at her.

"I recall now, that the three young men were wearing hoodies and on the back were the words 'Seatown University'!" Dora exclaimed, breathlessly.

For a long moment, everyone was silent.

"Oh dear." Nora said, with dawning realisation. "Ah. Now, unfortunately, this is making sense."

"Please enlighten us, Miss Jolly." PC Plod said, curious.

"I think it's an inside job." Nora replied.

James looked interested.

"Ahem." Nora cleared her throat and turned to enter The Secondhand Bookworm, her feet crunching on broken glass, which was, as she suspected, sparse on the mat and flagstones. It only took Nora a few moments to run about and investigate.

She felt like Enola Holmes as her investigations led her to conclude that the alarm had been stopped with the code. It had simply gone off because the code hadn't been entered in time and that was why Dora had only heard it briefly. She also saw that the loo door was not broken or forced and that the bunch of bookshop internal door keys with the loo door key included was now hanging on a different hook than usual. Briefly she concluded that nothing else but the loo rolls had been taken.

The rest of The Secondhand Bookworm was as Nora and James had left it, although there were three different right handprints in James' tacky white paint on the ground floor stair banisters. The robbers must have entered with a shop key and then smashed the window on the way out to pretend that it was someone *without* a key to throw the police off their scent. Unfortunately for them, the glass being on the pavement outside rather than inside showed clearly their plot.

Back in the front room, Nora addressed Paul, James and PC Plod. Dora was peering in through the bay window, watching.

"I think I know who could have orchestrated this." She announced.

"Fleur and Peaches?" James asked, having guessed, too.

Nora nodded.

"Yes, Fleur and Peaches."

"Who are Fleur and Peaches?" Paul asked from the doorway.

"They worked here on Saturdays. Georgina upset them both a couple of weeks ago by announcing that she wouldn't be able to pay them any wages over Lockdown. It was a bit of a situation. She let Peaches go and afterwards Fleur sent through her resignation to Georgina. They both live in Seatown in a flat with six college boys. Both of them still have shop keys. It's the college hoodies that makes me think they had something to do with it. Either that, or their flatmates swiped their keys, but the fact that the loo door key was used makes me suspect that one of the girls, or both of them, gave their flatmates instructions."

"Well, that makes sense." Paul agreed.

"The robbers didn't take any books because Fleur and Peaches are too nice to pilfer Georgina's books stock. I don't expect they had any use for them." Nora mused. "They just came for the loo rolls. I don't want to be a meanie and point fingers, but I think it would be worth checking them and their flatmates out as number one suspects."

PC Plod was already on the case. After asking Nora for the college students' address, he turned and picked up his phone to start his own investigation and Nora heard him telling his colleagues to organise a squad car for a trip to Seatown.

Meanwhile, Nora telephoned Georgina to let her know.

"That does sound like the most likely explanation. Rats! How ungrateful. What a betrayal. I shall want to know the reason behind their audacity in sending three of their flatmates to rob me of toilet rolls!" Georgina moaned.

"Well, PC Plod is heading over there shortly to investigate. If it is confirmed it was Fleur and Peaches and their flatmates then he will find out why."

"I know why. They were annoyed that I refused to pay them during the Lockdown." Georgina grumbled bitterly.

"They didn't take any books, which is why I thought of them as well as the Seatown college hoodies clue. They always showed such a love and respect for the books and the bookselling business whenever I worked with either of them. So we shall see. Meanwhile, James and I will have a clean-up and check for certain that nothing else was taken."

"Thank you, Nora. Please give PC Plod my direct number. I'd like to hear first-hand the outcome."

"Okay." Nora agreed.

After giving PC Plod Georgina's mobile number, the policeman left with Paul. Dora Magic returned to her flat too, spouting affirmations to Nora and waving until she became a distant form.

James and Nora looked at one another, biting back smiles, and set to work.

It took Nora and James a good couple of hours to repair the door, repaint the staircase banisters, have a careful sweep up outside, and inside, and check the stock. Georgina called with confirmation that The Great Toilet Roll Robbery had indeed been orchestrated by Fleur and Peaches.

"But I feel sorry for the foolish girls and their flatmates and I won't be pressing charges." Georgina declared.

"Oh. That's er…nice of you." Nora replied, surprised.

"Well, apparently all eight of them are living just on baked beans and couldn't afford toilet paper so have been using old college text books to wipe their bottoms during Lockdown."

"Oh dear!" Nora snorted, grimacing with compassion.

"Hmm. Both girls apologised. I told them to keep the loo rolls but made it clear I was changing the locks and alarm code so their keys won't work anymore should they decide to start wiping their bottoms using the stock of The Secondhand Bookworm. I'll send Humphrey to change everything this afternoon. Then I'll post out copies of the new keys to you all."

Once Nora and Georgina had ended their call, Nora told James.

"I'll send a large hamper over for them." He decided.

Nora smiled.

"We probably shouldn't be rewarding them for breaking in to The Secondhand Bookworm and stealing." She chuckled. "But I'll add six bottles of hand sanitiser, too."

Once everything was back up to scratch at The Secondhand Bookworm, ready for Humphrey, Nora locked up and she and James turned to set off up the hill back to the castle.

A human train of old people sporting bright animal masks was heading towards them, singing loudly, throwing out their bent or spindly old legs, while holding onto one another.

"*Do-do-do. Come on and do the conga. Do-do-do. It's conga night for sure.*" They sang.

Nora filmed them with her iPhone, laughing and nodding with approval until they had passed them by.

"I shall have to order some masks when we get back." Nora giggled, watching them turn the corner at the post office.

"I'd like the one that looks like a dog's nose and mouth." James said.

Nora grinned.

Back up at the castle, James spoke to Paul who told him there was a fake news report going around that James the Duke of Cole had contracted the Arctic virus. So after dinner, Nora linked their live feed to Castletown TV where Roy asked James in a live interview if this was true.

James assured everyone watching that he had done a swab test a couple of days ago at the request of his official royal office and it had come back negative and that he was remaining in Lockdown at the castle, self-isolating with Nora, until it was safe out in the world once more. He encouraged everyone to remain patient and to continue isolating too.

Nora then hosted a video about making your own hand sanitiser.

That evening, Nora and James sat in the library working out Humphrey's book emoji quiz. The first one was a bell emoji with a red line through it followed by three sheep.

"The Silence of the Lambs." Nora decided.

"Of Mice and Men." James pointed to number two which had a mouse emoji, a plus sign and then a man emoji.

Some of them were a little tricky but most of them were easy, concluding with The Lord of the Rings. Nora sent their answers through to Humphrey and settled back with their yet unnamed Quarantinis.

A video of Milton doing football tricks on TikTok came up on Nora's iPhone.

"Hmm. I think we'll call this drink *The April Fools Quarantini*." Nora decided, taking a sip while watching her brother dribbling a toilet roll down the hall of her old family house with great skill. "All of my family seem to be April fools."

James snorted on a laugh and took a sip of the Quarantini.

"April Fools it is." He grinned and they touched the rims of the glasses in a toast and settled down after an eventful day of Lockdown at The Secondhand Bookworm and the Duke of Cole's castle.

6 A BOOK CLUB IN LOCKDOWN

Nora's hand sanitiser was in great demand so she quickly established a routine with Karl, who picked up four boxfuls from Jeeves at the castle gates every three days and set off delivering them about Castletown in his yellow Tuk-Tuk. Jeeves kept Nora's enterprise in good supply by bringing boxes of freshly ordered rubbing alcohol, aloe vera and lavender oil for Nora each day.

The kitchen smelt perpetually lovely. Nora and James seemed to spend most of their time in the large room, concocting potions and drinks, trying out new food recipes, making videos and reading books while filling themselves up with teas, cupcakes and Quarantinis. Of course, there were regular excursions to the stables where the donkeys were thriving under the care of Mrs Booth and Jeeves, and weekday mornings spent working in The Secondhand Bookworm together. The shop was becoming so organised, catalogued, neat and tidy that it was soon almost unrecognisable!

It seemed as though Humphrey and the Duke of Cole were in competition as to who would look like the most convincing vagrant. Like James, Humphrey had not shaved at all and they now both sported beards, moustaches and tousled dark hair, the latter of which touched the collars of their shirts. Georgina thought it was horrible but Nora quite liked it and decided that kissing a bearded James goodnight was like sipping a glass of bubbly champagne.

"So when you kiss me without a beard it's like a glass of champagne without bubbles?" James chuckled, pressing his lips to hers

"Precisely." Nora nodded.

They did a livestream video about beards and moustaches with call in comments and questions and a vote as to whether or not the Duke of Cole should keep his after the month of April. It was decided that the Duke of Cole was more popular as a royal without facial hair, and that Nora would trim the Duke's hair and give him a Turkish shave to raise money for townspeople in need at the end of April, so, meanwhile, Nora made the most of his bubbly champagne face.

Because of Lockdown, people remained confined to their houses with small trips outside for exercise. Nora and James took up walking around the Duke's estate every couple of days, visiting and filming the Tamworth pigs, wild ponies, fallow deer (all being cared for by Spike, the Duke's head gamekeeper), the lakes, forest trails and rewilding fields, but spent most of their time indoors.

James taught Nora how to play poker. They also dug out old board games from their childhoods such as Connect Four, Guess Who and Ludo, and amused themselves (and their livestream viewers) with Dress-Up evenings. This included wearing the vintage and antique clothes that were displayed in glass cases about the public castle rooms, to partake in Quarantinis and discuss the history of what they sported.

Nora's favourite was an 18th century wedding dress worn by one of the Duke of Cole's ancestors. It had puffed silk trimmings, brocade and lace and dated back to 1745 and, although it smelt of moth balls, Nora felt like a princess as she carefully modelled it. James had an intense look in his eyes behind the iPhone camera as he observed her, so the next day Nora thought it best to model a suit of armour in case he got it into his head to drop down on one knee during their following livestream (not that she would have minded!).

The evening of *The Secondhand Bookworm Zoom Book Club* finally arrived. After dinner, Nora took her laptop into the main library and settled down with James and their copy of The Man in the Iron Mask, waiting for the start time of the Book Club.

"I think we should have a separate Zoom Book Club to share the novels of Dora Magic if we remain in Lockdown for the unforeseeable future," Nora mused with a chuckle as she finished the last page of 'The Vampire and the Caterpillar Farmer'.

James choked on his *The Lockdown* Quarantini.

"Could you imagine that?" He chuckled, shaking his head.

"It would be extremely entertaining," Nora decided, closing the book and keen to start volume three which was called 'The Vampire who ate the Nazi invaders'.

James gave her an amused look.

Cara was the first person to 'arrive' for the Zoom book club. She popped up in her box grinning, with her bulldog Arthur on her lap.

"HELLO!"

Nora yelped as Cara's loud voice filled their corner of the large room and quickly lowered the volume.

"Hi, Cara." Nora greeted. "Hello, Arthur."

James saluted with his quarantini. Arthur gave a pig-like snort.

"Are we the first to arrive?" Cara asked as Seymour rolled into view on a wheeled computer chair, stopping beside her.

"Yes, you are." Nora nodded.

"Evening." Seymour greeted, just as another box appeared, revealing Humphrey.

"Hi, Humphrey." Cara and Nora chorused.

Seymour leaned into his screen for a closer look at Humphrey's new look and his face filled his and Cara's box.

"How's the weight lifting going?" Cara asked Humphrey from behind her husband.

Humphrey rolled up his left sleeve and flexed his bicep which bulged firmly.

"Oh!" Nora blinked.

"You look like a very fit Jon Snow." Seymour decided, leaning back.

"I do, don't I." Humphrey bragged and looked smug. "I hear Nora's cutting your hair and giving you a shave at the end of April, Your Grace." He said to James.

"She is." The Duke sighed regretfully, rubbing his beard.

"You're not going to pretend to accidently cut his throat with fake spurting blood are you?" Seymour asked, keenly.

"Ewwww! Seymour!" Cara and Nora rebuked.

"What? The Jolly's are really into the April Fool's Tradition and for us it stretches through the whole month."

Humphrey looked interested and was about to comment when two more screens logged on. Betty and Danny filled one, sitting neatly together in matching jumpers with several bottles of wine on their desk; Felix filled the other.

"Oh golly!" Felix remarked when he noticed James and Humphrey and their matching tousled long hair and beards.

"Welcome to 10,000 B.C." Nora jokcd.

Felix snorted with laughter and leaned forward sniggering and guffawing so his curly hair bobbed about at the bottom of his screen. Cara giggled.

"Are you calling us cavemen?" James smirked and nudged Nora's arm.

"Good evening everyone." Betty greeted, eyeing Humphrey lustfully.

"Hello, Betty. Hello, Danny."

"Evening all!" Danny replied cheerfully, pouring wine into two glasses.

"Uh-oh." Cara grinned and gave Nora a look about the prepared brewery.

Lucy and Lee arrived next, keen to get started.

"Hi! How are you all?" Lucy wanted to know.

As everyone replied and a conversation began about how much weight everyone was putting on during Lockdown, Amy arrived with Finn.

"Hallo!" Amy greeted cheerfully.

"Hi, Amy! Hi, Finn." Nora welcomed.

Finn became a source of interest and happily chatted about himself and the latest painting he was working on until a box appeared and revealed Miss Raven.

"Is this working?" She asked, blue eyes flashing impatiently.

"Loud and clear." Nora assured her with a smile. "Glad you could join us, Miss Raven."

"Hmm." Miss Raven replied, dubiously. "You call this a story? I was most confused." She waved her copy of The Man in the Iron Mask up to her webcam.

"Oh dear, I'm so sorry to hear that," Nora regretted.

"Did you persevere though?" Cara asked, hopefully.

"Yes." Miss Raven scowled, begrudgingly. "But I had to read my Chalet School books in between. I hope we can read children's books in future. I'm persevering with being out of my comfort zone and joining this club so I have a break from just listening to mother wheeze and fart all day long, but it is going over my head."

Felix leaned forward sniggering loudly the same time Cara and Amy laughed but then cleared their throats and disappeared behind their copies of The Man in the Iron Mask when Miss Raven's blue eyes shot daggers, not amused.

Fortunately, Spencer logged on, sitting at a dark oak desk in what Nora realised was his Gothic Tower reading room.

"Blessed Be." Spencer greeted, sitting with his hands folded neatly on what looked like a book of spells before him, his white hair glowing in the candlelight, a fire burning behind him in a black hearth and a large painting of Aleister Crowley staring at them all demonically from over Spencer's shoulder.

Nora gawped.

"Ooer." Felix blinked, sobering in an instant.

"Hello, Spencer." Nora greeted politely.

"Wow. Are you in a Coven?" Humphrey asked, leaning forward.

"This is my reading room." Spencer smiled, sinisterly. He then did a quick wave of his hand and a puff of blue smoke crackled and fizzed into existence, hiding the room and Spencer in his Zoom box, before dispersing. Spencer was revealed as before, watching them sinisterly through his round, piercing blue eyes.

Miss Raven gasped.

"Oooh, spooky!" Cara clapped, chuckling.

"Do I need the Holy Water?" James whispered with a small smile.

"Perhaps." Nora mused, pleased when another box appeared and Roger arrived.

"Good evening." He greeted flatly. "Good evening, Your Grace."

"Hello, Roger." Everyone chorused.

Spencer waved his hand once more and produced another cloud of fizzing blue smoke. Apparently he was practising magic tricks during Lockdown.

Mrs Booth arrived next.

"Hello all. I'm so sorry I couldn't send you all these wonderful book club snacks in time for our meeting this evening. Look. I baked twenty 'sausage and sweet potato spiced biscuits' using left over sausages, butter, flour, sweet potato, milk, salt, pepper, garam masala and cinnamon with currents and carrots. They're eaten usually at breakfast, but I thought the fat and vitamins would do us all good during the Lockdown. I wasn't able to get them to you all though."

"What a shame." Roger said sarcastically.

Nora shuddered with revulsion.

"You can leave mine on my doorstep." Spencer suggested, seriously.

Everyone was genuinely baffled.

Luckily, Heather and Milton logged on and stopped the disgusting conversation followed by Georgina and Troy, the last members of the Zoom Book Club.

"Hi!" Heather waved enthusiastically.

"Hello, all!" Georgina greeted, followed by the pop of a cork being pulled by Troy from a champagne bottle.

Humphrey jumped and looked over his shoulder. He had heard it in real life because Georgina and Troy were in the kitchen while Humphrey was across the hall in the lounge.

"Oooh, what's the occasion?" Amy asked.

"What are you celebrating?" Lucy asked.

"Why the champagne?" Cara asked.

"Are congratulations in order?" Betty asked, winking lecherously.

Troy looked blank as he poured the bubbly liquid into the first flute.

"Not yet." Georgina smiled tightly and almost snatched the glass, giving Troy a dark look. "We fancied something different from our usual table wine."

"Their excuse is that they're drinking the contents of the wine cellar for the antioxidants." Humphrey smirked.

"It's true. We're keen to prevent damage to our blood vessels, reduce bad cholesterol and prevent blood clots. Thus lowering the risk of heart illnesses and strokes." Georgina agreed and took a long gulp.

Nora chuckled.

Humphrey rolled his eyes.

"We won't live forever. Will we lovie?" Georgina added, her eyes flashing hintingly.

"Just propose already." Roger muttered, picking up his newspaper.

Fortunately, hardly anyone heard him.

Crossword-Lady bit into one of her biscuits. Nora hoped she wasn't going to work her way through all twenty or else her stomach would turn.

Deciding she had best get the meeting started, she cleared her throat loudly and everyone in their boxes settled down, ready for the Zoom Book Club to finally begin. Nora thought it was quite comical to see thirteen boxes with eighteen people staring at her, as though they were framed photos. Until Roger sneezed loudly and sounded like an air horn.

"Well, I must say I'm glad this is a virtual Book Club!" Miss Raven said, curling up her nose in disgust and edging backwards so that she wobbled precariously on her stool.

"Wipe your webcam, Roger." Georgina suggested with a grimace.

Everyone cringed and 'ugh-ed' when a brown handkerchief filled up Roger's box for a whole minute as the small lens was cleared of snot. Roger then blew his nose like a fog horn and settled down.

"Ahem. Now we're all here and ready, may I welcome you all to our first Zoom Book Club!" Nora smiled warmly.

Amy 'whooped', Finn cheered, Cara clapped (sending a startled Arthur scrambling off her lap), Felix howled with laughter, Heather leaned forward giggling, Lucy and Lee looked highly amused, Roger disappeared behind his newspaper with a loud angry rustle and Spencer stood up so his groin suddenly filled his screen. When everyone noticed, they all instantly sobered. Spencer was wearing very tight black, sparkly trousers.

"Er…" Nora glanced at James who was watching it all with intense fascination and amusement.

"Spencer?" Cara called, her lips twitching with mirth. He sat back down again.

"Just throwing a spider out the window." He revealed.

"Lovely." Nora grimaced and lifted her book. "Ahem. As I was saying, welcome to our first online Zoom Book Club. I hope everyone is well and safe and that we all managed to read our book this week, The Man in the Iron Mask."

"I didn't manage to finish it." Crossword-Lady stepped in.

Everyone groaned as Mrs Booth commandeered the meeting as usual.

"Oh, that's a shame." Nora attempted to regain control but Crossword-Lady forged ahead.

"I got bored after a few pages so instead I read 'The Grinny Granny Donkey'. It was delightful." A bright purple children's book emerged and filled Mrs Booth's screen, showing a drawing of a donkey wearing spectacles hugging a smaller donkey on the cover. "Listen to the beginning. It starts: *There was a sweet donkey who lived on the heath, she was so funny with her false teeth. HEEEEE HAAAAAWWW!!! But her teeth kept falling out*!"

Nora edged back at the very loud, very realistic impression of a donkey's hee-haw, while Felix almost died from laughter, Roger looked extremely unimpressed, Georgina, Troy, Danny, Finn and Miss Raven looked comically amazed and Amy doubled over.

Humphrey grinned.

"I think we should read that one next week." He suggested.

Nora gave him a look, while Heather and Milton's sniggering and snorting came from their box.

Before Mrs Booth could continue, Nora interrupted firmly.

"Well, I'm sure that was a delightful read." She said, glancing at Lucy and Lee in their box as they recovered from their own shock and laughter.

"Give me a break!" Roger muttered rudely from behind his newspaper.

"BUT we are gathered to discuss The Man in the iron Mask." Nora reminded Mrs Booth and gave Roger a glare. He couldn't see her because he was reading the news.

Mrs Booth put her donkey book aside.

"I look forward to learning all about it." She smiled and leaned forward, expectantly.

"Okay, then." Nora said and popped on her reading glasses.

Georgina smiled at Nora, amused and impressed at her perseverance. She hadn't been at The Secondhand Bookworm Book Club over the past Christmas and New Year so this behaviour was all new to her, but she wasn't surprised.

"The Man in the Iron Mask was chosen as our first book to read and discuss together simply because it was a classic and it had the word 'mask' in its title." Nora explained.

"Clever." Roger said, sarcastically again.

He had lowered his newspaper and was sitting neatly with a bored expression.

Betty clicked her tongue disapprovingly, slipping on her spectacles.

"We thought it would be light-hearted due to the mask wearing in the Lockdown." Cara defended with a roll of her eyes at Roger.

"I thought it was a lovely idea, Cara." Betty praised and saluted with a very full glass of red wine, which sloshed over the rim and covered her book. "Oh, fish! Fish, fish…"

Betty and Danny both spent a few minutes mopping up the wine before sitting down once more.

"The Man in the Iron Mask is the final episode in a cycle of novels featuring the author's celebrated foursome of D'Artagnan, Athos, Porthos and Aramis, who first appeared in the novel The Three Musketeers." Nora explained cheerfully.

"Never read them." Danny admitted.

"Oh. Did you find this one difficult to read then?" Nora asked.

"We never finished it, Nora, so sorry, but that's us all over." Betty apologised.

"I didn't finish it, either." Miss Raven said.

Nora noticed she was now sucking milkshake up from a large glass through a swirly red straw.

"Did anyone else find it difficult and not finish it?" Nora asked.

Finn and Amy put their hands up.

"I found it quite boring." Finn confessed with an apologetic grimace.

"I didn't get the story because I hadn't read the others." Amy confessed. "But they're on my bucket list."

"Well, The Man in the Iron Mask can be quite a challenge." Nora agreed. "It's the last novel in the series, and set thirty-five years on. Well, in the story, the Musketeers' friendship is strained as they end up on different sides in a power struggle that could change the face of the French monarchy forever. I thought the best book cover was the Wordsworth paperback with what looks like a mad selfie by the man in the iron mask barring his teeth."

Cara laughed and held hers up.

"It really is!" She agreed.

There was a murmur of concurrence and then a ten minute conversation followed in which The Secondhand Bookworm Zoom Book Club shared the covers of their books and voted on the best. Nora was right, The Wordsworth cover was the most popular, although Miss Raven complained that it gave her nightmares.

"The Man in the Iron Mask," Nora continued, "was actually a real person, called *L'Homme au Masque de Fer* in its original French."

"Oooh, sexy." Humphrey said.

He then cleared his throat and smiled awkwardly at James who smiled back.

"*Merci, Monsieur.*" Nora fluttered her eyelashes playfully at Humphrey and then continued.

"It's about an unidentified prisoner arrested in the year sixteen sixty-nine or sixteen seventy and then held in a number of French prisons which include the *Bastille* and the Fortress of *Pignerol*."

"*Pignerol* is modern *Pinerolo* in Italy." Cara added, helpfully.

"Ha. Pig." Felix said and sniggered.

"The prisoner was held in the custody of the same jailer, Bénigne Dauvergne de Saint-Mars, for a period of thirty four years." Nora continued.

Humphrey took a large gulp of his energy drink and fanned his face, obviously finding Nora's French quite endearing.

"The prisoner died on the nineteenth of November in the year seventeen hundred and three under the name *Marchioly* during the reign of King Louis XIV of France." Nora explained.

"Who reigned during the years sixteen hundred and forty-three to seventeen hundred and fifteen." Heather added.

"Yes, that's right." Nora nodded.

"Oh thank you, Heather. How clever you are." Betty praised.

"Thanks. I like French history so I enjoy these novels." Heather explained.

"Save the chit-chat for later." Roger frowned, although his eyes were twinkling.

Betty poked her tongue out at him.

"No one is known to have ever seen the face of the prisoner because it was always hidden behind a mask of black velvet cloth, so his real identity still remains a mystery to this day. Various theories have been explored in books and films."

"Such as the movie with Leonardo de Caprio." Cara said.

"Pwarrrrr!" Amy purred.

Nora laughed.

"My favourite will always be the one with Richard Chamberlain, Patrick McGoohan, Jenny Agutter and Ian Holm." Lucy shared.

"Me too!" Nora agreed, pleased.

James stared at Nora and blinked.

"Really?"

"We used to watch it when we were kids." Milton told the Duke. "It was made for TV."

"Nora made us watch it over and over." Heather grinned.

"It's based loosely on the third novel in the series, The *Vicomte de Bragelonne*." Nora explained. "Richard Chamberlain plays both King Louis XIV and Phillipe, his brother."

"I see." James chuckled.

"Although it's a made-for-TV film they used actual locations in France including the Château de Fontainebleau and Fouquet's actual chateau of Vaux-le-Vicomte for the final ball scene." Heather enthused.

"Oh Heather, you make it sound so romantic and educational, we'll have to watch it." Betty decided.

"Perhaps we should change this to a Zoom *Movie* and *History* Club." Georgina suggested, amused.

"I like that idea!" Cara nodded.

"No, no, no." Nora laughed. "We'll stick to books. But, hmmm. We could do an additional Movie club."

"Count me out." Miss Raven objected with flashing eyes. "And I'm within two minds about continuing this book club if the novels we're going to read are going to be dreary."

"In 1987 there was an episode in the cartoon *DuckTale*s called 'The Duck in the Iron Mask'." Humphrey chipped in, ignoring Miss Raven.

Nora paused and then burst out laughing. James found it funny too.

"I quite enjoyed *Dogtanian and the Three Muskehounds*." Lee chipped in.

"We used to watch that." Milton laughed.

Nora hastily continued.

"Well, the real Man in the Iron Mask has appeared in many works of fiction, most prominently in this one we chose for our first Zoom Book Club, which was published in the late 1840s by Alexandre Dumas. Here the famous prisoner is forced to wear an iron mask and is portrayed as Louis XIV's identical twin. Alexander Dumas also presented a review of the popular theories about the prisoner extant in his time in the chapter "*L'homme au masque de fer*" in the sixth volume of his non-fiction Crimes Célèbres. It appeared first in serial form between 1847 and 1850. So, there you have the history of the novel." She concluded.

Amy, Lucy and Betty clapped.

"So, shall we work our way around the boxes of our zoom screen from left to right, row by row and give our reviews?" Nora suggested.

The reviews began, some of them detailed, some of them simple.

"With treachery, tragedy and swashbuckling battles I found it a quality read." Spencer said, surprising everyone. "I know, I know: no warlocks or séances, but it had a *grimness* about it that I liked."

Nora curled her nose.

"I actually found it fast-paced and straight into the action so I loved it." Heather confessed.

"I thought it was a fitting conclusion to the epic saga of the musketeers." James decided.

"If you were lucky enough to have read the prequels." Roger grumbled.

"I have always found this novel to be a sad ending to a great series." Georgina mused. "I like to read it on occasion."

"You've already read it?" Miss Raven looked unimpressed.

"Erm…yes, it's a classic." Georgina smiled thinly.

"If I read it again I'd count how many horses died. Numerous times they were literally ridden to death in the story." Seymour ruminated.

"How ghastly!" Crossword-Lady lamented. "Were any donkeys killed?"

"No, I don't think so." Seymour pondered.

James and Nora exchanged small smiles.

"If you were expecting the novel to be like the Leonardo di Caprio movie then you'd be sorely disappointed." Amy sighed, sadly. "I simply couldn't picture any of the men as hunky."

Cara giggled.

Georgina gave a detailed and intelligent review, followed by Felix who seemed determined to outdo her. His was likewise detailed, thorough and full of insights and anecdotes so that it ended in a round of applause.

Georgina snarled jealously and Felix looked smug.

Milton, Lee, Lucy, Crossword-Lady, Miss Raven and Roger gave the novel negative reviews even though Georgina protested it was a classic and that was scandalous. Nora was last and confessed that she probably appreciated it more because she was able to read from an early edition, in a castle, with the Duke. Everyone wanted to feel jealous but they were all happy for her instead. Troy looked as though his positive, enthusiastic review was a fake because of Georgina sitting staring at him with folded arms.

Once everyone had given their reviews, those who wished to read passages they had chosen and then explained why they had chosen them so as to spark conversation. This took some time and Roger fell asleep. Nora was among those who enjoyed this segment and there were lots of fascinating insights and topics, with unusual conclusions drawn by Spencer, Crossword-Lady, Miss Raven and Lucy. Once this was done, the meeting concluded and then several members announced they probably wouldn't continue unless the books they read were interesting.

"The whole point of a book club is to go out of your comfort zone." Georgina pointed out, amazed.

"And read something that you wouldn't ordinarily read." Cara added enthusiastically.

"Bah. I'd rather spend the rest of my years doing something I like." Roger, who had finally woken up, decided. "So count me out unless it's a decent read."

"And I only want to read children's books!" Miss Raven announced shrilly.

"Any books that include donkeys?" Crossword-Lady asked mildly.

"What about something risqué?" Spencer suggested with gleaming eyes.

There were some strong words exchanged between several boxes, with Betty waving her fist at Roger, Miss Raven clicking her tongue, shaking her head and moaning, Spencer rummaging through various suspicious and unsavoury books on his tower bookcases, Betty drinking straight from one of her bottles of wine and Heather and Felix laughing.

"Shall we read something along an isolation theme again?" Seymour proposed.

"Oh yes, we must keep it in line with our Lockdown experience." Lucy agreed.

"Anyone can send me their proposals through for what to read next and I'll pick one." Nora decided.

"Who put you in charge?" Roger asked.

"Me." Nora retorted.

"And I'm second in command." Cara piped in.

"Just tell me what to read and I'll give it a shot." Spencer said cheerfully. "Until next time…" And he logged off in a flash of blue smoke and glitter.

Everyone was silent for a moment.

"I was going to suggest we organise a Zoom Movie Club, too." Nora frowned.

"Do you really want to watch online movies with him?" Humphrey asked.

Nora's lips twitched.

"Well, I'll send around an email with a proposal about having a Book Club followed on by a Zoom Film Club everyone." She announced.

"Wonderful, Nora." Betty enthused.

"How would that work, Nora?" Georgina asked.

"We'll choose a book to all read that has also been made into a film. We'll read the book and have another Zoom Book Club about it and then watch the film together as an online Movie Club, maybe a day or two later. I read that another bookshop has been doing that while in Lockdown. I happened to see that Amazon is sorting out something called a 'Watch Party' with their movies on Prime. Or there's Netflix, I saw that you can all log on together and watch the same film with the ability to chat and discuss it together. It will be fun and social."

"Yes, I am feeling very isolated." Roger confessed forlornly.

Cara proposed that they read and then watch a zombie book and movie because there were rumours going around that *Polar Bear 9* had turned the entire populations of villages in Russia and Tibet into zombies. Crossword Lady was aghast and worried it could cross into animals (it had originally been in Polar Bears, hence the name, but had mutated and was currently only affecting humans) so Cara spent ten minutes convincing her that the donkeys wouldn't turn into zombies.

In the end it was decided that if they were all still in Lockdown within the next few weeks then Nora would contact them all with the chosen book suggestion, probably zombie related (that got the most reactions so would be interesting) and they would organise the online gatherings.

"And with that, thank you all for participating tonight and keep safe." Nora concluded.

Everyone clapped.

"I shall be in touch with any bookshop updates." Georgina told the staff members.

"Thanks, great, bye all." Lucy said hastily and logged off quickly. Nora suspected it was out of fear of Georgina letting her go.

Gradually everyone said goodbye and logged off so that it was just Cara and Seymour, Milton and Heather, and Felix left online with Nora and James.

"I really did enjoy that, Nora." Cara grinned.

"I did, too." Nora agreed with a chuckle.

"It was as fascinating as always." James smiled.

"Are we really going to read a zombie book followed by a zombie movie?" Heather asked, hopefully.

"Erk. That sounds scary." Felix grimaced.

"It would be brilliant." Cara enthused.

"It's a little out of my usual reading or watching but it would certainly be different for everyone." Nora agreed, glancing at James.

"I'm happy to give a zombie novel and movie a go." The Duke smiled.

"Then zombies it is!" Cara cheered. "We'll have to come up with some choices."

"Send through any suggestions and we'll take a vote." Nora decided, beginning to tidy up around her laptop. "I'll have a rummage on the shelves of The Secondhand Bookworm here and see what I can find."

"I'll write a list." Felix mused. "I'm sure there are also lot of isolation themed films too, in case you decide to go for that theme."

"And plenty of apocalyptic films." Seymour added.

"And pandemic films." Milton assured them.

"Oh dear." Nora chuckled.

They said their goodbyes, arranged to keep in touch via social media, and soon Nora was closing down her laptop and flopping back into the sofa next to James. Marlow jumped up beside Nora. She tickled his ears affectionately.

"A round of Quarantinis?" James suggested, easing himself up.

"How about *The Zombie*? I invented that yesterday." Nora proposed.

James' lips twitched. He stood up, shaking his head.

"The Zombie it is." He grinned and set off for the bar leaving Nora already planning their next Zoom Book Club meeting.

7 HOW TO SURVIVE THE ZOMBIE APOCALYPSE

Easter was celebrated in Lockdown with church services live streamed over the internet throughout the United Kingdom. Nora and James tuned into the Vatican for Mass and special intercessory prayers for people throughout the world who had contracted *Polar-bear-9*. They then had their own Easter lunch with roast goose and all the trimmings, followed by Zoom conversations with members of James' family and some of his friends and then Nora's family and friends. At the end of April, Nora gave the Duke of Cole a shave and a haircut live on Castletown TV. The event drew thousands of viewers and was covered on mainstream media.

April soon passed into May and plans were being made for the nation to commemorate VE Day in Lockdown. Meanwhile, Crossword-Lady was still convinced people who had contracted the virus could become Zombies. She also kept a suspicious eye on the donkeys after sharing her theory with Jonathon who agreed that animals could become Zombies, too.

Plans for the second Zoom Book Club were underway and people expressed interest in a Zoom Movie Club, too. Everyone seemed keen except Miss Raven who sent Georgina a rude snail mail letter saying she certainly didn't want to read any more adult books and would stick to her fairy tales instead so was quitting the Zoom Book Club. Nora thought that was a shame and hoped she would change her mind and set about organising the next Zoom Book Club and a matching Zoom Movie Club, trying to keep a literary theme by contemplating movies that had been made from novels.

"I'm favouring the Zombie theme." Nora told James as they headed into town one Tuesday morning in the first week of May. "Mrs Booth seems obsessed with them. And I think those of us joining the Zoom Movie Club will enjoy that sort of thing, too. And Cara seems to have set her heart on *World War Z*."

"Was the *World War Z* movie originally a novel, then?" James asked, slipping on his animal face mask as they neared the shops at the bottom of the steep hill.

"Yes, it was written by Max Brooks and published in 2006. The original title of the novel is '*World War Z: An Oral History of the Zombie War*'." Nora explained.

"Sounds delightful." James grimaced.

Nora glanced at him and stifled a laugh at his grinning dog's mouth mask with accompanied furrowed brow.

"I have to say; you look like one of Spencer's hybrids in that mask, Your Grace." She laughed, rubbed anti-bacterial hand gel over her hands and stepped into the delicatessen.

James snorted and followed her inside.

The delicatessen was allowed to open for two mornings a week by appointment only with most customers having their food delivered to their homes, and with select people being allowed to collect their orders in time slots.

Georgina was hoping to organise some sort of book delivery service once *that* was allowed, so had been asking advice from the sellers who were able to open their premises in Castletown and Seatown.

Meanwhile, Georgina had told Nora not to bother going into the bookshop more than once a week because it was so sparkly and clean now that it was losing its smelly old book charm. Instead, Nora had to simply check on any answerphone messages and post out any books to customers who were supporting The Secondhand Bookworm by shopping over the phone during the Lockdown. Currently, there was nothing to post out because Georgina had dealt with a flurry of sales herself. She had had both phone lines redirected to her house on Monday, Wednesday, Friday and Saturday mornings. It was keeping her from going insane.

Nora and James were supporting the local businesses of Castletown by shopping from their websites, having deliveries sent to the castle from the butcher shop and the cake shop and collecting items from Alice when they popped down to check on The Secondhand Bookworm.

So, once James had finished mending and painting and Nora had dusted, polished, cleaned and straightened all 27,000 books on the shelves, they had organised to pop down every Tuesday morning to give the interior a check over, run the water and pick up their groceries from Alice in the shop opposite. Georgina was hoping that the government was going to start their furlough scheme soon so that she would survive paying her staff their wages with both premises still closed.

"Oh!" Nora suddenly found herself facing a wall of plastic screens fixed to the till areas of the shop once she was inside.

"Yes! Hi! This is now mandatory." Alice gestured cheerfully from behind the screen.

She was sporting an animal mask made by the people in the retirement home. It was a bunny mouth with large buck teeth.

"I'm glad to see them so quickly assembled." James said, examining them closely.

"Good morning, Your Grace." Alice dipped down in a curtsey with a knowing wink at Nora. "Yes, thank you for this. I hear it was your influence at the town council that organised them for all the shops."

"And paid for them." Nora added proudly. "And had his company fit them."

"Thank you, Your Grace!" Alice appreciated. "We all feel very safe behind them now and it has meant we can open for trade a little each week."

"That was the plan." James nodded, giving her a warm smile behind his mask.

Alice sighed dreamily at the Duke before clearing her throat and fanning her face with her hand, shooting Nora an apologetic look.

Nora grinned.

"Well, every shop allowed to open in Castletown now has them." Alice sang happily as she turned to fetch the boxes of groceries for Nora and James. "It's really helping out a lot of the businesses."

"I'm glad to hear it." James nodded, examining a box of very expensive Cuban cigars.

Nora gave him a curious look.

"For my brother." He winked.

"Wow." Nora examined them, too.

"It's a shame you can't open The Secondhand Bookworm for trading yet." Alice mused. "People are lost without it."

"I agree." Nora sighed. "But it really would be dangerous to have people squashing in there together, handling grubby old books which are a petri dish for bugs and bogies anyway. I'm sure we'll be able to open soon. Meanwhile, we're brainstorming ideas for delivery systems and phone orders."

"Sounds hopeful!" Alice nodded, pleased. "We're having arrows placed on the floors in here for when we can open generally, hopefully soon. It'll keep the flow of customers in one direction." She carried a box around the counter, placing it on the floor and returning to behind her new plastic screen. "On a related note, I hope you don't mind me asking, but have you downloaded the NHS app called 'Track and Trace'?"

Nora watched Alice hold up her phone.

"I heard of that." James mused.

"What does it do?" Nora asked.

"Apparently if you have the app and you come in contact with someone who has tested positive for *Polar-Bear 9* your phone will ping a warning."

"You will then have to isolate for ten days to two weeks to make sure you haven't contracted it." James added.

"I'm not sure if I'd rather not know." Nora grimaced.

"That was my thought, but then, being open and having people come into the shop made me think I'd like to be extra cautious."

"It sounds quite sensible." Nora agreed.

"Hmm. I've downloaded it but it only works of the person infected has downloaded it and registered as positive. And surely they won't be out and about until they're contagion-free! I'm not sure the idea will catch on."

"Most people are remaining indoors anyway." Nora reassured. "So it's unlikely an infected person will come along and ping you."

"We can but hope." Alice said.

James picked up their box of groceries, they bade Alice goodbye and set off so that Mr Rutler, a local man who bought architecture books from The Secondhand Bookworm, could head into the delicatessen to collect his groceries.

He was wearing a face mask that was a printed shark's mouth, wide open. Nora did a double take and clutched onto James' sleeve in fright, leaving Mr Rutler chortling, waving politely and entering the shop.

"At least the locals are providing some interest in face wear." James decided, leading the way to the kerb at the side of the road, opposite The Secondhand Bookworm.

"When will the barbers and hairdressers be allowed to open do you think?" Nora asked as her gaze drifted towards Johnny's barber shop on the corner across the road to the right of the bookshop.

"Hmm. It's too intimate a trade at the moment. Probably not for a while." James answered, leading the way across the deserted road.

"Shame. We all have mad hair." Nora pointed out. "There's only so much skill I have in cutting a Duke's mane."

James winked at her.

"I'd only allow *you* to." He admitted.

"I read that when the producers made *The Walking Dead* TV series, they put conditioner in the actors' hair to make it look greasy. It smelt lovely on set." Nora recalled, taking out her shop keys.

James was bemused.

One the bookshop door was unlocked and opened, Nora hurried across the room to punch the code in the alarm pad while James shut the door, turned and locked it only to be faced by a man in a mask that said '*Will only remove for beer*'. The man knocked.

James stepped back but kept the door between them. He took off his mask.

"We're closed through Lockdown." He pointed out.

The man gestured with both hands to the window.

"There's a hook in your window!" He said loudly behind his mask.

Nora joined James and assumed the man had said '*book*', not hook.

"You can telephone us and we can organise for it to be delivered to you." Nora called.

"EH?" The man's eyebrows shot up.

Nora took off her mask.

"YOU CAN TELEPHONE US AND WE CAN ORGANISE FOR IT TO BE DELIVERED FOR YOU!" Nora repeated, pointing at her mouth for him to understand her clearly. "THERE ARE BUSINESS CARDS IN THAT HOLDER THERE."

The man looked, spotted them and stamped a foot.

"I can't see why I can't pie it frown!" He hollered.

Nora and James looked at one another.

"Buy it now?" James translated.

"I think so." Nora said, trying not to laugh.

The man pressed himself against the glass. Nora yelped and both she and James edged back.

"I'll post a tenner through and you post the hook out ya letterbox?" He suggested.

Nora looked questioningly at James who shook his head.

"Bah!" The man rapped the glass with the balls of his fists and snatched a business card. "No wonder the Spindle is on the Lies!"

He stomped off, past the window, leaving Nora and James staring after him.

"Kindle is on the rise." Nora finally translated.

"Huh." James said and shook his head once more. "People don't like to stick to the rules."

Nora giggled. James was certainly a stickler for rules.

"It's a shame we couldn't have done that, though." She said. "Pass him the book through the letterbox."

"I won't risk your health just for a book." James reminded her.

"Hopefully Georgina will come up with some plans for resupplying the bookworms." Nora decided and turned back to face the front room.

"I'll measure up for the plexiglass to be fitted around the counter." James announced, taking a measuring tape from his pocket.

It had already been discussed with Georgina who was keen to have some installed in both shops with the hope that she would be allowed to open for trade as soon as possible.

"This will be wonderful." Nora gushed happily. "No more spittle and space invaders from bookworms when we open. I think we should keep it up permanently."

James huffed on a laugh at that and agreed. He picked up a pen from the broken mug that served as a pen pot and set about measuring, while Nora checked the answerphone messages. Georgina dealt with all phone calls redirected to her home telephone line but sometimes messages were left on the shop phones. This morning there were twelve! Nora sat down on the stool behind the counter and the more she listened to them the more her throat tightened, her eyes started to water and she closed her eyes, until finally she bent over double in gales of laughter.

James stared at her, surprised.

"Oh, oh dear. It's Felix's favourite customer, Mrs Tentpole." Nora finally revealed, wiping the tears of laughter from her eyes. "I wish he had taken her with him to his charity bookshop in Seatown."

"What has she been saying?" James laughed, writing down measurements on the shop message pad.

Nora restarted the recorded messages and pressed speaker so that they could both hear.

1)   'Hello? Hello? I know it's the bookshop. Why is no one answering? I'm looking for Enid Blyton books and I want to read them during this pesky Lockdown. Hello? Call me back in ten minutes.

2)   Hello? It's me again. Are you still in bed? I always thought you were a lazy young man. I asked you to phone me back. This is getting serious. Call me!

3)   I know you're there. I thought you were supposed to be supplying books! I want several Enid Blytons. I have to go and watch my soaps now so I'll have to try again tomorrow. This is not on!

4)   This is Mrs Tentpole. Is anyone there? I think they're still in bed. Lazy good for nothings.

5)   It's me again! Aren't you up yet? I'm looking for books by Enid Blyton. Call me back as soon as possible.

6)   Hello? Hello? Are you still even a bookshop?! I called yesterday and the day before for some books! I've got nothing to read during this quarantine. Hello? Do you need hearing aids?

7)   Hello? Where's that young man who sounds like he's constipated all the time? He always finds me an Enid Blyton book and if he doesn't, well it's my time he's wasted. I'm warning you! I need a book NOW. Call me!

8)   Hello? Hello? I've been trying to get hold of the booksellers. Is anyone there? Ugh. Still in bed asleep I expect. Fools.

9)   It's me again. I'm trying to wake you up. What's the point of having all those books if you won't sell them? I'm looking for Enid Blyton books and I would like to know the ones you have on your shelves. I've bought from you before. Have you changed hands? Call me!

10) Hello? Hello? I used to buy Enid Blyton books from the people who used to run this as a bookshop. I think they've all deceased from Polar-Bear 9. No one's getting back to me. Can you call me back please? I'm waiting.

11) Hello? You still haven't called me back. Are you still a bookshop? Where's the boy with the constipation problem? I'd like some Enid Blyton books. Call me back and give me your list. I'd like something to read in Lockdown.

12) Hello? Is that the bookshop? Are you still in bed! Lazy blighters. I await your call.

James was staring at Nora in stunned amazement, his tape measurer held in one hand, a pencil in the other. Nora burst out laughing.

"Yes. That says it all. Our customers turn you to stone."

James closed his mouth.

"I really don't know what to say." He confessed.

"Well, the last message was left five minutes before we arrived so…"

The telephone started to ring. Nora winced and gave James a look. He glanced at her with an admiring smirk, leaving her to deal with who was probably Mrs Tentpole as he went back to his measuring.

"Good morning, The Secondhand Bookworm, Castletown." Nora answered politely.

"Is that the bookshop? By the beard of Zeus! I've been trying to get hold of you!" Mrs Tentpole yelled.

"I'm sorry about that. We're not allowed to open during Lockdown and you happen to have caught me here while I'm checking on the shop." Nora replied, heading for the staircase to take the phone up to the children's room.

"Not allowed to open?! Not allowed to open? I've never heard of anything so ridiculous. This is a time of global crisis and we need our books. Don't you have any books anymore then?"

Nora began to climb the creaky staircase to the next floor.

"Oh yes. We have plenty." She said cheerfully. "Is there anything in particular you would like? I can post any books out to you."

"I'm looking for some Enid Blyton books. Now, I know you have some because that boy who works there, the one with constipation,"

Nora smothered a laugh.

"…he always reads them out for me."

"That would be Felix. He doesn't work here anymore." Nora explained, reaching behind a travel guide for Russia on the travel guide shelf at the top of the stairs and flicking on the hidden light switch.

"Doesn't work there? Humph. Well, can *you* read them out for me then?!"

"I certainly can." Nora assured her and creaked into the children's room as the upstairs lights all flickered on. It was stale and smelly in the children's room and looked as though everything needed a dust again. Nora was amazed because she and the Duke of Cole had spent a good deal of time cleaning, tidying, mending, polishing, painting and making the whole shop look sparkling clean. It seemed that books had a tendency to create mess and radiate stale air when not rummaged through by humans. She easily located the Enid Blyton tomes.

"What titles do you have then?" Mrs Tentpole demanded.

"I shall read them out to you. Right, we have, Bimbo and Topsie."

"No!"

"Mr Meddles Muddles."

"No!"

"Noddy and the Runaway Wheel."

"No thank you!"

"Noddy and the Invisible Paint."

"No!"

Nora wished she had some invisible paint for Mrs Tentpole.

"The Put-em-Rights."

"Certainly not!"

"Six Cousins at Mistletoe Farm."

"Forget that!"

"Five give up the Booze."

Silence.

"Er…" Nora hastily picked the book up, realising it was one of the popular spoof Enid Blyton books that didn't belong there. She continued quickly.

"Five have a Wonderful Time."

"No thanks!"

The list went on. The Enid Blyton section was practically a whole case, so by the time Nora reached the end of it, James had finished his measuring and joined her, listening and then laughing when Nora passed him the spoof book 'Five give up the Booze' with a grimace.

"And the last one, Naughty Amelia Jane." Nora concluded.

"No way! Is that it?"

"That's all of them."

"Bah, humbug. What guff." Mrs Tentpole moaned. "Thanks for wasting my time! I'll call back when you've got some new titles in. When would that be?"

Nora thought the woman was mightily rude.

"We won't be going on any calls or buying in any new stock until Lockdown is over and who knows when that will be?" Nora replied politely.

"I've never heard such hot air!" Mrs Tentpole said.

Nora blinked.

"Thanks for nothing." Mrs Tentpole concluded and hung up.

"What a rude old boot." Nora decided, ending the call too.

James sympathised.

"You should have sent her this." He held up the spoof book.

Nora giggled.

"That belongs in the humour section here. Shall we choose some zombie books then for the Zoom Book Club? I know Cara will be game." She suggested.

"If you insist." The Duke smiled and Nora led the way, slipping the Enid Blyton spoof onto one of the humour shelves as they headed for the paperback room, up the second staircase, turn right and up some steps into the attic.

Once inside the paperback room, Nora opened the window to give the space an airing.

"Zombie novels are usually found in the Horror section." Nora gestured to the correct area. "And sometimes fantasy."

"Any titles come to mind?" James asked, crouching down before the shelves.

"Hmm, let's think." Nora crouched down beside him and ran her finger along the spines. "I'll recognise them when I see them. Ah. *I Am Legend* by Richard Matheson." She spotted. "It's a 1954 horror novel and tells the tale the story of Robert Neville who is the only survivor of a plague that has killed or turned the rest of humanity into vampire-like creatures."

"Sounds like something Spencer would read." James supposed.

"I'm sure he has read them." Nora nodded. "This would be a great one for our Zoom Clubs. The novel has been adapted into three films: The Last Man on Earth, The Omega Man and a film by the same name as the novel, I am Legend. We could watch them as part of the study."

"Lovely." James winced.

They found several more zombie books just for good measure and then James left Nora browsing while he oiled the window hinges and closed them up. Once she had an armful of zombie related books that had been made into movies, they made their way downstairs, checking the rooms for leaks or ghosts and turning off the lights.

While James checked on the kitchen and the yard, Nora laid out the books on the counter top, picking up and examining World War Z and an accompanying guide by the same author, both of which seemed to be the most appealing for a Book and Movie Club.

A loud tapping sounded on the window. Nora looked up and across the room to see Dora Magic standing with her nose pressed against the glass, waving madly and blowing kisses through her blue surgical face mask.

"Oh dear." Nora muttered, returned the books to the counter top and walked around to the door.

"Hello! Hi! Hello there, Nora Jolly. You are special. You are appreciated! You are…"

"Hello, Dora!" Nora interjected quickly. "As you can see we're closed."

"Ah yes, yes, very wise too, you must keep safe, Nora Jolly, safe and well and ready to embark upon your future mission, when *you* will run The Secondhand Bookworms and everyone will see you for the heroine you are, you are wonderful, you are admired, you are a source of inspiration and magnificence…" She stopped to gasp for breath through her mask, having run out of oxygen with her very loud gushing.

Nora stared, alarmed and slightly creeped out.

"Is there anything you need, Dora?" She finally asked.

Dora drew a heart with her arms which then lifted into the air and her hands became claws. She began to walk on the spot with stiff legs, making a strangling sound. Nora gawped.

"Yes, yes. Can you guess? I am writing a NEW series of novels for you, Nora. It's about Zombies!" She shouted through her mask.

"Zombies?" Nora repeated, amazed that Dora had the same theme in mind as Nora's Zoom Book Club and Zoom Movie Club.

"Oh yes, Zombies! Of course. Such a wonderful topic. It will be a romance,"

Nora smothered a laugh.

"…but also about survival and hope. There will be wars and battles and many, many feasts on brains, but in the end, the survivors come through!" Dora gushed and clapped her hands together excitedly.

"Wow. That sounds…amazing."

"Who knows, perhaps you would like to read them with your friends in a Zoom Book Club or something?" Dora added.

Nora stared at her.

"How did you know about that?" She asked.

"Oh! Oh I just *presumed*, Nora, yes that's it. I presumed. You are so trendy and interesting and I just *knew* it would be the kind of thing you would do. Yes, ahem. That's it." Dora said. "So I shall be writing my Zombie series and will be able to share it with you next week. Who knows, when you run The Secondhand Bookworm, *soon*, mark my words, you are loved, you are appreciated, you are important… (gasp for air)…you will stock my books and my many fans will fill your shop seeking my signing and meet-and-greet…"

Fortunately James returned from locking up the kitchen. Dora spotted him and her eyes became dreamy.

"Erm, well that all sound very lovely, Dora. I wish you luck with your writing." Nora said, glancing over her shoulder at James who saw Dora and stopped still.

"Oh thank you, thank you, thank you, Nora, thank you! You are loved, you are famous, you are watched, you are important. I'll let you finish up and return to the castle. Yooooooour Graaaaaace." She said and sunk to the pavement in a curtsey that saw her disappear behind the lower wooden part of the door.

"Are you alright down there?" Nora called.

"Yes, Nora Jolly. It's quite comfortable thank you." Dora said before finally hoisting up her rotund frame. She then stood and drew another large heart with both her arms, followed by a zombie impression, before bowing and heading off back across the square.

Nora turned around.

"Dare I ask?" James chuckled, shrugging into his jacket.

"Best not." Nora laughed, but as she walked across the room to gather the books and her bag, she cast a look warily around, thinking how it was becoming very suspicious that Dora Magic seemed to know everything she did and said. She then shrugged.

"I think that's everything checked for Georgina." James decided, gathering his measuring tape, piece of paper with the measuring details on and hoisting up their box of groceries from the delicatessen. "I'll send it through to my company tonight and then organise with Georgina the future fitting of the plexiglass."

"You are so good and helpful, Your Grace." Nora said with appreciation.

He smiled.

"It's my pleasure. And it's all about keeping you safe, Nora, when The Secondhand Bookworm opens once more."

Nora blushed, pleased at his continued affection for her. She cleared her throat.

"Well, I think we can return to the castle. The coast looks clear out there." She popped her collection of books into a blue plastic bookworm bag, turned off the lights, replaced the telephone handset to its cradle, chuckled quickly about rude Mrs Tentpole with a reminder to herself to text Felix the details, set the alarm and they hurried to the door, closed, locked up and breathed sighs of relief.

The town was quiet. It seemed as though the local police had finally 'driven' away the Hell's Angels motorbike menaces, and there was also no sign of Dora Magic lurking outside. Next door to The Secondhand Bookworm, the antique shop looked completely deserted, as though the owners, rudely referred to as Pig-Goat and Hatchet-Face by Felix (it had stuck), hadn't popped in at all and had in fact abandoned it to be taken over by *Shelob*. Great cobwebs had appeared across the windows and it looked like they reached into the depths of the cluttered old rooms. Nora suppressed a squeal.

The sound of stomping came from further up the hill. Nora and James saw one of Nora's customers, known as Drunk-Boy, plodding along the pavement with a can of beer in his hand, acting like a zombie.

Across the square, Nora spotted Pip and Merrie who had been due to open their new Prosecco shop and host a festival in April for a week of merriment and wine celebration. That had sadly been postponed until Lockdown was over.

James was in regular contact with Pip and his wife Merrie, both of whom had worked with the Duke for permission to reopen the old brewery factory buildings by the river and make Castletown a base for the County of Cole's main Prosecco trading.

Everyone in Castletown was depressed it hadn't managed to open before Lockdown because they could all do with an entire warehouse full of Prosecco to keep up their spirits.

Nora waved. Pip and Merrie headed nearer, keeping a wide distance that still allowed them to speak across the cobbles.

"Nora. Your Grace!" Pip nodded, sporting a Venom mouth mask from the DC Movie. He looked horrific.

"Hello Nora, hello Your Grace." Merrie greeted, sporting a simple flowery face mask and bobbing a curtsy.

"Hello. How are you both?" James enquired.

"Just surviving. Thank you once again Your Grace for the financial assistance. We're managing to keep the shop, and the breweries are almost ready for a future opening." Pip shouted.

Nora looked at James.

"You're very welcome." He nodded.

"We'll aim to have the Prosecco Festival once this wretched pandemic is over." Merrie assured them optimistically.

"We look forward to it." James encouraged.

"Well, we'd better head home, we just came to continue painting and preparing the shop but we'll get arrested by PC Plod if we're spotted talking to you both. Look forward to your next Livestream, Your Grace, Nora." Pip called, gave a small bow and with a wave from both of them, they headed off.

Nora met James' gaze.

"What other secret things are you up to, Your Grace?" She smiled behind her mask, curious and impressed. "Are you personally keeping the town afloat from your own coffers?"

James snorted and shrugged his shoulders.

"Only until the government is able to give furlough assistance. Which I am told will be soon." He confessed. "According to Paul the *Polar-Bear 9* Job Retention Scheme is about to be presented to Parliament and will provide grants to employers so they can retain and continue to pay staff during the Lockdown. They will be granted eighty percent of their wages. Meanwhile, I'd like to do as much as I can to keep local businesses alive."

Nora shook her head, amazed and admiring of him.

A taxi went past. Nora barely noticed the driver wearing a mask that just had the word 'STILL?!' printed on the front. Taxis and buses were back on but all vehicles sported huge plexiglass screens and only allowed one person per taxi or three people per bus. Many elderly people spent their time travelling about aimlessly on the buses for company, shouting at one another across the roped-off seating.

Nora and James headed up the hill, pleased to see Drunk-Boy advancing down Market Street in his usual crapulous state. As they approached Spencer's house to pass by, they noticed Spencer throw open the window of his gothic tower and lean out, surrounded by blue smoke that streamed out from behind him. Nora dreaded to imagine what he was up to in there – hopefully just playing Dungeons and Dragons by himself.

"Greetings Nora and Your Grace." Spencer called down.

Some flashes of light illuminated his wild white hair from behind.

"Hello, Spencer." Nora waved.

James saluted politely.

"You've managed to avoid *Polar-Bear 9* still, then. That's good news." Spencer said. "Of course, Vampires probably have a natural immunity." His piercing blue eyes burrowed into James' with a suspicious and interested look.

James looked blank.

"The virus is now transmitted by houseflies and mad people." Spencer added.

Before Nora could bid him a hasty goodbye a sudden voice joined in from behind them.

"I heard that too, Gina."

Nora and James turned to see Crossword-Lady on the path at a distance. She was heading for the castle paddock to see the donkeys. Since she was a regular visitor with Jeeves, the latter of whom only mixed with Nora and James, Mrs Booth was considered part of the Duke's bubble, but Jeeves still insisted Mrs Booth observe all of the social distancing protocols around James, so she remained back along the street.

"Oh, hello Mrs Booth." Nora greeted politely.

"I am still *very* concerned about the donkeys contracting *Polar-Bear 9* and becoming zombies." Mrs Booth shared. "*Very* concerned."

"That's always a possibility." Spencer called down. "You should protect yourself from the zombie strain."

Nora groaned.

"What would you suggest?" Mrs Booth called up to the tower, blinking as more flashes illuminated Spencer's white hair and more blue smoke billowed out the window from behind him.

"I don't think…" Nora began but Spencer looked keen.

"Oh, I would recommend many adventure skills that would come in useful should *Polar-Bear 9* mutate into a full-blown zombie apocalypse." Spencer called down.

James glanced at Nora. She could see his eyes sparking with amusement and amazement.

"What, what should I do?" Crossword-Lady called up.

"Firstly, turn up the heat! Build fires and make sure your house is very warm." Spencer suggested.

"Yes, yes? What else?" Crossword-Lady called.

"Make sure you drink carefully. Deploy water safety. Check it isn't infected."

"What next?"

"Forage! Forage for food in forests. I've learned a lot from fairies and goblins about that."

James almost dropped the grocery box.

"What else?" Crossword-Lady had produced a pen and paper and was scribbling it all down.

"Learn to catch your dinner. Go fishing in clear rivers but beware of ZOMBIE LEECHES!!" Spencer called out, disappearing for a moment in a billow of blue smoke and coughing and fanning his face.

"Yes, yes." Crossword-lady scribbled madly.

"Take care of your house. Keep it protected and fortified from Zombie Donkeys or men. And then become a pro at map reading. Always useful for running away."

"Erm..." Nora tried to interject, but Spencer continued.

"Become fit. Try trail running; it will help you outrun zombies and also Lemures."

"Lemures?" Crossword-Lady asked.

"Fearsome spectres of the dead, usually grotesque and horrifying, manifesting themselves from Roman times. And finally, climb! Learn to climb! Climb hills and towers and walls. It's an important skill to have."

"Yes, yes thank you. This is very useful." Crossword-Lady nodded. "I have already been planning my survival route. I have chosen Jeeves as my emergency contact and I have a list of police, emergency and fire department contacts."

"We really should think about organising a local Zombie Response Team." Spencer suggested.

"Well, none of this will happen." Nora hastily assured Mrs Booth. "And you don't need to fear zombies or the donkeys."

"You have my word, Mrs Booth." James joined in solemnly. "Castletown is quite safe from the undead."

Nora's lips twitched behind her mask but she nodded keenly.

"Ah, thank you Your Grace Jim, thank you Gina. And with this additional information I shall certainly feel safer."

"You are safe." Nora said and went to glare up at Spencer, only to find he had become bored, or a housefly had been spotted, and he had closed his window.

"Would you like us to accompany you to the paddocks?" James offered Mrs Booth.

"Why thank you, Your Grace, Jim." She replied.

Your Grace, Jim had been a title Mrs Booth had started using at the Book Club Nora had run in The Secondhand Bookworm, when James had been incognito. Unfortunately it had stuck, but the Duke didn't mind.

James nodded and he and Nora set off for the castle gates, Crossword-Lady walking behind them at a distance, humming.

"I'm wondering if this zombie theme is really a good idea." Nora mused, admiring a large chalk NHS rainbow some children had drawn on the castle walls.

"I think it is." James confessed with a hidden smile.

Nora bit her lip and grinned.

Back at the castle, Nora finished off making a fresh batch of natural hand sanitiser for Karl to pick up the following day and received a new email quiz from Humphrey. This time it consisted of photographs of crisps of different shapes and shades. The challenge was to guess the flavour. For instance, some of the crisps were covered in dark yellow powder or lighter powder and could be cheese, steak flavour, prawn cocktail etc… Nora thought it was ridiculously hard but James pored over it, fascinated.

Meanwhile, Nora texted her cousin Felix to tell him about Mrs Tentpole.

'Har-har-har! Glad I left her behind, the old goose! Xx' He gloated in response. *"Hope you had lots of fun with her! Ha!"*

Nora decided she would point Mrs Tentpole to Felix's shop the next time she called.

After dinner, Georgina telephoned Nora as she sat reading through her zombie books.

"I think this one is Truffle and rosemary, this one Wagyu beef with honey and English mustard, this one parmesan and port and this one Champagne and Serrano chilli." James was musing as he examined the email crisp guessing quiz from Humphrey while stroking Marlow's head.

Nora didn't have the heart to tell the Duke it was unlikely the crisps were from the premium crisp brands stocked in Harrods. She answered her phone.

"Hi, Georgina."

"Hi, Nora! Sorry to call you in the evening. Are you busy at the moment?" Georgina enquired.

"No, not really. We're in the library." Nora smiled.

"Ah, how lovely! And how were things at the bookshop today?"

"Fine. James checked over everything and I dealt with twelve telephone messages from Mrs Tentpole."

"Oh *her!*" Georgina hissed. "Rude old Snollygoster. Did you find anything for her?"

"Nothing she wanted." Nora confessed.

"Good. She's more trouble than she's worth. You could consider sending her Felix's way." Georgina proposed and sniggered.

"I've already planned to." Nora laughed.

"Excellent."

Felix had once worked for Georgina, starting at The Secondhand Bookworm on Saturdays before being promoted full-time. However, Felix had felt persecuted by Georgina, who often phoned him late at night to tell him off for trivial things such as leaving the shop toilet light on, not putting a pen back in the pot, eating one of her biscuits, shedding hair on the counter top (he had had a haircut one lunch break), putting ugly books in the window display, not emptying the bin, laughing when someone fell down the stairs, hoovering up her gloves, putting a book in the R section instead of the S section in the paperback room, and much more. In the end, Felix had snagged a job as manager of a charity shop in Seatown and handed in his notice. Georgina had been quite miffed about it, so there was now some bitter bookshop rivalry between them, although they were both passive aggressive to one another whenever they met, with false smiles and loud pleasantries.

"Now, the reason I'm calling you is to ask for quite a favour." Georgina continued.

"What is it?" Nora was curious.

"If it's not too much of a bother, would you mind going down to the bookshop this evening and getting that lovely Folio Society special edition copy of *American Gods* by Neil Gaiman for Troy? I shall be coming through the town early tomorrow morning and could pick it up from Jeeves at the gatehouse. I know it's silly and dramatic but I don't want it stolen in *another* robbery overnight and Troy really, really wants it. I don't want to be seen opening the shop in the morning either and being questioned again by the nosey locals about how the shops are faring during lockdown. Is that alright?"

"Of course! That's no problem. We could go down now." Nora agreed cheerfully.

James looked up from his laptop, inquisitively.

"Ah thank you, thank you so much! You're such a good friend."

"It's the least I can do." Nora assured her, ever grateful to Georgina for paying her wages during the Lockdown.

"Wonderful. Let me know when you have it and I can put Troy's mind at ease. We can't come over now because we're currently in the bath and once we're out we like to settle in our jim-jams."

If Nora had been drinking her quarantini she would have spat it out at that image. As it was, she grimaced to picture Georgina's current setting while speaking to her, more so when she heard splishing and splashing sounds in the background.

"Erm…okay, really it's no problem. I'll let you know when I have it." Nora said and smothered an urge to laugh.

"Oh! By the way. I have a funny story for you. Percival was fined for having a barbeque on the beach today. He was foaming at the mouth about it when he phoned to tell me." Georgina shared, referring to one of her more specialist book customers, a millionaire who collected rare tomes, mainly about trains.

"What was he doing having a barbeque on the beach?! That's very out of character for him." Nora was amazed.

"He does a lot of commonplace things, it often surprises me!" Georgina confessed.

Once they had said their goodbyes, Nora told James about Georgina's request. He closed his lap top, stood up and held out his hand. Marlow jumped down from the large sofa, looking up at them expectantly.

"I could do with an evening walk." James smiled.

Nora took his hand and stood, too.

"Do you think Jeeves would mind placing the book outside for Georgina in the morning?" She asked.

"Not at all." James shook his head. "He would relish it, I'm sure. I'll grab Marlow's lead on our way out."

"Good idea!" Nora agreed. "We might need the protection."

James laughed.

Marlow seemed to understand he would be going with them and spun three circles with a happy yelp, following close at their heels.

They made their way through the castle, stopped in the kitchen to collect Marlow's lead (it was hardly used because the miniature schnauzer usually had the run of the massive castle grounds when James and Nora went for a stroll) and enjoyed the walk through the darkened castle grounds to the gatehouse.

James phoned Jeeves to tell them they were coming so he opened the door, bowed them through and told Nora it would be a pleasure to give Georgina a special book for Troy in the morning. Nora gave him Georgina's mobile number so they could arrange it and then they stepped through the small side room next to the gates and out into the street.

"I'll rap on the window when we're back, Jeeves." James said.

"Certainly, Your Grace." Jeeves bowed, watching them head off.

Nora had Marlow's lead in one hand so James linked his fingers with those of her other, drawing her close.

"It's been a long time since we took a moonlit stroll around Castletown." He said, taking in the scene from the top of the hill.

The streets were deserted. Lights twinkled from the windows of flats above shops or townhouses along the main street.

"Do you think we'll spot any zombies?" Nora teased. James nudged her arm.

"You have zombies on the brain." He laughed.

"Don't mention that word." She teased and mouthed 'brains'.

James was most amused.

However, there certainly was a strange and eerie atmosphere in the darkened, empty lock-downed town. The Duke and Nora were relieved to spot someone walking their dog down on the cobbles. The dog walker wore a black mask and was walking a large black Labrador. He gave a wave and hurried off down Market Street, leaving Nora, James and Marlow alone.

In the bookshop, once the alarm had been turned off, Nora kept the lights off so as not to attract attention. It was dark and shadowy inside and she had the distinct feeling that she was being watched.

"Are you alright in there?" James called from the doorway with Marlow.

"Yes, I won't be long." Nora assured him, scanning the rare and specialist bookshelves behind the counter for the *Folio Society special edition copy of American Gods by Neil Gaiman*. It was a collector's item in very good condition so was priced at one hundred and eighty pounds. Bound in blocked cloth with a slipcase, there was a frontispiece and eleven colour illustrations that included three double page spreads.

Nora found it and popped it in a bag, grumbling to herself because it was heading out of The Secondhand Bookworm without manufacturing a sale. Georgina often pilfered good stock for herself or friends and family.

The alarm was reset and as it beeped, Nora ran across the room, up the step, closed the door and locked up.

"I have it." She showed James.

"Wonderful. Shall we head back home?"

Nora smiled. She liked the sound of the Duke of Cole including her in his sanctuary. She blushed red.

"Ahem. Yes, let's go home."

James grinned and took hold of her hand once more.

"I could get used to this." He admitted.

"Me too." Nora agreed.

The Duke looked thoughtful a moment, glancing at Nora, as though he wished to say something, but he changed his mind, squeezed her fingers and they set off up the hill.

Michael Jackson '*Thriller*' could be heard playing out of someone's window. Nora arched an eyebrow and met James' eyes.

"Zombies?" She grimaced.

"Zombies." He nodded and, chuckling, they quickened their pace.

Once they were back in the safety of the castle, having given Jeeves the book, Nora texted Georgina to let her know, kicking off her shoes and settling back into the large sofa next to the Duke of Cole and Marlow.

'That's wonderful! Thank you, Nora. Have a good evening xx' Georgina sent back.

Nora smiled, placed her phone on the coffee table, linked her arm with James and snuggled close to him, confident they might survive the zombie apocalypse after all.

8 THE REBELLIOUS BOOKWORMS

It was decided that the Zoom Book Club (minus Miss Raven) and the complementary Zoom Movie Club would read (and then watch) *World War Z*. In addition, the companion book by the same author *The Zombie Survival Guide* would also be read alongside. Nora created a special *Watch Party* system that allowed people to binge watch a TV series together or a movie by logging into their Netflix accounts online and synchronizing video playback, also adding a means for group chat. Nora and Cara had been watching *Stranger Things* together during the Lockdown while James and Seymour had been busy so they knew how it worked. And everyone confirmed they had Netflix accounts and laptops and Chrome browsers. Nora would send out the URL and they would click on it and then on the Netflix icon to join in. A chat room would appear along the right-hand side, like the Skype chat they used in The Secondhand Bookworms, so they could discuss and comment as they watched.

So, copies of the books were organised and ordered and posted out or delivered (by Georgina) and they all set about reading the book and the guide in between their Lockdown adventures so as to all meet up on the virtual plane to have their online Book and Movie Club.

Mrs Booth was especially excited because she said she wanted to witness first-hand what a Zombie attack would look like so that she could be prepared.

It turned out that when Miss Raven heard that the topic was zombies (from Georgina), she opted in, having thought that her old mother had become one earlier in the week when she had found Mrs Raven in the kitchen one morning with her arms out straight and a horrendous groaning sound coming from her wide opened mouth, her eyes staring dead ahead.

In reality, Mrs Raven had just been sleepwalking and ended up in the kitchen. But Miss Raven was as determined as Mrs Booth to be prepared. She had even had Humphrey talk her through setting up a Netflix and Chrome account, the first of which she wished to only keep as a children's profile, but which Humphrey set up just this once for her to watch *World War Z*. Nora wondered if this was a good idea.

On the 8th May, when VE Day arrived, Nora and the Duke, under the supervision of Jeeves, hung bunting along the castle walls and played wartime music with the flags all flying from the keep and the towers and the turrets. The townspeople were delighted.

Street parties were put on with neighbours keeping their distance but managing to socialise. There were cream teas and music of the World War II Era, VE day scarecrows and fence panels between gardens used as table tops. Children played *Air Raid Statues* which was a game like musical statues but instead of pausing the music and standing still, people played air raid sounds instead. This echoed about Castletown and sounded eerie but commemorative. There were also games of Tin Can

Alley and marbles taking place in people's social bubbles.

The Duke and Nora joined in a VE Day Morse Code Challenge and played 1940's Bingo with Cara and Seymour online. Rather than using numbers Cara had designed 1940s films, icons and events instead.

There was also a socially distanced wreath-laying, a two-minute silence, and re-broadcast of Winston Churchill's speech on the BBC.

"To those who gave so much, we thank you!" James toasted with one of Nora's quarantini's as they sat watching the commemorations.

Nora baked red, blue and white cupcakes and James made delicious bread and butter pudding. They also did a special 'Make your own VE Day Party Hat' livestream two days before.

Together, Nora and James used old newspapers, PVA glue, balloons and paint and showed how to do Papier-Mache hats. Nora also used a flower pot covered in cling film for the basis of a top hat for Marlow. Several balloons popped but they had fun layering newspaper and glue over each one when they finally stayed inflated.

The next evening the balloons that had been covered in Papier-Mache were popped on the Livestream, and the top hat shapes removed from the flower pots. They made brims too, one bonnet brim for Nora's balloon and a cowboy hat brim for the Duke's balloon, with a short one for Marlow's top hat.

Finally, James painted his and Nora used crepe paper for hers and Marlow's, adding outrageous but fun red, blue and white glitters, ribbons, feathers and flowers.

It was a great hit online, especially with the school children, who were delighted when James read 'Goodnight, Mr Tom' to them while wearing his cowboy VE Day Party Hat and Marlow sitting on his lap with his top hat.

A new nationwide endeavour was announced that involving the continued scrupulous hand washing, use of face masks and social distancing when stepping outside of homes or using shops, hospitals etc…It was known as 'Flattening the Curve'. This would hopefully start to see a major decline in the spread of *Polar-Bear 9*. Everyone was invited to dedicate themselves to this task.

But it meant that everyone still had to stay at home with the intention of curbing the spread of the permafrost virus and reducing the strain on hospitals, healthcare providers, and the health of friends and family. Nora didn't mind. She was enjoying spending all her time with the Duke of Cole and having a break from the bookworms!

After lunch every day the Duke and Nora spent an hour or two chatting in the castle library while playing chess or reading to one another. They also researched the Duke's new property he had purchased from Humphrey's former firm in London, acquired as part of a recent acquisition that Humphrey oversaw. It was a large estate and country house in need of restoration on the north edge of Cole, about forty minutes from Castletown. Humphrey had discovered it had links to the Ravenstones, James' family, and was a former abbey dissolved in the 16th century. There was a lot of history, ruins, and grounds to explore and because James was renowned for doing up estates and castles and restoring buildings to a magnificent standard (like his castle in Castletown), he had eagerly purchased the property and wanted Nora to be involved in every part of it.

Nora secretly hoped that the Duke of Cole intended it to be a future home for them, but she kept that to herself, not even telling him she thought she had had a *sweven* (a vision seen in a dream) as to that future just the night before that saw them happily living in the restored estate and house. She told Cara though. Her sister-in-law squealed so loudly that Arthur, the bulldog, tumbled off the chair beside her and rolled about like a stunned beach ball.

In the heart of the continued Lockdown, everyone kept in touch via Zoom which had really taken off worldwide. Milton was also becoming a TikTok star. He sent Nora a video of an old veteran he had filmed in Little Cove, where Nora had grown up, running around his garden to raise money for the NHS. He also did live coverage of his nineteenth birthday. Because he, Heather, their mum and dad were quarantining together in the family home, Nora's mum, dad and sister set up a nightclub for Milton in the garage for his birthday party. Nora's dad was a bouncer and her mum a barmaid while Heather was his dance partner. They had bought cut-outs of famous people which stood around as party guests. The videos were super popular.

Meanwhile, Humphrey worked out in his new gym (Nora suspected he was trying to win her back because he kept sending her photos of his muscles) and had regular online chats with Nora, sending through more email quizzes such as *Guess the Chocolate bar* from photographs of pieces of chopped up chocolate.

Georgina and Troy were having relationship problems. Humphrey gossiped that Georgina kept hinting she wanted Troy to propose marriage to her before they left for the USA but Troy changed the subject each time. There had been three bust-ups that involved Georgina shrieking that Troy didn't really love her but only wanted her for her body and then lobbing her entire miniature book collection at Troy's head, as well as Georgina accusing Troy of loving her Guinea pigs more than her and so making him sleep on Mrs Pickering's sofa in her attached annex, and also Georgina accusing Troy of cheating with her mother, romantically, and banishing him to their caravan in the drive for a week. Nora and Cara suspected the move to America might not go through after all. However, with that said, Georgina kept cheerful and professional when dealing with the Bookworms and kept her employees busy with book-related work as much as possible, glad when the government released their furlough scheme which paid their wages almost in full.

Nora continued to potter about The Secondhand Bookworm in Castletown, while Amy transformed the branch in Seatown with endless cleaning, tidying, sorting and shuffling; Cara worked on accounts, forms and paperwork; Roger kept the database of regular customers abreast of stock and tempted them with titles; Lucy's blogs and social media work brought the shops to larger attention and Betty, who had listed and sold books on EBay before working for Georgina, did just that for a lot of the special books in the rare and antiquarian cases in both branches. She managed to sell quite a few.

Down in The Secondhand Bookworm, Castletown, one morning in the middle of May, Nora stood before the window. James was busy with Zoom meetings and had an important one with an overseas charity he was patron of, so Nora had left him at the castle and headed down for the morning in the bookshop, planning to finish at lunchtime.

She had dealt with several answerphone messages and notes posted through the letterbox; including her usual *You are being watched* note. Now she was changing the window display, emptying it of books, polishing the wooden framework and shelves and choosing a selection of fresh books with signs on the window facing outwards saying:

See a book you like?

We can post it to you.
We take cheques or telephone orders.
Keep reading during Lockdown.
Phone us on….

"In you go, *Our Man in Havana*." Nora told the Graham Greene book as she stood in the window next to the wooden display unit.

The glass rapped.

"Eeek!" Nora almost fell backwards.

"Sorry!" Clive mouthed after pulling his mask down.

She waved and laughed before walking around to the door.

Clive operated an internet bookshop from his property down Market Street. He listed titles online for specialised collectors and readers who mainly collected and read sci-fi and fantasy books, but occasionally people arrived in town to seek out its premises and assumed that The Secondhand Bookworm traded under the name Bellerophon Books online.

"Hi, how are things?" Clive asked, keeping distant from the glass.

"Not too bad. How are things with you and Bellerophon Books?" Nora asked him.

"I've started a skateboard delivery service." Clive said.

"Oh! Are we allowed to do that?"

"Just about." He nodded. "My younger brother does the deliveries on his board. The books that are sold locally are placed in plastic bags and left on customers' doorsteps. It's been really successful. You should get started. Word among the nation's booksellers is that the government is going to allow us to do deliveries, but not open the premises yet."

"That's brilliant." Nora was relieved. "We do have some ideas."

Clive stuck his thumbs up.

"Glad to hear it. Let me know if I can help. I've been watching your livestreaming. I also have to confess I tune into the Duke of Cole reading to the local school children. My sister is a teacher and she lets me log on."

Nora chuckled.

"He is a good reader." She nodded.

"He is indeed. I didn't see any reports but I wondered if you or His Grace have caught *Polar-Bear 9* yet?"

"No, thankfully." Nora assured Clive.

"I had it. Ugh. It knocked me out for about four weeks. I tested positive for twelve days. Then I could finally move but I still feel a bit tired."

"You poor thing!" Nora sympathised.

"The common thought is that everyone will get it at least once, but the vaccines are on the way and then it should mutate and be less threatening." Clive relayed.

"I hope so." Nora grimaced. "What a terrible thing it is. I feel so sorry for those who are at risk and those who have died."

"Me too, Nora. Well, take care and keep safe. See you soon!" He waved and set off towards the delicatessen.

Nora went back to her display, only to hear knocking on the door window a moment later. She put down the copy of *White Teeth* by Zadie Smith she was about to place into the shelving and came face to face with Dora Magic at the door window.

"Nora!" Dora greeted, waving with both hands like a mad woman.

"Oh. Hello, Dora." Nora smiled politely.

"I saw you talking to Clive. Don't worry! You are loved, you are special and admired, YOU are the greatest bookseller in the town, indeed the WORLD! You are watched and studied and are the greatest person. You are amazing. You are better than *him!*" Dora gushed.

"Er…thank you." Nora said warily.

"What a wonderful window display you are doing. Such talent and such thoughtfulness have gone into it. And such a fascinating selection of books. Might I suggest The Caterpillar Wars? I expect they would be a hit! Now, as promised." She dove headfirst into her carpet bag, rummaging around and muttering until she hoisted out a stack of books, at least ten of them, wrapped in a red ribbon. "The Zombie Saga."

"Oh, wow!" Nora was delighted.

"All twelve volumes ready for you to enjoy, especially since you have had such a zombie theme going lately."

"Thanks." Nora said with appreciation, suspicious of Dora's constant nosey knowledge of her every move.

"I was going to write my romance series based upon you and His Grace, but I thought this would be more appropriate, and it contains romance of course! Plenty of it. And wars and battles and books and rivalry and brains, lots of brains. And violence. I'll place them here and when I've crossed the road you can disinfect them and bring them into your shop. Ah, what an adventure awaits you, Miss Jolly. I am sure you will recognise many familiarities and allusions to those things and people that surround you. But don't worry! The heroine, based on you of course, gets her Duke and keeps her bookshop even in the midst of the zombie conflict. Georgina becomes a zombie of course." Dora added with a sly snigger.

"Oh dear." Nora couldn't help but be amused. "Well, thank you, Dora."

"You're welcome Miss Jolly. I must say, it's nice to see you in the bookshop regularly again. It's looking wonderful, and all your own handiwork. And that of the Duke of Cole's of course!" She sighed, pressing her hand to her ample bosom over her heart.

"Hmm, yes. How did you know that?" Nora asked her, beginning to suspect that Dora Magic was her note stalker.

"Oh! Oh I have such sharp eyes, Miss Jolly. Yes, that's it. I always know when you are down in the town, working your bookshop magic. Yes, yes. Well, I must return to my typewriter. I have another series underway that you will like, in addition to my romance series about you and the Duke. It's a Western series set here, right here in Castletown. There are cowboys and Indians and stage coaches and settlers and outlaws and gold and treasures and the taming of the Wild South Coast. Oh yes, I know this is England, but it's a hybrid work, Nora, one of my magical infusions; they don't call me Miss Dora Nora *Magic* for nothing! Heh – heh! In this series, the castle is a fort and all the townsfolk are settlers. There are surrounding rugged lands and vast plains and the South Downs are vivid mountain ranges. And one day a wicked woman rolls into town to open a bookstore. But she gets her comeuppance when a beautiful heroine named Flora, who is under her servitude, manages to bring her down and falls in love with the Sheriff who is up at the fort. He and a gunslinger, the brother of the wicked bookstore owner, have a duel in the main square. The Sheriff wins of course and sweeps Flora off her feet. Sadly, zombies attack, but all will be well in the end! Goodbye, Miss Jolly, goodbye, ta-rah, cheerio, you are loved, you are magnificent, you are…*eeeeek*!"

Dora had been walking backwards and almost fell into the road off of the kerbside, dropping her carpet bag with a thud.

Nora covered her mouth with both hands on a gasp, but Dora whipped her arms about like a windmill for a moment and stepped back onto the pavement just as a taxi beeped her and trundled past.

"WATCH IT YOU GIT!!" Dora shrieked out, balling her fists and shaking her arms at the retreating vehicle as the taxi headed off past the barber shop and towards the bridge.

Nora gawped, amazed at this new angry side of Dora that was hidden beneath her usual gushing and fawning.

Dora smoothed her large flowery skirt, shook out her brown bouncing curls and turned back to Nora, smiling brightly.

"Take care, Miss Jolly! And enjoy the books! Goodbye, goodbye!" She resumed, picked up her enormous carpet bag and then hugged it to her bosom and made a run for it across the road and the cobbles.

Nora stared mutely before looking down at the Zombie book series left on the step. She looked up, and Dora was nowhere to be seen. Nora debated calling the police on the madwoman, but really wanted to look at the new novels, so unlocked the door, picked them up, brought them in and placed them on the desk.

They were all paperbacks and were of varying colours, mainly in the orange, red and black range, with blood-spatter effects and titles in bold black block that read:

Book One of the Zombie Saga: Arrival of the Zombie-Christ

Book Two of the Zombie Saga: Love in the time of Zombies

Book Three of the Zombie Saga: The Devouring of Georgina

Book Four of the Zombie Saga: A Royal Dish of Brains

Book Five of the Zombie Saga: The Zombie Head Smasher Heroine

Book Six of the Zombie Saga: Humphrey the Zombie Bait

Book Seven of the Zombie Saga: The Melting of Clive
*Book Eight of the Zombie Saga: The Battle for
Zombie Fort*
*Book Nine of the Zombie Saga: Zombies in the
Bookshop*
*Book Ten of the Zombie Saga: A Feast of Legs and
Arms*
*Book Eleven of the Zombie Saga: Kiss me, I'm a
Zombie, too*
Book Twelve of the Zombie Saga: A Zombie Wedding

Nora stared, her lips trembling with mirth. She took
out her iPhone and snapped a photo to send to Amy,
Dora's only other fan, giggling to herself and shaking
her head. She then set about disinfecting them and
wondering what on earth madness they contained.

"Ah, Dora. You really are lunatic." She said to
herself, finally popping them in a blue carrier bag and
placing it with her own bag to take with her when she
had finished.

Back on the window display, Nora found she was
interrupted regularly. Even though it was supposed to be
the *Flattening the Curve* endeavour and the nation was
still in a state of strict Lockdown, people were taking
advantage of being allowed out to exercise. Numerous
locals, pretending to jog, stopped to see the new books
being displayed in the window of The Secondhand
Bookworm.

Spencer arrived and knocked on the window.

"Morning, Nora. Any new occult books for me?" He
asked, loudly.

Nora screwed up her nose.

"We haven't been on any book calls since Lockdown
started!" She reminded him. "So we don't have anything
new in stock."

"Can you have a check for me and let me know, though?" He asked.

"When was the last time you had a look yourself?" Nora wanted to know.

Spencer placed the tips of his fingers together.

"Hmm. I had a look when Mal was visiting, you know, *Mal*, my medium friend, after we had followed that gnome trail across the Duke of Cole's rewilding land to the folly, while checking for his vampire lair." He told her musingly.

Nora sighed, inwardly.

"Yes, I remember that. Nope, we wouldn't have had anything new in since then. It was only a few days before Lockdown."

"Well, keep an eye out for anything for me, Nora. And let me know of any strange happenings in the bookshop, or with the Duke of Cole. I still can't believe you haven't discovered his coffin yet."

Nora rolled her eyes.

"James isn't a vampire, Spencer." She repeated for the umpteenth time.

Spencer looked knowing.

"Ah, I think you'll find he is. Next time he walks past a mirror, have a look." He advised her and glided off, his cape billowing out behind him, like his long, white hair.

A familiar man replaced him.

"Any regimental histories?" Don asked with his mask lowered, almost pressed against the window.

Nora edged back.

"Not since you last looked." Nora assured him, popping a copy of Calypso by David Sedaris on a window shelf.

"Ah, they come along, they come along." He nodded and set off.

"Argh. I thought this was supposed to be Lockdown." Nora grumbled and then nearly fell out of the window again. Harry was heading over, wearing the tightest shorts she had ever seen. She hastily averted her eyes and set about placing a nice copy of Heartburn by Nora Ephron onto the shelf (Cara had suggested popular novels so that people would be more likely to buy them to read rather than collectable and rare books during the crisis), aware of his shadow casting over her, big and hulking and running on the spot.

A few taps.

"Hello, Harry." Nora greeted politely.

"Hiiiiiiiii!" Harry winked and dropped in a sumo squat. "Any new Beano and Dandy annuals for my nephew?" He asked when he was back up, flexing his biceps and then squatting once again.

"Ahem. No, we haven't been able to go on any calls since Lockdown started." Nora explained to him, keeping her eyes fixated on the window frame above his head so as to avoid his tighter than tight shorts. She was beginning to think a tally chart would be in order to keep a record of how many times she had to tell people they weren't going on book calls to buy peoples collections or bookcases of books during the pandemic. Surely it was obvious?

"Ah, shame, shame. I've been enjoying your livestreams." Harry said loudly through the thin pane.

"Great." Nora smiled politely.

"Any chance you're going to do one modelling swimsuits?" He asked.

"I'm sorry Harry, I can't hear you." Nora feigned, cupping her hand to her ear and shrugging.

"Oh. I said, ANY CHANCE YOU'RE GOING TO MODEL SOME SWIMSUITS ONLINE?" He yelled.

Nora's lips pursed. On the cobbles Sherrie, who ran a kiddie's boutique in the town, dropped the bag she was carrying in shock. She then tittered and waved.

"NO CHANCE!" Nora shouted back, waving to Sherrie.

"Oh, shame, shame. Nora, can I ask?"

"No."

"When this Lockdown is over, do you want to go for a drink?"

"No."

"Fair enough."

"Bye, Harry."

"See you online soon." He winked, flexed an arm and turned and jogged off with his chest out.

Nora growled like a bear.

"Annoying man." She spoked aloud, unable to help but stare at his very firm buttocks in his very tight shorts as he jogged up the hill.

Her forehead hit the pane of glass as her eyes trailed him of their own accord. She shook her head, tutted to herself and placed the last few novels in the window, followed by a blue clothbound run of Dickens novels, deciding that being on show to the residents of Castletown really was asking for trouble.

The telephone started to ring. Nora jumped down from the window, crossed the room and grabbed the receiver, finished with her window display.

"Good morning, The Secondhand Bookworm, Castletown." She greeted politely, dropping into the swivel chair.

"Hello, is that the bookshop?" A gruff voice demanded.

"Yes, it is." Nora replied patiently.

"Do you buy books? I've been having a sort out and have loads I'd like to sell."

"Yes, we do buy books but…"

"Good. Shall I bring them along today or do you want to call round? We're only allowed one trip out a day so if I bring 'em to you I hope it'll be worth my while, love."

Nora's lip curled.

"It's Lockdown. We're not allowed to make visits to people's houses to look at books or receive customers into our shop." She said.

"What? What bilge!" The man objected, angrily.

"It can't be helped." Nora pointed out. "But if you're happy to wait I can…"

"Wait? Now there's a load of baloney if ever I hear it. These are trying times and I need cash. Your advert says you buy books!" He argued.

"Yes, we do. But these are extreme circumstances at the moment. The owner of our shops would be happy to keep your name and telephone number for when the Lockdown…"

"Forget it!" The man interrupted rudely and hung up.

Nora sighed and leaned back in the swivel chair.

"I don't miss this." She told a photo of White-Lightning Joe that was tacked to the wall close by. "Hmm, and I don't miss *you*, either."

White-Lightning Joe was a banned customer. He had been banned for stealing books and then trying to sell them back to The Secondhand Bookworm one Christmas. A greasy little man, he had once worked in The Old Hotel not far up the street, but had been made redundant. He collected ephemera and books all about Castletown and had coined the sobriquet 'White-Lightning Joe' due to the bottles of 'White-Lightning Cider' that he always had with him. Seymour had once employed him at his theatre out of charity and found him amusing, but he disgusted Georgina who remained adamant he was banned from The Secondhand Bookworm for life. His photo was up on the wall in a sign that warned anyone working there not to serve him. And to kick him out.

Turning slowly in her swivel chair back to the counter, Nora finished off her paperwork, tidied up and was glad when lunchtime arrived so she could return to James and the Duke of Cole's castle. A text message arrived. It was from Amy.

'Oh! That is so hilarious. What a treasure she is! Please, please, please can I read them after you? Xx' The message said, referring to Dora Magic's Zombie Saga.

Nora laughed.

'Yes of course! Glad to share the madness xx' Nora sent back.

As she shrugged on her coat:

'Wonderful. And I'll pick up The Caterpillar Wars from Jeeves when you've finished. Looking forward to Zoom Book Club tonight. See you online later xxx'

'See you tonight xx' Nora smiled.

She was about to set the code when her phone started to ring. Nora smiled to see that it was James.

"Hello. I'm just finishing up." She greeted, popping pens into the broken mug pot on the desk and closing the notebook.

"Hello, Nora. Good, I miss you." The Duke admitted.

Nora grinned stupidly.

"It's only been a few hours." She chuckled.

"That's a few hours too many." James confessed. "How was it this morning?"

"Very *Bookwormy*." Nora winced.

"I'm looking forward to hearing all about it, Nora."

Nora laughed.

"I'm glad you find it amusing, James."

"I do. I'll put the kettle on and then drive a golf buggy down to the gates to meet you." James decided.

"Okay, I'll be about five minutes, unless I meet a mad bookworm on the way up. I've already met plenty through the windows today."

James laughed.

"Well, keep covered up and away from them all and stay safe. You've no idea how much I've missed you this morning. I'll see you in a bit."

Nora smiled.

"See you in a bit." She said fondly and rang off.

She set the alarm, turned off the lights, picked up her bag and the bag containing The Zombie Saga, chuckled to herself, ran across the room, up and out into the street, shut the door and locked up, heaving a sigh of relief that she was free of bookworms for the rest of the day!

The night of the Zoom Book Club arrived.

After having spent a busy afternoon and evening cleaning the part of the castle they used, while James' phonograph collection blared through the empty halls and rooms; ironing (Nora ironed her The Secondhand Bookworm blouses, glad she wasn't having to wear them during Lockdown at the shop); cooking; reading online to the local schoolchildren; studying a handwritten tome that James had brought down from James Hall, one of his properties in Norfolk, written by an ancestor and called 'The Ghosts of Castletown Fortress'; taking a walk around the grounds to climb the Godwin Tower; and kissing (Nora concluded that James had recently developed *basorexia*, an overwhelming desire to kiss – it was a medical term she had discovered), they settled once again in the Duke's private library ready for their Zoom Book Club at seven thirty.

"Perhaps I shouldn't have read up on the castle ghosts again." Nora decided, glancing around the vast room, much of which was cast in shadows.

The fire was alight in the great stone inglenook fireplace that stood against the north wall and several lamps had been lit around them as Nora and James sat in one of the enormous red velvet sofas with their feet up on the walnut-wood coffee table. Outside, the rain pattered sharply against the great arched, mullioned windows.

The Duke was an avid collector of book subjects that interested him as well as a preserver of many manuscripts and books he had inherited. He had special collections of mountain climbing and exploration books, cartography, classic and ancient history, antiquities and architecture. There were also rare letters, manuscripts and journals in the main library in the part of the castle that was open to the public.

The books in the Duke's private library were in cases and most of them bound in leather, kept behind wooden and glass doors. Filigree woodworked arches with carved wooden pillars surrounded the centre of the room, supporting an upper gallery of books all around, even between the windows. In the centre, two enormous red velvet sofas faced one another with a walnut-wood coffee table in between. Six armchairs arranged with them faced a magnificent stone inglenook fireplace that stood against the north wall. The carpets were rich, red striped with gold, and numerous lamps stood upon tables.

James leaned into Nora and kissed her cheek.

"Are you referring to the sixth Duke of Castletown's admirer, the woman spurned by his love, whose ghost is often seen walking through this very library for she threw herself from the keep, clutching her favourite book?" He asked with a smile in his voice, quoting the manuscript.

Nora turned to him.

"Yes." She grimaced. "Have you never seen her, Your Grace?"

"Never." James assured her, kissing her again, this time on her lips.

EMILY JANE BEVANS

Nora wrapped her arms around his royal neck. Five minutes later she drew away, chuckling.

James, his face close to hers, arched an eyebrow.

"Does my kissing amuse you?" He feigned affront.

"No, assuredly not, Your Grace." Nora promised, shaking her head. "I just think I'm right about you having contracted *basorexia*."

James threw back his head and laughed.

"Ah yes, your kissing disease."

"Overwhelming desire to kiss." Nora corrected.

James nodded.

"I concur. I must have *basorexia*." He decided and spent another five minutes proving the point.

A clock on the mantelpiece chimed seven thirty, drawing Nora and James apart.

"The Zoom Book Club!" Nora remembered and turned to her laptop on the coffee table, drawing it towards her.

James smiled and stood up to pour them both some port. He gave the logs in the fireplace a poke so the flames rose with a pleasant crackle. He then leaned against the marble mantelpiece looking every bit like a Duke to contemplate Nora as she logged onto Zoom for the Book Club.

Once it was ready, Nora met the Duke's steady gaze. She smiled.

"You bring back a memory." She told him.

James nudged himself from the mantelpiece, picked up the glasses of port and joined her once more on the sofa.

"Memory?"

"The Autumn Supper and Festival you held here; when we put on a Black Friday book sale at The Secondhand Bookworm. Before the supper in the grand hall you invited the bookshop party up here to see 'The Ghosts of Castletown Fortress'…"

"Which you read from." James recalled, passing Nora her port, their knees touching.

She nodded.

"Yes. You had just abseiled down Godwin Tower and scared me half to death." She confessed.

James took her free hand in his.

"I did?" He was more pleased than concerned.

Nora snorted on a laugh.

"Yes. You certainly did, Your Grace. But I knew you to be a proficient mountaineer so I didn't doubt your safety."

"Good." He nodded, easing closer to her. "I could hardly wait to invite you here to show you the book. I knew you would love it."

"You were right."

"And as you read it…I so wanted to kiss you." He confessed, his lips now touching hers.

Nora chuckled against his mouth.

"*Basorexia.*" She murmured making him laugh as he kissed her.

It was how Cara found them when she logged onto Zoom first.

"Don't mind me!" Cara's voice sailed out of the laptop, amused.

Nora jumped and eased quickly from James, turning to see Cara and then Seymour in their Zoom box.

"Evening." She said, glancing at James and biting the side of her lip with a smile.

Smiling too, James took a sip of port before saluting them with the glass.

"We can always come back later, you know." Seymour teased, sitting down next to Cara.

James liked that idea but Nora gave her brother a look, drawing her copies of '*World War Z: An Oral History of the Zombie War*' and '*The Zombie Survival*

Guide: Complete Protection from the Living Dead'
towards her from the coffee table.

Another box appeared. Georgina had logged on.

"Good evening! Good evening, Your Grace." She gushed enthusiastically.

Nora wondered why she was in such a joyful mood.

"Hello, Georgina."

"Oh blast! Where did I put my books?!" She then realised and stood up, becoming smaller as she headed across her kitchen and into the hall.

Troy walked past, paused and noticed the Zoom conference. He waved.

Nora, James, Cara and Seymour waved back.

Humphrey then logged on, in the middle of calling out places where Georgina might have left her books.

"Try the downstairs toilet!" He yelled. "You were in there for a good half an hour earlier."

Nora smothered a laugh. Cara and Seymour looked at one another before chuckling. James remained politely silent, although his eyes twinkled with amusement.

"Hi, Humphrey!" Nora greeted,

Humphrey turned to his screen and grinned.

"Evening, all."

"How's the weight-lifting going?" Seymour asked him.

Humphrey pulled the sleeves of his t-shirt up to his shoulders and then flexed his biceps, like Harry. Nora stared.

"Looking good, mate!" Seymour nodded.

"Oh my." Cara fanned her face.

James glanced at Nora, who met his gaze and winked at him. He smiled, knowing she only had eyes for him.

Another box appeared. Roger was so close to his screen again that Cara squealed. He looked like a Porg from Star Wars.

"Is this working?" Roger asked grumpily with a downturned mouth.

Georgina had returned with her books (possibly from the toilet).

"Sit back, Roger!" She demanded, taking her seat.

"Humph!" Roger grumbled and took his place. He then picked up his newspaper with a rustle and disappeared behind it.

Betty arrived.

"Good evening, everyone. I've had a hell of a time with this flippin' thing. Somehow I logged onto Danny's Zoom chat he had just had with his eldest son, the one who fancies me, and I had to fight off his advances for a good ten minutes. And then this blooming machine crashed and I had to do some sort of Norton update. I finally got it working. That's me all over. Thanks for listening." She said.

Cara was highly amused.

"Glad to see you, Betty." Nora grinned.

"Ah, hello Nora, how pretty you look this evening. Your Grace." Betty greeted and ogled the Duke with a leer.

"Hello!" Amy arrived, followed instantly by Lucy.

"Hi!" Lucy greeted, disappearing for a moment behind an enormous glass of wine.

Finally, Felix, Spencer, Heather and Milton and Miss Raven logged on. The last arrival was Mrs Booth. Greetings were exchanged, taking a good five minutes, until Nora finally announced they had better start the Zoom Book Club.

"Good evening, everyone. How lovely it is to see you all and be together once again." She said.

They all concurred.

"We've been enjoying your livestreams." Lucy said, gazing at Nora and James.

"As have I!" Amy nodded.

"Are you going to ever do a tour of the cellars? And dungeons?" Spencer asked.

Nora knew he was fishing for suspected coffin discoveries.

"Erm…no, probably not." She said.

Spencer leaned closer to his camera, filling up his box.

"How are you feeling today, Your Grace? What with the full moon tonight." He asked.

James looked blank.

"Are you implying the Duke of Cole is a werewolf?" Georgina asked flatly.

Miss Raven let out a gentle shriek at that idea.

"I thought you suspected His Grace was a vampire, Spencer." Amy recalled, amused.

Felix sniggered and covered it with a cough.

"Who knows? Who knows?" Spencer smiled, leaning back and disappearing behind some white smoke.

Nora shook her head.

"Once Lockdown is over I shall give you a tour of the cellars and dungeons here, Spencer." James offered with an amused smile.

Spencer re-emerged through the smoke.

"Hmm. But you would have moved your coffin in advance, Your Grace." He decided.

Felix leaned forward, sniggering and snorting.

"We'll throw holy water over him and press silver crucifixes to his skin, then." Nora said and waved her hands for him not to press the subject so they could get on with the Book Club.

Amy, Heather and Lucy were laughing. Finally, everyone settled down again. Until Crossword-Lady interrupted, just as Nora opened her mouth.

"I didn't finish World War Z." She decided to share.

Roger groaned loudly.

"In fact, I found an even better book. Look!" She announced and held up a large paperback.

Everyone leaned in for a closer look.

"*The Zombie Donkey*. By Mr Brown." Nora read. "Uh-oh…"

"It was very interesting! I know the signs to spot now when I'm dealing with the donkeys." Crossword-Lady said, pleased. She opened the book. "Listen."

"Save us!" Roger lamented and covered his head with his newspaper.

"Er…" Nora tried to stop her, but Mrs Booth forged on.

"*There was a buzzard flying down the road and it saw…a…wait…it looked zinky, it looked zonky. Was it a donkey? Was it dead? It was a zinky, zonkey, zombie donkey. BRAAAAAAAAAAAINS!*" She read, accenting loudly and drawing out the *Brains* part.

Cara gasped on a laugh while Lucy and Amy covered their mouths. Seymour leaned in closer to listen. Spencer was interested, Milton riveted, but Betty shook her head and rolled her eyes, making rude hand gestures. Miss Raven looked terror-stricken.

"Mrs Booth, I…" Nora began.

Mrs Booth continued.

"*There were a couple of buzzards flying down the road and they saw…a zombie donkey! BRAAAAAAAAAAINS!*" She read.

Felix sniggered and snorted so hard that he disappeared headfirst under his laptop.

James was spellbound. Georgina looked annoyed.

"*He was wagging his bum. He had no tail. His tail fell off! He was a tailless-lifeless-donkey. He was a zinky, zonky, zombie donkey! BRAAAAAAAAAAAAINS!*" Mrs Booth read. She then showed them the paintings. "It goes on, explaining all the stages of donkey zombification, such as gums and eyes and feet falling off, so now I am prepared." She concluded, happily. "What a clever fellow this Mr Brown, the author, is."

Nora was glad it was over.

Amy was laughing silently, wiping the tears from her eyes. Miss Raven let out a howl.

"Oh! Oh how terrible! I have been dreading this. I wondered when the animals and birds, other than the polar bears of course, would suffer this fate. I wondered if the virus would turn us to zombification, like what almost happened to mother!" The latter bewailed.

"Miss Raven! It is fiction!" Georgina rebuked her sternly.

"Like heck it is." Spencer objected. "I think we all learned a lot from the books we read for the Zoom Book Club. If *Polar-Bear 9* does indeed mutate into a full blown zombie apocalypse we are now all prepared. I thought the books were spectacular."

Nora seized the opportunity to take control again and to lead the conversation into a discussion on the actual books they had read for the Zoom Book Club.

"And on that note!" She said loudly.

Everyone in their boxes looked at her.

She cleared her throat, smiled and slipped on her reading glasses.

"Let us start our Book Club."

"Here, here!" Humphrey stuck up his thumbs.

"About time!" Roger glowered, removing his newspaper from his head.

Felix climbed back onto his chair and picked up his books.

"Now. As we all would have learned as we read World War Z…"

"Is it not World War *Zed*. Like the English pronunciation of the letter?" Seymour asked.

"Oh. I assumed it was World War *Zee*, like World War *Three*." Nora mused. "A play on the term."

"World War Zed? World War Zeee." Heather tried out thoughtfully.

There was a murmur from all the boxes as people tried both pronunciations.

"Continue!" Roger interrupted.

Nora smiled.

"I'll stick with *Zee.*" She decided and resumed. "As we would have all read, the main character in this book interviews people about how life was between the discoveries of the zombie virus and when something called *The Great Panic* happened. The book's narrative is constructed of short interviews or stories narrated by survivors of the zombie war. The accompanying guide, *The Zombie Survival Guide: Complete Protection from the Living Dead* purports to draw from reams of *historical data, laboratory experiments, field research, and eyewitness accounts*, giving us a comprehensive and illustrated guide to face the greatest challenge mankind has ever encountered. It teaches the reader how to identify cases of infection by the zombie virus, Solanum, and recognize the hourly progression of symptoms, choose the right weapon and defend your home, among other things." She bit back a mirthful laugh.

People shuffled with their copies, nodded, smirked, chuckled or murmured.

"So, shall we work our way around the boxes of our zoom screen from left to right, row by row and give our reviews of the books as we did before?" Nora proposed.

Everyone agreed. Felix was first.

"Ahem. I often receive copies of these books in donations at my charity bookshop, so I am very familiar with them, having also read them both before of course. But I was happy to read them again in the spirit of the Zoom Book Club." He said.

Georgina's eyes narrowed into slits.

"I found myself saying on almost every page of World War *Zed*, 'I just don't believe it would happen like this'. I'm sorry, but being a zombie expert and an expert in this literature genre, I have to say, I would have written the interviews differently. Fair enough, some of the stories are brilliant - the pilot comes to my mind as a stand out example of this, but I found that I wanted know what happens to each person. However, the author jumps to the next interview and we never hear from the person again. As to the accompanying *The Zombie Survival Guide: Complete Protection from the Living Dead*, I found this to be highly enjoyable."

Nora stepped in.

"The Zombie Survival Guide is your key to survival against the hordes of undead who may be stalking you right now." She read from the back of the said book. "It covers everything you need to know, including how to understand zombie physiology and behaviour, the most effective defence tactics and weaponry, ways to outfit your home for a long siege, and how to survive and adapt in any territory or terrain."

Spencer was after Felix so dove in, saying:

"The top ten lessons for Surviving a Zombie Attack were especially helpful as we prepare for the Zombie Apocalypse."

Cara giggled.

"Organize before they rise!" Spencer continued, dramatically. "This is most important aspect. I think we would have learned from both books that this is a LIFE SAVER. For instance, I have found out in my online research that *the mutation* is starting to happen, RIGHT NOW. While walking along the lakeside after midnight last night…"

"Are you supposed to be out at night during Lockdown?" Betty asked.

Spencer ignored her.

"…I happened to come across the lair of a zombie. Someone locally, who obviously contracted *Polar-Bear 9* in its mutated form, had had to flee their isolation and hide in the woods by the lake. Are they a full-blown zombie yet? I think so. I heard groans and moans and shuffling in the bushes. A recent report online said that deep below in Siberia's permafrost, scientists found *thirteen* ancient zombie viruses preserved in the ice. That's where our current pandemic came from. So it must be related and will probably become a full blown zombie outbreak. We can now ARM ourselves against the somnambulists."

Mrs Booth and Miss Raven cheered. Roger groaned, like a zombie.

"And what about a review of the books?" Nora hinted in the midst of everyone else's stares or sniggers or shaking of heads.

"World War Z could almost be read as a series of short-stories or mini episodes. I believe they were written by a medium, or someone like Nostradamus, who knows the future and could see it as it will happen in his crystal ball." Spencer mused.

"Or *Palantír*." Cara chipped in.

"Those seeing-stones in Lord of the Rings?" Lucy asked.

"Yes, they're for scrying and telepathic communication." Cara said, hiding her smile.

"Where could I get one of those?" Spencer asked.

"I think we've gone off topic!" Georgina interjected.

"Call me later." Spencer told Cara.

"What's scrying?" Betty asked. "Sorry, Georgina."

"An object used for seeing or peeping." Nora explained. "Ahem, and to continue."

Amy dove in before Spencer could give his review of the survival guide. Nora gave her a grateful look.

"Use your head! Cut off theirs!" Amy declared dramatically.

Nora burst out laughing.

"And so, I quote the Zombie Survival Guide. But, World War *Zee* first." She began. "Each report contains enough emotions to make it very personal, I don't know if anyone else found that too, and so I was drawn into each one and caught up in the account. I thought this was an ingenious way of telling a story and I really enjoyed picking it up each evening to read an interview. What I liked was that it was not a story of just one person or group of people. It became a story of *humanity* told from various paths of life, countries, of different religions and beliefs. This makes it credible, well balanced and extremely readable. As to the guide, *ooooh*, what wonderfully useful advice." She winked. "And also very entertaining. I liked where it says, *this book is your key to survival against the hordes of undead who may be stalking you right now without your even knowing it*. Precious! Finn and I are now well prepared."

"And they *are* stalking us. Down by the lake." Spencer added.

Miss Raven was next.

"As you know I DO NOT enjoy reading adult books. This was truly a terror to endure. But I am grateful for the experience for I can now keep an eye on mother. I DO NOT wish to re-live my thoughts and emotions on each book but I will say that I thought the books were disgusting and gross and revolting and ghastly. The end." She said, pulled her brown jumper up and over her head and sat there.

Nora and James looked at one another. Fortunately Betty stepped in and gave a graphic and rather scandalous review of each book, on purpose, for entertainment and to shock Miss Raven, who seemed to be in a trance under her jumper, and then everyone else had their say.

"And to conclude…" Roger finished up, being the last one. "I began to suspect that I might be becoming an undead since increased dementia and loss of muscular coordination appear to part of the signs. I would have to say I would chose a section of lead pipe as a weapon and I intend to reinforce my house with steel rods and cinder blocks. Frozen zombies, zombies under the sea, zombies falling from the sky, ships full of refugees arriving from distant shores, wait… make that *zombies*."

Nora, Heather and Cara were giggling. Roger's eyes twinkled with sarcasm.

Once everyone had given their reviews, as before, those who wished to were invited to read passages they had chosen and then explain why they had chosen them so as to spark conversation. This took about an hour and during the readings Miss Raven had a very loud argument with her mother, who approached from behind Miss Raven like a zombie; Roger went off and made a cup of coffee, Georgina took a phone call, Milton made a TikTok video and Betty fell asleep. Danny woke her up by giving her a very wet, loud kiss.

James decided the entire meeting was extremely entertaining.

Nora was among those who enjoyed the reading segment and once again there were fascinating (and insane) insights into zombie wars and take-overs and apocalypses, with the usual wild conclusions drawn by Spencer, Crossword-Lady, Miss Raven and Lucy. Once this was finally over, Nora proposed they should each give the books a separate rating. Everyone gave their assessments from their zoom boxes in a left to right order once more.

It turned out that the average rating for the books was three stars out of five. This was pleasing because the topic was certainly out of everyone's comfort zone and it had been Cara who had proposed that they watch *World War Z* together for their first Online Movie Club because there were rumours going around that *Polar-Bear 9* had turned the entire populations of villages in Russia and Tibet into zombies. She was chuffed the books had been a success.

It seemed as though the second Zoom Book Club was just coming to an end when Crossword-lady cleared her throat.

"And may I just add." She began.

Everyone stiffened.

"It would be wise for us to start using natural toilet paper. The ancient Greeks used stones and pieces of clay. I would recommend this."

Everyone stared.

Roger dropped his book.

Lucy's mouth dropped open.

"Is that what you've been doing then, dear?" Betty cackled, looking down on Crossword-Lady from her Zoom box.

"As a matter of fact." Crossword-Lady smiled, dreamily.

James spluttered on his quarantini.

"Well, erm…ahem." Nora tried her best not to start laughing again. "Thank you everyone, I think you will agree that was all very interesting and also highly enjoyable. Well done for persevering and joining the club again. Thank you for your reviews and for undertaking this literary genre. I think it was a challenge and a great diversion to have read the two volumes together and engage in such an interesting discussion this evening."

Everyone clapped, having all enjoyed the discussion, even though it had been quite ridiculous and taken three hours.

"The Movie Club will take place tomorrow night at eight o'clock. I will email the URL around for everyone."

"Count me out!" Miss Raven shrieked and logged off.

"Oh. Oh dear." Nora grimaced.

"Ha-ha." Betty laughed.

"I'll telephone her when we've finished." Georgina said, slightly amused.

"Try not to have nightmares everyone. And stop going out at night hunting zombies, Spencer." Nora concluded.

Spencer smiled sinisterly and disappeared in a puff of green smoke, logging off. Nora laughed. Once Crossword-Lady had bid her goodbyes and Felix, Heather and Milton had logged off too, Georgina rapped her screen for attention.

"On a final note to my bookworms." Georgina then announced.

Everyone looked at her.

"Go ahead, Georgina." Nora nodded.

"It appears that the recent *Flattening the Curve* endeavour has helped the nation. I have just received word that all independent bookshops will be permitted to set up delivery systems and mobile sales initiatives as of next week."

"Hurrah!" Cara cheered.

"Hooray!" Nora clapped.

"Fantastic news!" Lucy applauded.

"Wonderful, Georgina." Betty toasted.

"This is marvellous news. At last!" Amy nodded.

"Great." Roger sang flatly.

"So I will be taking a meeting with Nora and Cara this weekend about their ideas for a new delivery system that will get our books out among the populace once more. I know Nora has some interesting plans. We will sort it all out, I will send around an email with details and rosters and all should be in effect by Monday." Georgina concluded.

There was a round of applause.

"Thank you, Georgina." Nora appreciated, pleased.

They all said their goodbyes, looking forward to the Friday night group movie viewing of *World War Z* and Nora was the last, ended the conference and closed her laptop. She leaned back, exhausted.

"Well done." James smiled, stifling a yawn. "That was one of the most fascinating evenings yet."

Nora laughed, shaking her head.

"I think I've just about had enough of zombies now." She confessed.

James leaned close to her and kissed her cheek.

"So have I." He agreed. "Now, what were you saying about *basorexia* again?"

Nora turned to face him, snuggling into the enormous sofa as he wrapped her in a strong and royal embrace.

"I don't remember." She chuckled dreamily.

"Oh, I think I do." James chuckled too and set about convincing Nora he probably did have her *sudden urge to kiss someone* desire.

"A little known fact," Nora said as his mouth covered hers.

"Hmm?"

"Sharks are always cranky because they all have *basorexia*, yet lack the lips necessary to act upon it."

James edged back and laughed heartily.

"Well, thank goodness I have lips." He said and descended eagerly.

"Yes, thank goodness." Nora agreed.

9 THE TUK-TUK DELIVERY SERVICE

On Monday morning, Nora sat at the counter in The
Secondhand Bookworm making note of the titles of
Penguin book mugs in stock while waiting for Karl to
pull up outside the door in his bright yellow Tuk-Tuk.
One of Nora's ideas for book deliveries, now that they
were allowed, had been to enlist him in a new book
delivery service endeavour around the town, seeing that
he had done such a good job with Nora's homemade
hand sanitiser and the castle's supply of toilet rolls for
the residents of Castletown.

While other booksellers and bookshops were listing
their stock online for sale, Georgina absolutely refused.
It was virtually impossible to even begin to list over
27,000 books in the Castletown bookshop on some form
of website, so they settled on supplying the regulars,
such as Mr Hill, Cat-Man and Miss Raven with books in
a phone and deliver system.

Georgina had *all* emails and calls from the
Castletown and Seatown shops rerouted to her home
computer and telephone now. She then organised lists of
requests for Nora to find on the shelves and then parcel

up and give to Karl for her locals. She already had
twenty parcels ready for Karl that morning.

Meanwhile, a new mobile bookshop service was
being organised using half of the Duke of Cole's fleet of
royal golf buggies. They were currently being renovated
to have bookshelves in the back where people could
come out of their house and buy any books, one person
at a time. The books left on the shelves would then be
wiped down. As a rule, people had to wear gloves as
they browsed.

There were six golf buggies. Three were being
refurbished for the project by Nora's brother Wilbur.
Nora's brother Milton and their sister Heather, as well as
Roger, were being enlisted as drivers. The service would
take place every Monday, Wednesday and Friday
morning. Everyone was excited (except Roger who
predicted he would run someone over). Nora was hoping
there would be loud sirens or tunes (like ice-cream
trucks) fitted on the buggies so the residents knew where
they were and could come out and browse and buy (but
that didn't seem likely).

In anticipation (and because they were bored at home
now that their college lessons were finished), Heather
and Milton moved temporarily into Nora's flat above
The Fudge Pantry.

Cara's plan for the Seatown branch was different
because The Secondhand Bookworm was in the midst of
a very large shopping area comprising of four long
streets that met in a sort of centre where a bandstand
stood. The houses and local customers were a bit further
afield, so Cara bagsied The Secondhand Bookworm van,
usually used for book calls, and set that up for their
delivery service and browsing library. This would be
driven by Amy who was thrilled.

The drivers of the buggies and van were to be given
special handheld PDQ machines to take card payments,

as well as cash. The vibe after the announcement had been made about the plans by the Duke of Cole on Castletown TV was one of excitement in the town. Nora was looking forward to getting started.

"And finally, three of Raymond Chandler's *The Big Sleep* Penguin book mugs." Nora concluded aloud in the front room of The Secondhand Bookworm and sighed. "I suppose I should pop one of you in the window display unit."

She slid off the swivel chair, stretched and picked up one of the green and white mugs. Once it was positioned nicely in the window, she stood back to admire her display, interrupted by a fast rapping on the door window.

"What the what?" She grimaced and headed over.

A large man stood waiting, sporting a green and white spotty mask which he whipped down.

"Do you have a copy of 'Interview with the Vampire' by Anne Rice in there?" He asked loudly.

"I'm afraid we're currently closed during Lockdown." Nora explained, politely. "If you take one of those cards and use that pen to write your request and leave your name and number, if I have it I can have it delivered to you."

"Huh. How efficient." He nodded, impressed.

Nora was surprised. Usually she was greeted with anger at not being allowed to fetch and sell books for people.

"Thanks." She nodded.

"Okay, I'll do that now." He turned to the said cards and pen underneath the business cards outside.

Nora's iPhone vibrated in her pocket. She took it out and saw that it was from James.

The Duke had several meetings lined up on Zoom that morning but was also organising work to be started

on his three golf buggies. He had sent her a text
message.

*'Wilbur has arrived. Jeeves has shown him to the
garages. I am about to start the town council meeting.
How are things? – James xx*

Nora smiled.

*'Quiet and boring, here. Good luck with your meeting
xx'*

*'Apparently there will be a statement released today
about a Party of Six initiative. Polar-Bear 9 cases have
gone down and a vaccine is imminent. The government
is planning on extending peoples social circles a bit –
James xx'*

Nora was pleased.

'That's excellent. Things are looking hopeful then xx'

The man posted his card.

"Thank you, I'll have a look and let you know if we
have it." Nora nodded.

He stuck his thumbs up, pulled his mask back over
his mouth and nose and headed off up the street.

*'It looks that way, Nora. I'll call you after the
meeting and give you an update. Miss you desperately –
James xxx'*

Nora read the message and sighed, dreamily, only to
be jolted out of her rapture by knocking on the glass
once more.

"Bah." Nora grumbled.

A wizened old man, gripping a check shopper on
wheels, was now standing there. His name was Mr Fink
and he fancied himself a bit of a local celebrity author.
He researched and wrote about the smuggling history of
Castletown and about the local taverns and inns. Once
there had been a scene because he had decided to let the
museum sell his books instead of Georgina, even though
the plan had been for The Secondhand Bookworm to sell
them. Fortunately that was all behind them now and

Georgina stocked copies of his book. He reminded Nora of Bilbo Baggins. Betty despised him because he had once referred to her as an *old lady.*

"Hello, Nora." Mr Fink greeted. "Wonderful to see a woman at work. Ah, the world today. Who would have thought it, eh?"

Mr Fink was a misogynist.

"Yes, it's amazing isn't it." Nora agreed, humouring him.

"Eh? Pardon? Who said that?" Mr Fink asked, spinning around and looking up and then down.

Nora rapped the glass.

"I did Mr Fink!" She called.

"Oh! Oh yes." He looked past Nora to peer deeper into the shop. Nora knew he was looking for Betty.

"Betty isn't here. It's only me during the Lockdown." Nora explained loudly.

"Ah, of course. It'd be dangerous for her to be out and about at her age. Probably resting those ancient old bones of hers." He surmised, rudely.

Nora was grateful Betty wasn't here. She expected all the protocols and rules of Lockdown would have been done away with and Mr Fink would have received a violent bop on the head from Betty's fist.

"Ahem. Is there anything I can help you with?" Nora prompted.

"Ah, yes, yes. I thought I'd let you know my new book will be available soon! '*Smuggling Love*', remember?" He enthused.

"Yes, I remember." Nora nodded, slightly amused.

During Valentine's Week last year, Mr Fink had spent his time giving walking tours of the local buildings and sites linked to the amorous history of Castletown. For instance, he had dedicated a whole ten minutes to describe The Secondhand Bookworm building, citing that among other things a pirate named Captain Thunder had once lived in the shop when it was a house, back in the late eighteenth century. So named for his thunderous voice, Captain Thunder was an amorous fellow. Ten of his fifteen children were conceived there. Nora wondered if Mr Fink knew about the attic being linked to Sweeny Todd.

"Jolly good." Mr Fink nodded. "I expect Georgina would like to stock the new title here when the shop reopens. Shall I put her down for five hundred copies?" He asked.

Nora blinked.

"Erm…it's probably best you discuss that with Georgina first." She said hastily.

"Hmm, yes I understand, you probably can't make an executive decision about stock. Ha. Women." He mused and chuckled to himself, like a misogynist.

Nora snarled.

"She will of course like the book, being that there is an entire chapter dedicated to this very building that now houses The Secondhand Bookworm." Mr Fink said arrogantly.

"Did you happen to mention anything about the Dukes of Cole in it?" Nora asked, hopefully.

"The Dukes of Cole? Hmm, ah, now I remember. Do you recall you asked me about the building at the top of the hill where The Fudge Pantry now is?"

Nora was impressed.

"I do, indeed."

"Yes, a fascinating story" Mr Fink nodded. "It had been the home of Father Diego Francisco Sánchez, a Jesuit priest who was chaplain to our Duke of Cole's great, great grandfather when the original castle stood mainly intact. You recall that he worked with smugglers to safeguard barrels of wine and spirits and that there was a tunnel from the property that led to the castle keep and dungeons where Father Sánchez hid the contraband.

He had to use good quality wine when offering Mass, you see, so he thought the smuggling of wines and spirits was justified. The fierce smuggler, Billy Black Teeth, married his bride Ada Hatt in the top room above The Fudge Shop. The marriage ceremony was performed by Father Sánchez and the Duke of Cole's sister was maid of honour. It caused a bit of a scandal at the time."

Nora recalled the tale vividly. She often thought of it when drifting off to sleep in her bed in her lovely flat, imagining Billy Black Teeth and Ada Hatt's secret marriage ceremony attended by the Duke of Cole's sister, and wondering what it would be like if James and she…

"I said there are also other romantic historical tales linked to the Duke of Cole's estate, Nora." Mr Fink repeated loudly.

Nora shook her head to clear her thoughts, having obviously disappeared in a fugue.

"Sorry, oh wow, really. I can't wait to read about it all." She nodded, pleased.

"I shall contact Georgina direct and arrange for the books to be delivered once you are up and trading once again. Meanwhile, I have started work on my next book. *The Historical Ghosts of Castletown*!"

Nora thought that was a brilliant idea. Her thoughts went to the Duke of Cole's book "*The Ghosts of Castletown Fortress*' but she couldn't be bothered to shout about it all through the pane of glass, so made a mental note to tell Mr Fink all about it when Lockdown was done with.

They said their goodbyes, Mr Fink turned and headed off, dragging his wheelie shopper behind him and another local stepped up to the door.

"Any Regimental Histories?" Don asked.

"Gah!" Nora replied and slapped her forehead.

Nora was happily looking through a scrapbook of Polaroid photos taken of the weird items found about the bookshop after every weekend when she noticed Karl's yellow Tuk-Tuk skid to a stop outside The Secondhand Bookworm.

"Finally!" She cheered, put the scrapbook aside, tugged on her mask and headed for the door.

"Good morning, Nora!" Karl greeted. "Ready for today's bookshop delivery expedition?"

Nora grinned behind her mask and stuck up her thumbs. She picked up the parcels and the sheet of details which she then carried to the back of the Tuk-Tuk. The parcels were placed inside and Karl given the sheet.

"May I take a photograph please? For the bookshop social media pages?"

"Certainly!" Karl nodded, taking the sheet of paper.

While he studied it, Nora snapped several photos with her iPhone, which she then sent over to Lucy, Georgina and Cara.

"Thank you, Karl. Have fun! And let us know how it goes." Nora said with appreciation.

"Will do, Nora!" Karl nodded and set off, chugging along the road and leaving Nora taking additional photographs of the funny little vehicle's journey.

"What an excellent idea!" Alice called over from the doorway of the delicatessen.

"Hi. Yes, let's hope it takes off." Nora nodded, watching Karl appear on the other side of the road next to the butcher shop having circled around the shops by the riverside, chug-chug along and turn down Market Street.

"Oh I'm sure it will take off. I believe Gray ordered a book from you and is going to have it delivered today." She said, referring to her son.

"He did." Nora confirmed. "And yes, it's on its way."

"Wonderful. I'll let him know. How are things going up at the castle, Nora? Wink-wink."

Nora laughed.

"Very well, thank you."

"We're all waiting. And hoping." Alice said.

Nora looked blank.

Alice wink-winked.

"You know what I mean, Nora! We're all waiting and hoping...For that *special* livestream. Wink-wink."

Nora still looked blank.

"Honestly, woman! I'm sure it will happen any day now. Everyone can see it in His Grace's eyes. The way he looks at you. Be still my beating heart. A *proposal* you ninny!" Alice cried out.

Imogene, who ran the organics shop and had organised Nora's kidnapping with Braxton last year, was crossing the cobbled square and dropped her box of vegetables she was on her way to deliver.

"Whaaaaat? The Duke finally proposed and I missed it. Are you engaged to His Grace now, Nora?!" She hollered.

The door of Lady Lane's antique shop opposite the bookshop opened. Lady Lane and her boyfriend Mr Sykes stood on the threshold in matching blue masks.

"A proposal?! At last!" Lady Lane cried, clapping her hands.

Mr Sykes stuck up both his thumbs, sucking on his pipe which was half wedged under his mask.

"A proposal?!!" Albert from the Print Shop shouted, so that his voice echoed loudly from beside the war memorial where his spaniel was doing its business. "Well done, Nora. At last!"

Nora suspected Alice was cringing behind her mask.

"No, no, everyone!" Alice yelled. "It hasn't happened *yet!*" She corrected.

Nora felt her cheeks getting redder and redder.

"Not yet?" My Skyes shouted in disappointment.

"He hasn't proposed yet?" Albert yelled.

"WHO HASN'T PROPOSED YET?" A familiar booming voice asked. It belonged to Billy who owned the antique centre with his girlfriend Jiao. He was standing on the kerb the same side as Nora, holding two Chihuahuas who were snarling and biting his watch strap.

"THE DUKE OF COLE!" Imogen yelled back.

The butcher shop door flew open.

"The Duke of Cole has finally proposed to Nora?" Tim the butcher asked, holding a headless chicken by its feet.

"Sorry, Nora." Alice grimaced.

Nora felt like melting into a puddle of embarrassment on the pavement.

"NO! HE HASN'T PROPOSED YET!" Mr Sykes corrected loudly.

Nora considered that everyone in the town could probably hear this conversation, possibly even James up at the castle.

"NOT YET? WELL, FINGERS CROSSED!" Billy yelled.

"ANY DAY NOW!" Tim shrieked.

"WE'LL KEEP AN EAR OUT, NORA!" Lady Lane screamed.

"ANY BOOKS ABOUT THE CHIP WAR: THE FIGHT FOR THE WORLD'S MOST CRITICAL TECHNOLOGY?" Albert bellowed, thus ending the topic.

Everyone went back into their shops and closed the doors, including a chagrined Alice, and Imogene hoisted up her vegetable box and continued on her way.

"Ahem." Nora supposed she was still as red as a bloodstained ruby. "I can have a look for you, Albert, and let you know." She called across the square.

He nodded, waved and set off.

Nora leaned against the doorframe of The Secondhand Bookworm, shaking her head.

"I think I'll go home soon." She told herself and then bit back a small smile. "Hmm, *home*. Ha. You never know." She said and disappeared back inside the bookshop, closing the door, hard.

Nora was packing away when James telephoned. When she saw his name and face on her iPhone, her stomach did several loop-di-loops.

"Honestly, woman." She rebuked herself.

The 'Proposal' shouting match in Castletown square was still echoing about her brain and Nora couldn't help but think of all the comments the local shop sellers had made about the way James looked at Nora in their Livestreams and that they all expected an engagement announcement imminently. She felt her cheeks redden again. Her finger swiped answer and she sat down in the chair.

"Hello!" She greeted, cheerfully.

"Nora, hello." The Duke of Cole greeted with his usual warm, affectionate tone reserved just for her.

"Get a grip." Nora whispered to herself.

"What was that, Nora?" James asked with a slight smile in his voice.

"Oh, oh nothing. It's been a crazy morning." Nora waved off.

"I can imagine." He chuckled. "Are you on your way to the castle yet?"

"Almost. I'm just closing up the bookshop."

"Wonderful. I'm finishing preparing lunch for us. I'll jump in a buggy and head on down to the gates to meet you. The meeting went well with the council. I also had a talk with the Prime Minister. I've lots to share with you." He explained.

Nora smiled.

"I'm looking forward to hearing all about it."

They rang off just as Nora noticed the Tuk-Tuk squeal to a stop once more outside The Secondhand Bookworm. Quickly, Nora hastened to the door, unlocked it and pulled it open.

"Hi, Karl. How did it go?" Nora asked nervously.

"A smash hit, Nora." Karl revealed. He passed her the bag of money from the delivery sales (several had opted to pay by cash upon delivery).

"Really. Whew!" Nora took the bag and leaned against the doorframe, relieved.

"All delivered and plenty of praise. Everyone's looking forward to the Duke's Golf Buggy Bookmobiles. Did I happen to hear on the air that His Grace has proposed marriage to you?"

Nora blanched.

"You *heard* that?!"

Karl shook his head, his shoulders jerking up and down with laughter.

"Na, I heard about it from Gray. Apparently his mum phoned to tell him I was on the way and relayed her mortification about the hullabaloo she had caused in the square."

Nora was relieved, but also felt sorry for Alice.

"Well, His Grace hasn't proposed marriage." She assured Karl.

"Yet." Karl winked.

"Ahem." Nora nudged herself away from the doorframe. "Thank you very much for today, Karl."

"No problem. I'm off to deliver some meat now from the butcher shop, all over Castletown. See you again on Wednesday morning. Beep-beep!" He honked the funny little horn and shot off.

Nora thought he looked like Bugsy Malone in a pedal car.

Once back inside The Secondhand Bookworm, Nora placed the bag of cash in the safe for Georgina to collect, finished up, turned off the lights, set the alarm and headed off 'home', glad the Tuk-Tuk Book Delivery Service was now a success.

10 THE MOBILE BOOKSHOP TASKFORCE

The Duke of Cole and Castletown Council revealed an easing up on the Lockdown measures as a new vaccine created to fight against *Polar-Bear 9* arrived at the end of May. The residents were invited to be jabbed at the town hall with the explanation that it would reduce people's risk of getting seriously ill or dying from *Polar-Bear 9*, of catching and spreading *Polar-Bear 9,* and protect people against different strains (variants) of the virus that were now appearing (none of them zombie). There was still the chance that people would get or spread the virus even after the vaccine, but its arrival meant life could start to head towards getting back to some version of 'normal' over the next few months. The aim was for Lockdown to ease and finish by the end of summer.

"I think this will encourage people not to be afraid of the vaccine." James said as he replied to an email from Paul at Castletown TV, arranging a time with him for a live jab broadcast on Thursday evening.

Nora grimaced and bit into her pancake. She didn't like needles very much.

"Are you sure you're happy to do this?" The Duke asked, looking up from his iPhone.

Nora nodded.

"Yes. Being vaccinated live on Castletown TV with you is the right thing to do." She assured him.

James reached across the table and laced his fingers with hers.

"I will go first." He promised her.

"You certainly will, Your Grace." Nora agreed.

He chuckled.

"And don't worry; I'll make it look painless." Nora added.

"Thank you, Nora." He looked uneasy too so Nora squeezed his fingers. "I'm not the only one who hates needles, am I?" She deduced.

"No, you're not." He confessed. "But I promised the Prime Minister we would do it. And Jeeves is a pro with administering injections."

"Glad to hear it!" Nora said and hastily filled her mouth with comforting pancakes and maple syrup.

Her iPhone beeped, notifying her of a text message.

"Mind if I read this?" She asked as James finished with his phone.

"Go ahead." The Duke nodded, standing to fetch the coffee pot.

The message was from Wilbur.

'Morning, sis. I told James I'd be along today to finish the last of the golf buggies. He mentioned you were both being stabbed on Thursday night on Castletown TV. Good luck! Tell him you hate needles and he'll make it up to you I'm sure, wink-wink. – Wilbur x'

Nora choked on her pancake, swallowing it awkwardly. James was crouched beside her in an instant, rubbing her back with concern.

"I'm okay." She chuckled, thumping her chest. "It was just Wilbur."

Nora showed James the message. He read it and grinned at the end.

"Hmm. I'm sure I will make it up to you." He said, kissed Nora's cheek and stood up to continue with their coffee.

Nora grinned too, watching him.

There was a polite knocking at the door, heralding the arrival of Jeeves with the morning post.

"Good morning, Your Grace." He bowed. "Good morning, Miss Jolly." He smiled fondly at Nora.

"Hello!" Nora greeted.

"Good morning, Jeeves." James nodded.

"Your Grace. I am about to go down to the gatehouse to prepare for the arrival of Milton, Heather and Roger." The valet informed the Duke. "I had a message saying they would be here at nine to continue practicing driving the golf buggies before the weekend, ready to set out on Monday morning. Wilbur will be completing the refurbishment of the three for the bookshop."

"Wonderful." The Duke smiled. "We'll join you shortly."

Jeeves placed the post in a holder on the table top.

"They have assured me they will be outfitted in masks and gloves once more." The valet then added.

"Let's hope Roger doesn't roll into a ditch again today." Nora said, biting back a giggle at the recollection.

The team of three drivers had already had one practice which had seen Roger ending up with his buggy on its side three times, almost running over a peacock which had chased him to Godwin Tower while hissing like a goose, and rolling neatly down a steep ditch and ending with his legs in the air.

James snorted on a laugh and cleared his throat at Jeeves' surprised glance.

"Ahem. No, I believe he will be quite capable in it today. I have the upmost confidence in him."

Jeeves' lips twitched.

"Wilbur will be painting The Secondhand Bookworm logo on the sides of the buggies for the bookshop." The valet explained. "He said he will be finished by lunchtime."

"That's good news." James said, pouring Nora a fresh coffee, his free hand resting on her shoulder.

"Mrs Booth will be arriving at ten o'clock to assist with the donkeys. If you need me, Your Grace, I shall have the walkie-talkie." Jeeves added and pointed to a device clipped to his belt.

The week before, Nora had brought the walkie-talkies from The Secondhand Bookworm to the castle so that James and Jeeves could have instant contact when needed rather than using their iPhones. Jeeves was spending most of his time busy in the gatehouse and grounds so the distance between the Duke and his valet was prolonged as James and Nora took care of themselves in the quarters aside for them in the large castle. Nora's idea was that keeping them in use would prevent the devices from degrading during Lockdown. James and Jeeves loved them.

"Channel seven, Jeeves." James said, picking the partner up from the worktop.

"Right you are, Your Grace." Jeeves nodded.

They both turned the dials to seven.

'Customer wants picking up from Windmill Road.' A voice crackled out loudly. *'It's the old prune with the blue rinse and plastic face visor again. She wants a ride to the dentist. Careful! She bites!'*

Jeeves looked bemused.

"Taxis." Nora said with a laugh.

"Ahem. Let's try channel eight, shall we?" The Duke suggested.

They fiddled with the dials. Gentle static filled the room, free of taxi drivers. Jeeves clipped the walkie-talkie to his belt.

"We'll be down later, Jeeves." Nora told him, sipping her coffee.

"I look forward to it, Miss Jolly." Jeeves bowed, took his leave of the Duke and headed off.

James placed the walkie-talkie on the worktop. He then sifted through his post.

A text message arrived on Nora's phone from Georgina.

'Boxes of books for the Duke's Golf Buggies are all ready for you to collect just inside the bookshop door with the blue platform trolley. Troy just wheeled it in for you.' Georgina had written. *'I've already dealt with Karl and loaded him up. Now I'm heading to Seatown. Enjoy getting ready for the mobile bookshop enterprise and don't worry about working in the shop today. I think you're doing enough with the practice driving at the castle this morning! xx'*

Nora read it out to James.

"We can go and collect the boxes of books once we've finished breakfast." The Duke suggested.

"Okay. But I get to pull the trolley." Nora said, eyes twinkling.

James pursed his lips.

"We'll take it in turns." He suggested instead, smiling with amusement.

"Deal." Nora agreed and they both laughed, eager to get started.

Castletown was bathed in sunlight as June dazzled on the horizon. Fresh rainbows and hearts and NHS logos drawn with coloured chalk covered the pavements and castle walls. The streets were empty of people and cars, still eerie and dystopian. But James and Nora were glad because they were able to hold hands without feeling on show as they strolled down the steep hill to The Secondhand Bookworm.

Once inside The Secondhand Bookworm, James loaded up the blue platform trolley with the boxes of stock for the backs of his refurbished buggies. Nora had chosen an interesting variety of novels and poetry with hopeful themes, as well as gripping and distracting fiction. She knew the tastes of many of the locals so there were all sorts of books included in the mix, including interesting and unusual tomes on war, occult, art, history, crafts and children's books.

It was a bit of an ordeal to get the heavy trolley up the step and onto the street. James and Nora heaved and hoed with no success. In the end, James disappeared into the yard while Nora spoke with Alice, who kept winking, until the Duke reappeared with a heavy sheet of wood and a selection of sand puddings. The latter were used as weights to stop the postcard spinners rolling into the road when placed outside. They were constructed out of builders sand and The Secondhand Bookworm blue plastic bags.

It took some arranging but it did the trick, a slope was constructed and James pushed while Nora pulled. The trolley wheeled up and out onto the street.

"We could have taken the boxes off and loaded them up in the street, you know, Your Grace." Nora pointed out, wiping her brow and leaning on the trolley handle.

James smiled.

"Yes, I thought of that first. But we were having so much fun." He confessed.

Nora laughed.

James leaned the wood against the topography shelves, Nora piled up the sand puddings on the flagstones, thinking uneasily about the ghost of the boy trapped down the well that was purportedly located beneath, set the alarm, locked up the shop and off they set, James pulling the trolley first.

"What a scoop!" A voice said from behind them.

Nora and James turned to see a member of the paparazzi running away, having snapped some photos of their escapade. They looked at one another and laughed.

"Do you think we'll make the national papers?" Nora asked, ironically.

"I expect so." James joked.

Nora joined the Duke, both pulling the trolley, which was very heavy. The roads and paths were extremely steep.

The old people from the retirement home danced by, sporting new masks they had made, pausing to clap and cheer Nora and James on.

Albert watched, fascinated, from his open shop doorway, and then Harry and Corrine came jogging towards them. When Nora saw Harry's muscles glistening in the sunshine she was filled with envy.

"Good morning, Nora! Good morning, Your Grace." Harry said, running backwards in front of them as they pulled.

Corrine stopped to stretch her leg against the castle wall, gazing at James with fascination.

"Morning!" Nora puffed.

James nodded royally, his cheeks slightly flushed.

"Are they boxes full of books for the mobile book service? Wow. Any Beano's and Dandy's?" Harry asked.

"Nope." Nora huffed.

James stopped pulling and they put on the trolley brakes for a breather.

"Maybe we should take up running?" Nora suggested, placing her hands on her knees.

James rotated his shoulders.

"Hmm. Might be an idea." He smiled at Harry and then Corrine.

"How are things at the castle?" Harry asked.

"Very well, thank you." Nora puffed.

"The ancient Romans shared a sponge on a stick before the invention of toilet rolls." Harry then said and winked at Nora, hintingly. Nora stared, mutely.

"Is that what…er…you two are doing?" She finally asked Corrine.

Corrine smiled thinly, standing on one foot while stretching out her hamstrings.

"We have our own wool and rosewater." She said frostily.

"Another ancient Roman method." Harry said.

"I heard corn on the cobs work well." James said.

Nora bit back a giggle.

"Is that what you do?" Corrine asked, eyes narrowed at Nora.

"The castle has…bidets." Nora corrected.

"Aw man! What luxury." Harry was amazed and jealous.

"I thought you would have been cutting up all your books and newspapers in the bookshop to use over Lockdown, Nora." Corrine said.

Nora noticed her eyes were twinkling slightly.

"I don't think Georgina would be too pleased about that." Nora pointed out.

Corrine smiled and then shrugged.

James released the brakes.

"Nice to see you both." He said, starting the trolley once more.

Nora joined in.

"Bye, Corrine. Bye, Harry." She nodded.

Corrine gave a small wave. Nora was pleased she wasn't looking with her usual daggers at Nora, commonly due to Harry's flirtation.

"Goodbye. Goodbye, your Grace." Corrine curtsied.

"Looking forward to your swimsuit modelling livestream, Nora." Harry said, winking broadly.

Nora's lips tightened. She sighed when Corrine's eyes narrowed.

"What was that?" James asked on a bemused laugh as they tugged the trolley past Nora's flat above The Fudge Pantry.

"The usual nonsense." Nora assured him.

"Oh...I'm not sure about that." The Duke said and glanced at Nora, grinning. "Although, I would have to insist on leaving out the livestream part."

"We'll see." Nora teased back.

James laughed and they were glad when they reached the castle gates.

The platform trolley was pulled slowly through the castle grounds to the garages while Nora and James chatted in the sunshine. The three refurbished buggies were in a neat row in the little compound by a large fountain. The three non-refurbished buggies were nearby. Wilbur was sign writing the bookshop buggies, chatting with Jeeves.

Milton, Heather and Roger had arrived and Milton was doing a driving impression, his hands gripped around an invisible steering wheel, giving advice to a grumpy looking Roger and making engine sounds. They were all wearing gloves and masks.

"Nora!" Heather waved, pleased.

Greetings were exchanged and Nora and James put on their masks.

"Wilbur said he is fitting cameras to the buggy cabs." Milton pointed.

Nora and James looked at a large black electrical case sitting on the grass.

"Georgina's idea." Wilbur said, crouching before a buggy and painting a large 'B' at the start of Bookworm. "She said she wants a live feed to be able to watch the buggies as they travel around."

"Wow." Nora was impressed.

"It's outrageous!" Roger protested, livid. "I won't have any privacy from Georgina's snooping and she's bound to criticise my driving methods. And what if I want to pick my nose?!"

Heather laughed.

"Just go ahead and do it." Milton suggested. "Mind if I film our practice again for TikTok, Your Grace?" He jiggled his iPhone.

"Go ahead." James allowed, amused.

"Bah!" Roger snarled behind his mask.

"I don't foresee any…mishaps today." Nora encouraged him, examining the buggies. "Just remember they will be a lot heavier loaded with books on the shelves at the back."

"Yes, sir." Roger moaned, climbing aboard.

Milton and Heather eagerly jumped into theirs.

It was illegal to drive a golf buggy on the roads so the Duke had acquired a special dispensation from Castletown council and Wilbur had made the necessary modifications to make the three bookshop carts street legal for the mobile bookshop service.

When the Duke of Cole had recently rebuilt his ancestral castle in Castletown he had purchased a brand new fleet of three golf buggies for staff to use around the grand estate. They were driven by tour guides, including one of Nora's regular customers Monica, who was an elderly lady with a penchant for cheap novels and the legend of the local Knucker Dragon. The Duke also used them to ferry lazy guests up to the castle from the main gatehouse when he put of events such as feasts and balls. He had added three more six months later totalling six of the vehicles.

The transmission powered the rear wheels and each buggy was virtually silent, operated by state of the art batteries. They travelled at 15mph and lasted for 25 miles with two or four people aboard. The rack and pinion steering on each buggy was light and precise, and braking was uncomplicated, using a combined pedal with anti-roll brake. Nora had to remind Heather and Milton that they weren't bumper cars.

"Oh yes. That's right. Better watch out Roger, just in case I forget." Milton joked.

He turned the key to start his buggy.

"I forbid you to film me. I'll sue if I turn up upside down in a ditch on that blasted Ticker-Tocker!" Roger retorted.

Milton laughed and started his buggy. Heather followed suit.

They set off along the winding paths of the Duke's estate, Milton filming with his iPhone with a running commentary, Heather singing loudly, Roger picking his nose.

"This may take a while." Nora decided, grinning as she watched them.

James led her by the hand to the grass verge.

"We may as well get comfortable." He said, drawing her down into the lush, dry grass.

"Aren't we supposed to be watching them?" Nora laughed as James leaned against a towering oak tree, wrapping his arm around her shoulder.

"Jeeves is on it." James pointed out.

Nora turned to see Jeeves using his arms to relay airport marshalling signals.

"I think that one means slow down." She deduced as Jeeves moved both arms up and down.

"And that one means emergency stop." James said next as Jeeves lifted his arms above his head.

"Oh dear." Nora grimaced, watching Roger spin around several times, overturn and roll down a bank.

"I'm fine! I'm fine!" Roger assured, climbing up and waving as Nora and Milton skidded to a stop at the top.

Nora buried her head in James' shirt, her shoulders shaking with uncontrollable laughter.

The morning passed quickly. After Roger's first blip, the rest of the driving practice went perfectly. Once the bookshop buggies were painted and fitted with the cameras, hand sanitising pumps, paper towels, carrier bags and free face masks and gloves, everyone organised the shelving with the books from the boxes Nora and James had brought up from The Secondhand Bookworm. Topics were divided between the three buggies, with Heather's buggy containing fiction, poetry and children's books, Milton's containing arts, crafts, theatre, cookery and hobby-related books (such as stamp collecting) and Roger's containing wartime, history, occult and religious books. Wilbur sent Nora the live streaming links for her iPhone and so she could set the feeds up on the shop computer. He then sent them to Georgina.

"It has sound, too." Milton explained.

"This is brilliant." Nora laughed.

"Ssss." Roger glared.

The drivers finished up and Jeeves ferried them in a buggy to the gatehouse leaving Nora confident that things would go well on Monday morning and that Roger shouldn't overturn when driving around a corner and spill books across the roads of Castletown!

Monday morning arrived after the usual routine of a
nation confined to weekends in Lockdown. After
breakfast the Duke of Cole and Nora set off down to the
garages to meet Heather, Milton and Roger.

"This is so exciting." Nora rubbed her hands together
once they were all together.

"Says you." Roger grumbled, donning his mask,
surgical gloves and a plastic apron (Georgina's idea). "I
feel like an insane surgeon about to remove someone's
brain."

"Zombie?" Heather teased.

Roger lifted his hands and made attack claws with his
fingers while groaning and rolling his eyes.

Nora giggled.

"Now, James and I will be down at the Secondhand
Bookworm watching you on the live feed and choosing
more books for you. Georgina said for you to finish up
in stages so you can each pull up outside the shop on the
pavement before the bay window and we can fill up the
shelving with replacement books – hopefully you'll sell
a lot – ready for Wednesday."

"If I don't get arrested for running people over."
Roger muttered as he climbed into the cab.

"Don't forget to finish up by lunchtime so that the
batteries don't run down and leave you stranded." Nora
instructed. "If you all finish at once, just wait your turn
on the cobbles. James has a dispensation for the buggies
to drive and park anywhere and everywhere so you
won't get a ticket from an angry traffic warden."

"Awesome!" Milton stuck his thumbs up before
climbing into his cab.

"Jeeves is waiting to let you out of the gates." James
smiled, watching Nora hand out printed sheets of the
routes they would drive through the streets of
Castletown. She also gave them a walkie-talkie each,
new ones purchased by Georgina especially for the team,

so they could call one another if a customer wished to browse through a different literary subject.

"There shouldn't be much, if any, traffic. It'll probably just be taxis and Karl to contend with." Nora added.

"Races!" Milton cheered.

"And we're off!" Heather declared.

Pedals were floored and the three buggies set off along the neat castle paths to the upper gates next to Jeeves's gatehouse.

"Wow. They look so smart and interesting. Thank you for this, James." Nora admired, leaning against the Duke affectionately as they followed on foot.

"It's a pleasure." James smiled, watching the fleet of refurbished golf buggies. "And Wilbur did an excellent job."

"He did." Nora agreed. "We'll see if we can bring up the live feed once we're down at The Secondhand Bookworm. I'm excited to find out if the mobile bookshop idea will be a success."

"I have complete confidence that it will be." James assured her.

When they reached the gatehouse the fleet had already departed. Jeeves let them out, praising the convoy and wishing Nora good luck.

Down in The Secondhand Bookworm, once the alarm was switched off, Nora turned on the lights and the computer while James gathered the post.

"Hmm. Another of those troubling notes again." The Duke said with furrowed brow, standing on the other side of the plexiglass that had been fitted around the counter.

Nora sighed.

"Yes. I do believe they're here to stay." She lamented.

James turned the note over, examined it thoroughly and then spent five minutes inspecting, scrutinizing, probing and prodding the ceilings, shelves, lights and walls around the front room for surveillance equipment.

"If it says *You are being watched* it is surely implying you are actually being watched, here, in the shop." James frowned, shaking his head.

"Or stalked." Nora said, no longer worried about it.

"That's not amusing, Nora." James was concerned.

"It's been going on for a while now and nothing's happened. I think it's probably a prank." She shrugged, bringing up the live feed on the bookmobile buggies.

James remained concerned but didn't pursue it, although Nora could see he was thinking of other ways to track the note-sender. He walked around the counter and joined Nora, blinking and then grinning to see the three boxes filled with the interior of each of his refurbished golf buggies.

Nora turned up the sound.

Milton was narrating loudly for his TikTok and Instagram viewers, Heather was singing cheerfully and Roger was driving, white-knuckled, muttering swearwords.

Nora giggled.

"Is Georgina watching?" James asked.

"Yes. She sent me a text message. Apparently she's already got some advice for Roger."

"Oh dear." James chuckled.

They watched Heather pull up to a kerb and jump out. Additional voices were picked up by the microphone and the buggy rocked and jolted as books were rummaged through and purchased from the back.

Milton did the same, followed by Roger. Heather jumped back in her cab and stuck her thumbs up at the camera. "I just sold eight books!" She announced.

Her walkie-talkie beeped.

"Heather! I've got some delightful children here requesting children's books, if you please?! Over." Roger's voice called, laced with sarcasm and annoyance.

Heather picked up her walkie-talkie.

'I receive you loud and clear, Roger. Where are you? Over.' Heather replied, sticking up her thumb and grinning at the camera.

'In Hell.' Roger answered.

Nora and James looked at one another and laughed.

Roger gave the address and Heather headed over. Nora and James watched as Heather sold five more books. Roger sold nine on his first stop and Milton twelve. They continued on. At one point, Roger ran something over that sent him bouncing high in the air from his seat so he hit his head on the roof. It turned out it was just a discarded old shoe, but Roger remained red in the face and delivering angry commentary until his next stop. Nora thought it was hilarious.

While Nora organised more books in arranged piles on the floor before the bay window, James put finishing touches on the plexiglass around the counter. Several people interrupted by knocking on the door window and making requests for books, toilet rolls or gossip, and Dora Magic payed a visit with her usual crazy veneration of Nora. Nora was glad when it was lunchtime.

The mobile bookshop service was a success. As the golf buggy fleet made its way back to The Secondhand Bookworm, Heather said she was out of stock! Every single one of her books had sold. Milton only had twenty left and Roger twenty three.

Heather pulled up onto the pavement outside the bookshop first, clapping her hands happily.

"That was such fun!" She said. "Oh. Here's the money!"

While Nora dealt with the takings, Heather and James loaded up the shelves at the back of her buggy from Nora's piles, while Milton and Roger waited their turn on the cobbles.

The whole process took another hour. Several locals came and praised the initiative and Heather sold four more books while waiting.

Once the buggies were restocked the drivers headed back up to the castle where the fleet would be safely stored until Wednesday morning.

Nora locked up The Secondhand Bookworm and she and James joined the bookworms at the garages just as the last buggy was driven inside and the doors closed and locked by Jeeves.

"Well done!" Nora praised, pleased.

"It was such fun." Milton grinned. "Although I almost kept running over a crazy old dude who was pulling a checked shopper. He was running around photographing people who were breaking Lockdown rules."

"Oh dear." Nora giggled. "That would be Mr Fink."

"Crazy old dude." Milton shook his head.

"I'm worn out." Roger said grumpily, rubbing his head.

"I'm not. I can't wait for Wednesday." Heather decided.

"Bah." Roger grumbled, but Nora suspected he had enjoyed himself really.

"Did Cara tell you about Seymour's plan for The Jolly Theatre, Nora?" Heather asked.

"No. What?" Nora was curious.

"Well, The National Theatre had made a lot of plays available for people to watch on YouTube during Lockdown so Seymour is going to sort out his bored actors and livestream some socially distanced plays every Friday evening on Castletown TV from The Jolly Theatre." Heather explained.

Nora was delighted.

"What a good idea," she praised.

James agreed.

"While I was on my rounds I learned that the townspeople have been doing some interesting things." Milton shared with them. "One man walks his dog every day wearing his wife's dresses, a different one each day, for the entertainment of his neighbours."

Heather laughed.

Roger stared.

"And, there are lots of boxes of junk out on the pavements in boxes with handmade signs that read 'FREE'." Milton added.

"There's a sign that says '*Rapunzel was in isolation and she was rescued by a prince*'." Heather remembered. "It was on a wall by someone's bedroom window."

"I saw a woman with a square plastic box over her head instead of a mask." Roger shared.

This time James stared.

The bookworms said their goodbyes and hopped into a non-bookshop buggy, driven by Jeeves, who set off to take them to the gatehouse after a successful, if exhausting, morning.

James took hold of Nora's hand, starting them walking to the castle.

"That seemed to go very well." The Duke smiled.

"It did." Nora agreed. "Georgina's going to drop into The Secondhand Bookworm and pick up the takings. She'll let me know tonight how much they made."

"I wonder how Seatown did." James mused.

"Me too." Nora nodded. "People seemed pleased to be able to shop for books in person again, rather than just online. I expect everyone will be glad when we reopen The Secondhand Bookworm."

"Well, bookshops are lanterns of civilisations and beacons of hope." James said.

Nora looked at him.

"Clearly you have never been to The Secondhand Bookworm, Your Grace. I would hardly call it civilised." She half joked.

James threw back his head and laughed.

"Perhaps you're right." He allowed, kissed the top of her head and they continued on to the castle.

That evening, Nora sat with her feet up on the large coffee table in the Duke of Cole's library, playing Animal Crossing on her new turquoise *Nintendo Switch Lite,* while James had a zoom meeting with the town council. He was up in the gallery above her, sitting in a red velvet chair at a small round reading table, looking very Duke-like surrounded by his magnificent books.

After setting up her own unique island, which she called Moonacre, and creating her avatar, Nora had met her two first villagers, a purple sheep called Muffy and a smiling cat called Rudy, and was currently picking up sticks for a campfire.

"So once you're set up and you have your airport established and running, it's called *Dodo Airlines*," Milton explained. "I'll be able to come and visit and bring you things, like a hot dog hat and some iron nuggets."

"Oops, I just shook a tree and some angry wasps are now chasing me." Nora said.

"You can't outrun them. You'll need medicine once they've stung you."

Nora shifted her iPhone to her other ear.

"Ow, that looks painful. My eye is now swollen." She told her brother.

"Ha. Yes. I sort of like that look."

"Hmm, I can see the appeal of this game. It's very relaxing. Apart from the wasps." Nora confessed, laughing as her purple sheep gave her a recipe for making medicine.

"It's brilliant. I visit loads of my friends' islands. Check out my tutorial videos on YouTube." Milton said.

"You really are cute, Milton." Nora grinned.

When they had hung up their call and Nora had saved her game and turned the console off, James called down.

"I'm just about to have a meeting with Spike." The Duke said, leaning his arms on the ornate gallery banister and smiling down at Nora.

She picked up her book.

"Okay. Shall I make us a pot of tea for when you're finished?"

"That would be lovely, thank you, Nora." James nodded. "After speaking with Spike I need to zoom with Kelly in Myanmar. I need to know how things are going with the locals since she's being spending Lockdown out there."

"Okay. I'll go to the kitchens now." Nora nodded, putting down her book.

James watched her go, turning when his zoom meeting with Spike began. Spike managed the Duke of Cole's rewilding estate in Castletown, including the Duke's popular lakes, forest, the area by the folly, the land with wild pigs and boars, ponies, bats and rare butterflies, the local Deer Rut Safari and he also organised special tours around the estate given in two pinzgauers, which were Austrian troop carriers.

As Nora walked to the kitchen, Georgina telephoned.

"Well done today!" Georgina praised.

"Thank you. It was interesting and quite enjoyable." Nora confessed.

"I was glad for the live feed in the cabs on the Duke's golf buggies. Troy and I were hooked. And what a success. Now, for figures. Cara and Amy took over five hundred pounds in Seatown."

"Oh that's wonderful." Nora was pleased.

"But Castletown took seven hundred and twenty three pounds altogether." Georgina revealed.

"Brilliant!" Nora smiled, opening the kitchen door.

"I've had lots of phone calls and email requests for books in the aftermath, so we're beginning to get busy again. We'll keep the bookmobile services on Monday, Wednesday and Friday for now, but if it proves successful we could consider doing it every weekday until we reopen at the end of Lockdown."

"Sounds good!" Nora agreed, reaching for the kettle.

"Thank you for all the work you've put into this, Nora. And please thank the Duke of Cole for me again. It's wonderful that he's lending us three of his golf buggies."

"He is wonderful." Nora agreed, dreamily.

Georgina laughed.

"Well, I can tell you're enjoying spending time with His Grace during this awful Lockdown." She said.

"I'm so grateful we've been able to quarantine together." Nora nodded, filling the kettle with water.

"Yes, it's very lovely. Unlike Troy and I. Ugh, that man."

Nora almost dropped the kettle. She grimaced.

"Oh. Oh, I'm sorry, are you having problems?" She asked, hesitantly.

"I know Humphrey's been sharing the gossip with you." Georgina revealed, sounding as though she didn't mind.

"Well…he did mention a few, erm…episodes." Nora admitted.

"Yes, well. He has a front row seat." Georgina allowed. "It's only that I do feel Troy should ask me to marry him. I don't think the man has any intention to ever do so. So I'm considering booting him out when we're free of Lockdown."

"Oh dear." Nora sympathised.

"It doesn't look like I'll be moving away with him to America after all. Oh, I just know I'm going to end up like Miss Raven, living with my mother as a bitter old spinster." Georgina lamented and let out an unladylike wail.

"Not at all. You're a catch." Nora assured her with a wince.

"Huh. If only Troy thought so."

"I'm sure he does. He might just be afraid of commitment?" Nora suggested.

"He is! Silly man. Oh it's probably just being confined with him during this Lockdown. It's testing all of our relationships. Anyway, I won't burden you with my moaning. Mother's always keen to listen to me. Now she's assured me she and Troy haven't been having an affair."

Nora paused, not sure whether to grimace or laugh at that idea. She decided to remain silent instead.

Once they had said their goodbyes, Nora finished the tea tray and carried it back to the library where James was now down from the gallery.

"Have you finished?" She asked the Duke as he rose to help her place the tray on the coffee table.

"Yes. A brief conversation with Spike. He had to help his wife wash all their shopping. Apparently he and his wife place all their shopping in the bath for seventy two hours before they will use it, in case it is infected with *Polar-Bear 9*." James explained.

"Oh." Nora was alarmed.

"Hmm. And I had a brief conversation with Kelly and my charity in Myanmar. They've asked if I'll go over there once the Lockdown is over."

Nora nodded.

"That's a good idea." She agreed, although she didn't like the thought of being apart from him for a prolonged time.

"Yes. But I can sort that out later. Who knows how long the Lockdown will continue? I'll be glad when we're all vaccinated."

Nora shuddered.

"Oh yes. The Jab." She remembered.

James smiled and wrapped his arms around her.

"Don't worry. It'll be fine." He assured her.

"Hmm. We shall see." Nora mused, dubiously.

Thursday and the day of the live vaccination arrived.

Nora had watched as groups called Pro-Jabbers and Anti-Jabbers emerged on the internet and social media around the world. It was being called an *'infodemic'*, with a lot of different information and theories about the virus and the vaccine being circulated.

Spencer Brown belonged to the Anti-Jabber party and warned Nora and James that the vaccine for *Polar-Bear* 9 had been made by an ancient federation from the Arctic that wished to make everyone into slaves before they took over.

"It's all to do with the *Gargantuan Retune* of the entire earth." He called down to Nora and James from his tower window. "The whole thing was engineered by the ancient peoples of the North Pole, the *Northpolians*, who are preparing to arise from their frozen city in the hollow earth with Godzilla and his fellow Titans once we are all transformed. There are already *Northpolians* among us in disguise. They made this vaccine using the blood of vampire bats and *pangolins*."

"Aren't they those scaly anteaters?" Nora recalled.

Spencer drew his cape around him like Count von Count from Sesame Street and hissed, disappearing in a puff of blue smoke.

Nora thought pangolins were being given a very bad rap.

When Jeeves arrived at the kitchen that evening with a sealed packet containing a syringe for the Duke and a syringe for Nora, she glanced at James beside her, remembering Spencer's theories.

"Ready for the *Northpolian* uprising?" James nudged her elbow teasingly.

"As ready as I'll ever be." She chuckled.

Roy appeared on the laptop having logged on with Castletown TV.

"Good evening, Your Grace. Good evening, Nora!" He greeted with enthusiasm. "We're ready to go on air in five. I'll introduce you first, and then, Your Grace, you can give the NHS explanation and history of the development and content of the vaccine. Then you can both receive your jabs. Good luck!"

Because the Duke of Cole was involved with many charities that also provided immunisation vaccinations, he had been able to acquire all the details of the process and ingredients, side-effects and effects of the vaccine for *Polar-Bear 9* and was satisfied it was safe and ethical.

"Thank you, Roy." James nodded, glancing at Nora who cringed at the needles.

"I am trained in field medicine and immunisation, Miss Jolly." Jeeves encouraged her warmly.

"Jeeves has inoculated thousands over the years on our trips overseas with several charities." James added, rolling up his sleeve.

A text message arrived on Nora's phone.

"Sorry, I'll just silence that." She said as Roy started his live programme, explaining the benefits of the *Polar-Bear 9* vaccination.

The message was from Spencer.

'Remember, the Duke is a Vampire. I hope he's made you one too, so you'll be immune to the powers of the jib-jab.' Spencer had written.

Nora felt her bottom lip tremble with mirth, silenced her notifications and sat down next to James where Roy welcomed her and the Live Jib-Jabs began.

As the vaccination approached, James took hold of Nora's hand out of view of the audience. At one point Nora thought all the blood had been cut off from her fingers when James squeezed her hand during the injection. He kept his royal composure, and fortunately Nora kept hers, although her eyes watered and she had to blink as inconspicuously as she could while Jeeves gave her hers.

Afterwards, James shared his experience with the audience on the benefits of vaccines from his work overseas, encouraging everyone to go to the town hall when called so as to receive their inoculations.

After questions and answers from the locals who emailed in, which Roy filtered out as usual with smirks and shakings of his head, (Nora assumed Spencer and Harry had been emailing), they said their goodbyes and logged off.

Nora and the Duke of Cole looked at one another.

"I am so sorry, Nora." James winced, lifted her squeezed hand to his mouth and pressed a kiss to her numb fingers. "Are you okay?"

Nora chuckled and tentatively touched her arm, followed by his.

"Yes. You?" She asked, concerned.

He nodded.

"Yes, thank you, Nora." He assured her, opening her hand and lacing his fingers with hers.

"I'm afraid you will feel the pinch for a day or two, Your Grace and Miss Jolly." The valet reminded them.

"Lovely." James said with a small, rueful smile.

"I shall be heading down to the town hall tomorrow for my vaccination." Jeeves said. "Is there anything else you need before I retire for the evening, Your Grace?"

"No. Thank you, Jeeves." James smiled.

"Then, good evening, Your Grace. Good evening, Miss Jolly."

"Thank you Jeeves." Nora waved.

"Goodnight, Jeeves." James nodded.

Once they were alone, Nora and James drew closer to one another.

"Poor Duke." Nora sympathised.

James pouted.

"That was rather painful."

"I know. I'll make us a batch of pineapple oat cookies to make us feel better. Cara sent me the recipe this afternoon and I know we have the ingredients." Nora proposed.

James looked delighted.

"Wonderful, Nora. I'll help." He said and went to stand. "OUCH!"

Nora laughed as he sat back down at the kitchen table, tentatively clutching his arm.

"What a pair of wimps we are." Nora giggled, wincing because of her own painful arm.

"I've always been a wimp when it comes to needles, Nora." The Duke confessed with a rueful grimace.

"Oh dear. Perhaps this will help meanwhile." She decided and pressed a bolstering kiss on his lips.

James sucked in a surprised breath through his nose, before cheering up considerably.

"Oh yes." He murmured happily, wrapping his arms around her and ignoring the pinch of the vaccine. "Yes this will do nicely."

"Indeed, Your Grace." Nora hummed against his lips, all thoughts of *Polar-Bear 9* and the vaccine melting away. "Indeed."

11 BOOKWORM CONTAGION

At the end of June Georgina sent an email to all the bookshop staff one morning to say that she and Troy had caught *Polar-Bear 9*. She said her ears felt like they were full of snow and the tips and lobes had turned blue; her tongue felt like it was white and hairy, her eyeballs were on fire with black lava; her blood had turned to ice and she felt massive, like a beached whale washed up on shore. Apparently bloating was a possible symptom.

'So Troy and I will be confined to bed for the next week or two, where we will probably spend the whole time arguing with thick, hairy tongues. That's if I don't pop. Humphrey has to self-isolate now because he's in our bubble, so he won't be able to do anything, and mother has locked herself in her annex. We have supplies and plenty of paracetamol but we have to just wait it out. I've redirected bookshop emails and phone calls to Cara so any questions ask her. Do what the heck you like with the shops. I don't care. Keep safe xx'

"Poor Georgina and Troy." Nora lamented.

Cara telephoned Nora while James was buttering toast, looking concerned.

"The poor thing." Cara sympathised. "She sounds like a bear. I phoned her and she just seemed to respond with a very deep, husky voice that went, *whuff, whuff, growl, chomp, woof, woof.*"

Despite the dire circumstance Nora couldn't help but giggle.

"Oh dear. Well, I suppose we'll keep things as business as usual where we can." She proposed.

"Yes. I'll deal with email and phone requests and find any books people want in both shops. I can also package them up and post them out. Amy will continue with the Seatown mobile bookshop van getup and Lucy is still on all correspondence and advertising. We'll keep Betty away because of her...*age*." Cara ended on a whisper.

"Agreed." Nora nodded.

"If you keep doing what you're doing in Castletown we should be fine. Let's hope Georgina gets better soon!" Cara concluded optimistically.

However.

Two days letter Nora woke up feeling like she had been placed in a vice overnight. Her ears were blue at the tips and lobes, her eyes looked like they had turned into black polar bear eyes or she was suddenly possessed by a demon, her skin crawled, as though she had bear fleas, her blood felt like ice and she was aware of an intensely stronger sense of smell.

"Oh rats." She rasped, but it sounded like she had in fact said, '*whuff, woof*'.

Although her arm felt like a lead pipe, Nora reached for her glass of water. She had to force it down. She then started shivering.

Next, she rolled onto the edge of her bed and hunted for her box of rapid tests. She shoved a stick up her nose, rolled it around and dunked it into the small bottle of clear liquid with a dropper at the end. Finally, she placed a drop of the solution onto the rapid test strip. A red line appeared at the top, indicating negative. But then…

"Oh *whuff, whuff.*" Nora groaned.

Another line had appeared, telling her she had contracted *Polar-Bear 9*.

She waited for the full half an hour just in case, but the way she was feeling was enough to have her know she had the dreaded Arctic virus. Still sitting on the rich rug next to her bed, Nora picked up her phone. She squinted and found James' name.

"*Whuff, woof?*" The Duke answered groggily.

"*Woof, Whuff!*" Nora lamented, realising he must have caught it, too.

It took them a while but after drinking and clearing their throats they could finally understand one another.

"I feared you had it, too." James rued, huskily. "I've already contacted Jeeves to tell him. He's insisting on coming to care for us."

"No, but he might catch it!" Nora was worried.

"He said he's part of our bubble anyway so he's probably already been exposed. Nothing I can say will stop him. Nora, I've asked him to bring you here, to my room." James explained, in between coughs and sniffs.

"Really?" Nora's eyes widened, painfully.

"It will save Jeeves walking the corridors between us and we can suffer together." The Duke explained.

"Shall I start crawling to you now?" Nora proposed.

"Oh my darling, I'd come and carry you here if I could." James bewailed.

"Stay right where you are, Your Grace. I'm on my way. Erm…where is your bedroom exactly?" She asked, moving onto her knees and then adding one hand to help move as she held the phone in her other.

James laughed and then groaned.

"Oh I feel so bad." He lamented and proceeded to give her instructions.

Once Nora was upright at the door (she used the ornate doorframe to hoist herself into a standing position), she kept a hand against the walls to steady herself as she made her way to the Duke of Cole's bedchamber. If she hadn't felt so rotten she would probably have had to hold onto the wall for support anyway. She couldn't believe she was going to James' private space.

"Get a grip, Nora." She said, although it sounded like '*Whuff, whuff, woof, growl*'.

At last, Nora turned into a wide, beautifully decorated stately corridor. At the end was a large open doorway. The Duke of Cole was leaning against the doorframe in his pyjamas.

"Nora." He greeted huskily and shoved himself away from his door.

Nora couldn't help but half laugh-half cry (the first with amusement, the last with suffering) as they made their way to one another along the great distance, each using the wall for support.

"It's not funny, my darling." The Duke of Cole rebuked with a pained grin as they finally met.

"I know. It's bloody awful." Nora corrected.

James huffed on a laugh that ended with a groan. He wrapped his arm around her shoulders, she wrapped her arms around his torso and with one another as support they made it to the Duke of Cole's bedroom.

Nora was briefly aware of a magnificent interior, with a fireplace, huge windows, panelled walls, additional doors (one ajar that led to a massive bathroom), sofas, a desk and the biggest four-poster bed she had ever seen.

They climbed aboard and both collapsed on their backs beside each other.

"That was a nightmare." Nora said when she was finally able to speak.

"Here." James passed her a glass.

"Ugh."

"We have to drink. It's para…parac…para…you know, that pain killer that brings down your temperature."

"*Parachetamol*?" Nora asked, reaching for the glass but grasping at the air.

"That's the Italian pronunciation." James said.

"What?" Nora was confused.

They both then dissolved into laughter, spilling some of the drink on Nora's neck. She finally managed to take the glass.

"I've had two already. It should help when it kicks in. It's the only thing that does anything." James said, lifting the glass to her mouth.

Nora drank it and cringed.

"Are they dissolvable?" She realised.

"Yes." James nodded, gently stroking hair from her clammy forehead with shaking fingers.

"Ugh. It smells disgusting."

"Your sense of smell is strong, too?" James realised. "Mmm, well you smell so nice. I could eat you all up."

Nora almost choked on her medicine as the Duke of Cole nuzzled into her neck. She giggled as he sniffed her.

"But I have no appetite." He lamented, making her finish the beverage of pain killers.

"Maybe that's a good thing." Nora said. "I value my neck. Are you really a vampire?"

James fell back into his enormous pillows, laughing a little manically.

Nora felt his forehead.

"Oh dear. You're on fire." She said and threw the empty glass onto the floor.

James jumped.

"I think we might be delirious." Nora then giggled.

"I can't feel my eyes." James was blinking repetitively.

"Here. Let me." Nora offered.

"Ouch."

"I'm so sorry, Your Grace, let me kiss it better." Nora apologised as her fingers prodded his eyelids.

She leaned over him but ended up kissing his pillow. James found that hilarious. He laughed so much that he got the hiccups. Nora found that hysterical. They were on their backs in uncontrollable laughter, while groaning and clutching their sides and then their heads in pain, when Jeeves arrived.

"Have we been invaded?" Nora asked, sitting upright, clutching her head and falling back down.

The Duke of Cole let out a yelp.

"It is I, Your Grace. It is your valet, Jeeves. Do not fear my appearance." A muffled voice consoled from inside what looked like a hazmat suit.

James and Nora stared.

"Jeeves? Is that you, old man?" James leaned up to stare as the figure moved slowly towards the bed.

"Your Grace! Has Miss Jolly been staying here in your bed all this time?!" The muffled voice asked, scandalised.

Nora and James looked at one another and dissolved into laughter, clutching one another and resting their heads on each other's shoulders.

"How dare you impeach my honour, Jeeves." Nora said between laughs.

"After the journey she undertook to get here." James joined in and wagged a finger at the hazmat suit, before laughing into Nora's shoulder.

"Forgive me, Your Grace. Miss Jolly." Jeeves apologised hastily. "Erm…it would appear to me that you both have the new *Polar-Near 9* variant."

Nora fell back into the pillows, which felt like marshmallows. She had a sudden urge to eat them.

"What?" James asked, falling back too.

"Your Grace. Nora. If you have the new variant then you will feel feverish and delirious for a few days. And then you will just feel exhausted. The worst of it all will be over soon." The valet explained, picking up the discarded glass on the floor.

"That's good news." James mumbled, clutching his forehead.

"I am here to care for you both, Your Grace." Jeeves assured them kindly. "Sadly all you can do is wait for the virus to run its course."

"Care for Nora first, Jeeves." James said, reaching for Nora's hand but taking hold of her nose instead.

Nora held still. They both then dissolved into laughter.

"Miss Jolly. Have you had any paracetamol?" Jeeves wanted to know.

"*Parachetamol?* Si, si signor. " She replied.

James found that hilarious.

"Good, good." The valet said and stood beside her. He felt her forehead, leaned over her and nodded, taking her pulse.

Nora stared mutely at the enormous square head swimming before her delirious eyes.

"Hmm. Yes. Alright then. Both of you must stay in bed, but…"

The next second a huge bolster cushion was suddenly plopped between them. Nora sat up straight and stared at it.

"James?" She asked, prodding it with a finger.

"It's a bolster cushion from one of the sofas, Miss Jolly. For propriety." The valet explained.

"I'm hardly going to ravish her in this state, Jeeves." James pointed out, still clutching his forehead.

"James?" Nora repeated, amazed, still prodding the cushion.

James noticed. He burst out laughing.

"Well, we had better maintain a level of respectability as you weather this virus together. In your bedroom. In your *bed,* Your Grace." Jeeves said, pointedly.

"Very wise, old man." James agreed, although he was hardly aware of what was going on.

Jeeves examined the Duke next while Nora lay back, shivering, but starting to feel a little better as the paracetamol kicked in.

"I will monitor you both but you will probably just want to sleep. Apparently that's what…"

Jeeves' voice trailed off as the sound of snoring started.

James was suddenly fast asleep.

"Are there bees in here?" Nora asked, looking around, before she suddenly fell asleep and started snoring, too.

Jeeves pondered them both, nestled either side of the long bolster pillow asleep. He smiled slightly, shook his head, turned and set off, worried but confident they would both do well in the end. They had one another, after all.

After three days of laying almost comatose, with the occasional fit of giggles and bizarre conversations, both Nora and James felt well enough (and no longer sounded like bears for the majority of the time) to speak with people via telephone calls.

Georgina, who was about four days ahead of them on the virus train, described how there would be relapses into delirium but that they would settle into a feeling of complete exhaustion until the wretched thing had indeed run its course. Probably by the end of two weeks.

"At one point I thought Troy was a balloon animal." Georgina shared. "I tried to pop him with my sewing needles."

Nora and James laughed for over an hour about that.

The rest of The Secondhand Bookworm staff remained in good health. The shop remained closed in Castletown but Roger opened up each day to restock the three golf buggies, which were a roaring success, and Jeeves continued to help out (from an enormous distance) as the little vehicles were collected from the castle estate each day and returned after trading. Jeeves also remained virus free. It was decided that he was a bionic valet.

When Spencer learned that the Duke of Cole and Nora had the variant of *Polar-Bear 9*, he sent an email recommending using an ancient cure for the black plague. He said to shave the bottom of a live chicken and strap it to their lymph nodes. When the chicken got sick they were to wash it and then return it to its place on the body.

Mrs Booth missed Nora's crossword assistance. She recommended that Nora slather ten year old treacle over her whole body to speed up recovery. James asked for some treacle from Jeeves when he came to change the bedding and make them take showers on the fourth day.

"I don't think that'll achieve anything, Your Grace." The valet assured them as Nora headed off for the enormous bathroom, taking it slowly and wincing because of her aches and pains.

On the sixth day, Nora and James regained their appetites, but were still exhausted if they moved. The bolster between them became their friend named 'Bolsty'. Bolsty was quite mischievous. Sometimes he would get up by himself and roll to the end of the bed, but he was always back between the Duke of Cole and Nora again at night time.

On the seventh day there was a relapse into delirium.

Bolsty became quite annoyed by it and rolled to the end of the bed.

Nora was pleased because now she could put her hands on the royal blue pyjamas covering James' chest.

"What is it like to have a flat chest? It must be very, very, very strange, Your Grace." She said and burst out laughing.

James laughed too, pressing his burning hot forehead to hers.

"It is. It really is!" He nodded.

When he saw Nora attempting to read book four in Dora Magic's zombie saga, but that the book was upside down, James fell off the bed laughing, dragging the duvet with him. Nora helped him climb back up.

"Shall we slather each other in treacle?" James proposed, feverishly.

Nora snorted and buried her face in the recovered duvet, laughing.

"What? What?" The Duke asked. "It was a suggestion from Doctor Donkey."

"Doctor Donkey?" Nora asked and giggled uncontrollably for five minutes.

By the time they reached the ninth day, the Prime Minister of England had contracted the variant and insisted on having a zoom meeting with James.

It was decided that they would use a tropical background and position the laptop so that the camera wouldn't show that they were in the Duke of Cole's bedroom. Unfortunately James pressed the potato head filter and had the whole conversation looking like a potato with a face. The Prime Minister didn't mention it because he assumed he was seeing things in his delirium.

On the twelfth day, both Nora and James tested negative for the virus. Although they still felt tired, it was decided they would spend the day in the kitchen and library and that Nora would return to her own room that night. James looked grim about that.

It was Saturday and Nora assured Georgina she would be happy to go back to work on Monday.

"I'm so glad." Georgina admitted. "The Secondhand Bookworm in Castletown really benefits from your magic, Nora."

"How kind of you to say so." Nora yawned with a smile.

"It's true. Roger has done his best, I'll give him that, but he doesn't have your knowledge of the locals' literary tastes. Good news from the houses of parliament though. Did you hear that Lockdown will be lifting for all businesses and schools at the start of September? That gives us the whole of August to continue with the Tuk-Tuk delivery service and the Golf Buggy mobile bookshops in Castletown and prepare the shop for opening at last!"

"I did hear that." Nora recalled, picturing the Prime Minister telling Potato-James. "I'm so glad."

"It will be weird to physically see one another again. I'm really looking forward to it."

"Me too." Nora agreed.

"Well, I'm glad you and His Grace are better, Nora. Speak to you soon." Georgina clapped and they said their goodbyes.

That night, Nora and James parted at the top of the grand staircase in the Duke's private wing. Nora wrapped her arms around James' neck.

"Although we felt so terrible, I had a lovely time spending twelve days and nights with you." She told him.

James hugged her tight.

"If only it could continue." He kissed her cheek and looked at her, smiling. "I don't think I ever laughed so much in my life."

"I know." Nora giggled, shaking her head.

James looked at her intently for a long moment, before drawing her close for another hug.

"Your Grace, I do believe we may be suffering from redamancy." Nora decided.

"That sounds agreeable. What does it mean?" The Duke asked, looking down at her, curiously.

"It is the act of loving someone who loves you; a love returned in full." She explained with a tender smile.

She felt James' hands tighten on her arms before he smiled too and kissed her, saying:

"Also from *Eudaimonia*." He murmured against her lips.

"And what is that?" Nora asked, easing back.

"I looked it up. It means a human flourishing; a contented state." James told her, stepping away.

"Perfect word use." Nora nodded and with that they bade one another goodnight.

Back in her room, Nora was about to climb into bed when she noticed a lantern light in the distance through her tall mullioned window. It was bobbing up and down along the moat that ran beside the castle walls in the road that led down to the Wetlands. She stared. She rubbed her eyes.

"It must be a little lingering delirium." She decided, closing the curtains and shrugging.

It was actually Spencer Brown, taking one of his nightly rambles and looking for leeches for his bloodletting.

12 THE BEGINNING OF THE END

Throughout the month of August The Secondhand Bookworm in Castletown kept to a successful routine of mobile bookselling and book deliveries using Karl and his Tuk-Tuk and the three refurbished golf buggies. Sales were increasing in all the local retail establishments and then general optimism improved as *Polar-Bear 9* gradually disappeared, going through several weird but less serious mutations until only a couple of new cases were reported a day in the nation. By the end of the last week of the month it was announced that the county of Cole had been totally free of new cases for one week and everyone in the town, except Spencer Brown, had been vaccinated.

With only one week to go before reopening The Secondhand Bookworm for trading once again, with temporary restrictions for a while or course, plans were made to retire off the Duke's mobile bookshop buggies (Wilbur was going to reverse the modifications that had been made on the following weekend) and Karl was returning to his former Tuk-Tuk taxi service. Nora set

about preparing the shop for opening on the first
Monday of September.

The local Catholic Church was open once more for
Mass but there was to be no singing until further notice.
Nora and James attended Mass on Sunday, pleased to be
back in their Christian community which was like an
extended family. When the Duke and Nora arrived they
wore their masks and were told that for the time being
the congregation, which was spread out sparsely,
shouldn't say any responses and neither could they shake
hands for the sign of peace.

Everything ran smoothly but there was a noticeable
lack of people. Nora hoped everyone would get their
social confidence back soon!

Meanwhile, on the Tuesday before the opening of
The Secondhand Bookworm, the British government
lifted restrictions on pubs, restaurants and social
gatherings with suggestions that cautions remain in place
for a few more weeks and people should still practice
social distancing.

The Duke of Cole and Nora headed down that
evening to support the pubs of Castletown and partake of
local beers and conversation.

"Mask on." Nora said as she and James stepped
though the private castle gate at the top of the hill. "Oh
look. Most people are still wearing masks even though
it's becoming optional." Nora pointed out.

"I expect mask-wearing will remain for a long time."
James mused, putting on his dog-face mask.

The Duke's Pie was a popular restaurant at the top of
the hill where Phil, who doubled as the local postman
and a waiter and was the town's notorious gossip, stood
encouraging people into the establishment.

"Good evening, Your Grace. Good evening, Nora!"
Phil greeted from behind his blue surgical mask. "Are
you here for an impromptu dinner?"

"No, we're just saying hello." Nora replied, pleased to see through the windows that there were people inside, sensibly spaced out, and enjoying hefty pies and mash. The waiters wore face masks and plastic visors as they poured drinks and brought meals from the kitchens.

"It's good to see you open and with patrons, too." James smiled politely.

"Yes, indeed, Your Grace." Phil nodded. "We have a current rule that our diners must book first and they must all bring their own cutlery. Most people have complied so far. Only two families had to run back to their kitchens to collect their knives and forks."

Nora giggled.

"And how are things up at the castle? Any good gossip to report for my popular blog? I'm into podcasts now, too." Phil announced and whipped out his iPhone. "I am here this evening with His Grace, the Duke of Cole and his girlfriend, the lovely Miss Nora Jolly, who runs our local bookshop The Secondhand Bookworm!" He said dramatically, holding up his iPhone and sticking up his thumb while looking at the camera. "Of course, you will all know the lovely pair from their regular Livestreams over Lockdown from the Duke's spectacular recently rebuilt castle. The question we are all desperate to know is…will there be an imminent *special announcement* from our very own royal and bookworm? Wink, wink! Nudge, nudge! We're all waiting with bated breath. So, I'll take this opportunity to ask His Grace and Miss Jolly. When can we…oh…?"

Nora and James had fled down the street, heading for the nearest pub.

It seemed as though the inns, taverns, pubs and cafes of Castletown were currently offering takeaway beers and beverages only. Landlords and owners stood in their doorways, wearing surgical gloves while handing glasses of beers or ale to queues of people who were cheering and imbibing keenly.

The crowds parted for the Duke of Cole and Nora, who were clapped, toasted and cheered when they were spotted. They stood and conversed with the locals (keeping a social distance), James accepting a Cole Brew on the house and Nora a Cole Ale on the house.

"I don't know how long we can keep this up before it starts to affect us." Nora whispered to James as they approached the fourth pub amidst cheers and claps.

"I was thinking the same thing." The Duke nodded and hiccupped.

"Oh dear." Nora suppressed a bubble of laughter. "This is not good."

It took a good two hours to do the rounds, or a Nora renamed it, their *royal pub crawl*, and both were quite tipsy by the end of it. Fortunately the delicatessen was open for take-away coffees, so James and Nora joined the queue, smelling like a brewery, and bought a double expresso each.

They sat and drank the hot beverages on a bench by the war memorial, masks down when taking sips, chatting with locals and posing for selfies, until they were so full of liquid that they said their goodbyes and walked quickly back to the castle and the royal privies!

Friday was the last day of book deliveries by Karl and his Tuk-Tuk and the last day of the Duke's mobile bookshop golf buggy taskforce. After waving the three drivers off from the castle, James returned to his study in his tower for zoom meetings and Nora headed down to The Secondhand Bookworm. Teddy bears and paintings were gradually being removed from people's windows. Many shop doors were open as preparations were being made for Monday's opening.

"Good morning, Gina."

Crossword-Lady was standing at the door of the bookshop, holding her daily paper.

"Oh, hello Mrs Booth." Nora replied politely from behind her mask, digging her keys out of her bag.

"Are you opening for trade today?" Crossword-Lady asked.

"No. I'm here to get ready for our opening on Monday." Nora explained.

"I won't keep you then, Gina." Crossword-Lady promised. She opened her paper. "Today's literary crossword puzzle clue."

"Go ahead." Nora nodded, sticking the key in the door lock. She frowned. It felt odd. There seemed to be bits of putty in the key hole. She wiggled it and finally managed to turn it. "Odd." She frowned.

"Ahem. 'The Lost *blank* by J. Meade Falkner." Mrs Booth read. "An 1895 gothic novel."

"The Lost *Stradivarius*." Nora answered, wiggling the shop key.

"Oh, that was easy enough. Thank you, Gina."

"It's a short novel about ghosts and the evil that can be invested in an object. The object being a very fine Stradivarius violin." Nora explained.

Mrs Booth smiled mildly.

"Well, I'd best get up to the castle. As you know, the donkeys will be leaving this afternoon and returning to the donkey sanctuary. Jonathon is preparing it all in anticipation."

"I hope to be back to wave them off." Nora nodded.

"Goodbye, Gina. Enjoy your movie role research." Crossword-Lady said and set off along the road.

Nora shook her head, opened the door, closed and locked it behind her, fled across the room and around the counter, punched in the alarm number and then looked down.

Stuck to the sole of her boot was a familiar piece of paper.

"Bah. You again." She muttered, stooping to pick it up.

She unfolded it.

"*Nora Jolly. You are being watched.*" She read aloud.

Slowly Nora screwed the note into a ball. She lobbed it into the bin and then scanned the room, feeling uneasy, as if she *was* being watched. She sighed loudly and her glasses steamed up as her breath shot up from behind her mask. Annoyed, she tore off the mask and flopped down in the swivel chair, thoughtfully.

There was no need to run around the shop gathering fresh books for the bookshop-buggies because they would be decommissioned at lunchtime. But Nora had a list of things from Georgina to do in preparation for Monday.

A text message arrived.

Nora dug her iPhone from her pocket. It was from Humphrey.

'Are you at the shop, yet? I'll be there in ten minutes with my tools and a box of hand sanitisers for the walls, six red bins, a gazebo for the yard, a table and a lorry of paper towels, tissues and anti-bacterial spray. Looking forward to seeing you after so long! Xx'

That cheered Nora up.

'Just arrived and unlocked. I'll be by the door waiting for you xx' She sent back.

The telephone started to ring. Nora blinked. She then picked up the receiver.

"Good morning, The Secondhand Bookworm."

Heavy breathing.

"Is that the bookshop?" A familiar voice asked.

Nora gasped. She then cleared her throat.

"Yes, yes it is." She replied, recognising Mr Hill.

"And who's that?" Mr Hill asked.

"It's Nora."

"Do you work there?" He asked wheezily.

"Yes!" Nora replied.

"Arora. This is Mr Hill."

"Yes, hello Mr Hill. It's actually *Nora*."

"Arora. I've got some books for sale." The madman said and coughed and spluttered for one whole minute.

Nora barred her teeth like a piranha.

"We're reopening on Monday." She explained.

Long, loud, frantic breathing.

"Monday, you say? I see. Never mind, then. I'll telephone Georgina. B-bye." He decided and hung up.

"You do that." Nora said to the dial tone and hung up too.

She waited for a few minutes, just in case he decided to call again, but the phone remained silent. Nora headed for the window to see if Humphrey had arrived. She saw his truck pull up on the pavement outside The Secondhand Bookworm followed by three beeps of his horn.

When Nora opened the door it was to the sound of reprimanding.

"It's half outside *my* shop!" Hatchet-Face from the antique shop next door was telling Humphrey's back as he rummaged in his truck.

"I've only got to unload and then I'll park over there." He told her cheerfully.

"That's not good enough!" Hatchet-Face's hands were on her hips. "I need to bring that penny farthing into my shop."

"I'm sure you can squeeze it between the side of the truck and your shop front." Humphrey smiled, lifting three enormous boxes at once with his new muscles and turning around.

Hatchet-Face fell silent. Nora wondered if she had swooned. She leaned out of the bookshop door to see.

Hatchet-Face had one hand slowly reaching towards Humphrey's right bicep, her mouth wide open.

"Go ahead." Humphrey told her smoothly.

"My, my. Take as long as you like." Hatchet-Face said, drawing her hand back so as to fan her face.

"Just a few minutes." Humphrey said and headed towards The Secondhand Bookworm, Hatchet-Face's stare trailing him like he was a magnet and her eyes were chrome steel ball bearings.

Nora was trying hard not to giggle.

When he saw Nora, Humphrey grinned, followed by a wink.

"You'd be amazed how much trouble my biceps get me out of now." He told her, carrying the boxes down the step.

Nora followed him, laughing.

"Oh Humphrey. It's so good to see you again." She grinned.

He deposited the boxes and turned to face her. He then closed his eyes and inhaled.

"I really missed that."

"What?"

"Your scent."

"Ewww. Are you Jean-Baptiste Grenouille?"

"That serial killer from the novel 'Perfume'?" Humphrey asked and laughed, partly offended. "No. I'm not going to bottle you up into a fragrance. But I wish I could give you a hug."

"Elbows." Nora said and they moved closer to touch their elbows together in greeting.

Gradually, they became aware of Hatchet-Face staring at them through the bay window glass.

"Is she drooling?" Nora whispered.

Humphrey snorted.

"I'll get the rest of the stuff and then move the truck for her." He decided.

Nora stood aside, watching him go. She then whipped out her iPhone to tell Georgina about her brother and Hatchet-Face.

When Humphrey returned from parking his truck in front of the butcher shop (usually a rare spot to claim but the town was still like a deserted settlement), Nora noticed lipstick on his cheek in the shape of Hatchet-Face's mouth. She gawped.

"That's all done." He announced, pleased.

"Have you become a gigolo?" Nora asked.

"What?" Humphrey gawped back.

Nora pointed at his cheek with a finger.

"Oh." Hastily, Humphrey rubbed it off. "I can't help it if bored housewives throw themselves at me. Blame the guns." He said and curled his biceps.

Nora doubled over laughing.

"I have to tell Georgina!" She was finally able to say.

"Hah. She won't be surprised."

"Do you have a new secret life I don't want to know about?" Nora asked, alarmed.

Humphrey just grinned.

"This might be a long morning," Nora muttered, her lips twitching with mirth.

They set about opening the boxes.

"I have to fix a wall mounted hand sanitiser dispenser to a space on a wall in each room and every corridor." Humphrey explained. "Can you help me find the spaces? You can fill the dispensers up with the anti-bacterial soap. Look how many Georgina sent over. Twelve!"

Nora calculated for a moment.

"Yes, that will do it." She nodded, picking one out of the box. "Oooh, snazzy."

"I also have to put this gazebo up in the yard."

"For the book cleaning station?" Nora recalled.

"Yes." Humphrey was bemused.

"I can see this is going to be fun for a while."

"Well, I have these laminated signs for you as well." Humphrey plucked out a folder. He held up a random sign. It read:

> IF YOU TAKE A BOOK FROM A SHELF
> THAT YOU DECIDE NOT TO BUY
> **PLEASE** TAKE IT TO THE CLEANING
> STATION IN THE YARD ON THE GROUND
> FLOOR THROUGH THE KITCHEN AND PLACE
> IT ON THE TABLE FOR WIPING DOWN BY A
> MEMBER OF STAFF!
> THANK YOU!

"People will start making themselves cups of tea again." Nora rued, grimly.

"Like they did during Black Friday?" Humphrey remembered.

"Hmm!"

"There are also these signs." Humphrey said, pulling out another.

> THIS IS A SNIVEL STATION.
> WIPE YOUR NOSE AND PLACE THE
> SOILED TISSUE INTO THE
> RED BIN. PLEASE SANITISE YOUR HANDS.
> THANK YOU!!

Nora grimaced.

"These are the red bins. Small but secured enough to keep snot inside."

"I expect they'll be kicked around the shop." Nora decided, grimly.

"I also have these face mask dispensers. And boxes of surgical gloves for the door."

"I expect a lot of people will moan about that." Nora prophesied.

"Definitely." Humphrey grinned. "I'm glad you have the plexiglass all set up." He noticed.

"Yes, thanks to James." Nora agreed. "Shall I make us a cup of tea each and then we can get started. It'll probably take us all morning."

"That sounds perfect!" Humphrey concurred, reaching for his drill.

It did indeed take all morning. Despite the gargantuan amount of books lining the walls throughout The Secondhand Bookworm, Nora and Humphrey managed to find spaces for the signs and hand dispensers.

There was a sanitising station set up outside the shop. Humphrey drilled into the wall next to the door for one of the dispensers that would still allow the cheap paperback boxes to be fixed either side of the door but also house a compulsory sanitising requirement before entering the shop. Hatchet-Face ogled him while he did so.

Additional dispensers and signs were fitted underneath the alarm pad in the front room behind the desk, in the small hallway at the bottom of the stairs, in the doorway to the back room and in the kitchen; on the humour section bookcase in the first floor landing, the doorway into the first floor, front room and the children's room at the back; next to the crime section on the second floor landing, in the doorway of the second floor, front room, the wall next to the steps leading into the paperback room and finally in the window alcove in the paperback room. All twelve. With additional signs, mask dispensers, red bins and tissues.

"Whew!" Nora had just sat down to recover when the first of the Duke's golf buggies pulled up outside The

Secondhand Bookworm. Humphrey was building the gazeebo in the yard.

"Over already?" She checked the wall clock and her eyes widened.

It was one o'clock.

Heather jumped out of the cab to meet Nora, who stepped out of the shop carrying two flat packed boxes.

"Hi! How did it go?" Nora asked her sister, curious.

"Oh wonderful. I'm so sad it's my last day." Heather confessed, opening the back of the buggy.

Nora joined her.

"Wow. You sold most of them?"

"Yes. And people were saying how pleased they were that The Secondhand Bookworm will be open once more on Monday."

"Well, people often show enthusiasm and then no one bothers to turn up, so I don't expect we shall be busy at all next week." Nora said, starting to fill up the box with the leftover books.

Heather chuckled.

"I see you're getting your bookshop mind-set back already."

Nora laughed.

"Oh dear. You're right. The bitter, pessimistic Nora Jolly of The Secondhand Bookworm returns."

Heather giggled.

The leftover books fitted in one of the boxes so Nora left the empty one leaning against the wall while she carried the full one into The Secondhand Bookworm. Milton was heading towards them so Heather jumped back into her cab.

"Here are the takings." She said, handing Nora a small pink tin. "I'd best drive up to Jeeves. He's at the gates waiting for us. What a fun job that was. Then it's back to your flat to start packing up. Milton and I will be going home this weekend." Heather explained.

"I hope you enjoyed your stay." Nora smiled.

"It was brilliant. Speak soon!" Heather waved and set off as fast as the buggy could go, now a professional at handling it.

As the next buggy neared, Nora did a double-take.

Milton pulled up alongside the pavement, almost rolling the buggy onto its side as he repetitively bumped the kerb. The reason why was that he appeared to have collected a young, female passenger who jumped out of the buggy after pressing several *mask-kisses* against his lips.

"Milton! Who is that and why were you kissing her while driving?" Nora asked, amazed.

Milton stepped out of the cab.

"As Albert Einstein once said, *any man who can drive safely while kissing a pretty girl is simply not giving the kiss the attention it deserves*."

Nora shook her head.

"Honestly!" She half-laughed.

They loaded up the box that had been leaning against the bay window. Milton handed her his green tin of cash.

"I really enjoyed this job. I almost hope we get another pandemic so we can do this again." He joked, climbing back into the buggy.

"Milton!" Nora rebuked.

"Ha. Just kidding. Right, I'll take the buggy back and then pack up my things from your flat. Maybe I'll see you on Turnip Yard later." He said, referring to his Animal Crossing Island.

"Maybe." Nora chuckled and waved him off.

Nora was able to retrieve two more boxes from inside the shop by the time Roger's buggy arrived.

"How did you do?" She asked her colleague as he stepped out of the buggy.

"I almost ran over a cat. And Mr. Fink." He replied glumly.

Nora bit back a smirk.

"Sell much?"

"About half of it. Glad it's over." He said, helping Nora load up the boxes. "I'm in Seatown with Cara on Monday. I hope Miss bossy-boots doesn't have me disinfecting the entire stock all day."

"It's possible." Nora grimaced.

"Bah. Poops to it." Roger scowled, although his eyes were twinkling.

The books were all unloaded, the blue cash tin added to the safe with the other two, and Roger set off in the last buggy to return it to the castle. Nora watched sadly, blinking back tears.

"Blasted hormones." She sniffed, wiping her blurry eyes.

When her vision came back into focus she did a double take. Georgina was reversing into a space a little further up the road in The Secondhand Bookworm calls van.

Nora slipped on her mask and watched, noticing a familiar dustcart parked not far from the space Georgina had chosen. It belonged to Hugh, the local street cleaner, a grubby man with a bad attitude, who was emptying a bin while muttering expletives behind his grimy face mask about doggie-do-do bags being left in the general waste.

He turned and noticed the van.

"Oy! You there! Maniac van-driving female! Watch where ya going!" Hugh hollered, shaking a fist full of doggie-doo-doo bags.

Georgina ignored him, knocking the front of his cart with her back bumper before straightening the van up alongside the kerb.

"Are you blind, you little pixie bat? Watch my cart!" Hugh hissed, shaking his broom in his other hand as well as the doggie-doo-doo bags.

Nora covered her mouth, smothering her laughter.

Georgina stepped out of the van, slowly put on her sunglasses, looked Hugh up and down, stuck her nose in the air, slammed her door and clip-clopped away from him, leaving Hugh contemplating lobbing a bag at her retreating form, but wisely deciding against it.

"Ridiculous man." Georgina said from behind her posh yellow face mask as she reached Nora.

"Hello! It's so good to finally see you in the flesh!" Nora greeted, aware of Hugh wheeling off his cart while pausing to shake the doggy-doo-doo bags at Georgina every few steps.

"I know, I know! It's been so long! Aw, we can't hug!" Georgina lamented.

"Ridiculous, isn't it!" Nora said but they touched elbows instead and laughed.

They stepped into The Secondhand Bookworm, closing the door behind them.

"Would you like a cup of tea?" Nora offered.

"Thank you but I'm not staying, Nora." Georgina refused, taking off her sunglasses. "Miss Raven still wants her books delivered so I've come to relieve you of several ladybird tomes and any Julia Donaldson and Axel Scheffler books you might have. She's looking for '*The Smeds and the Smoos*' and a book called '*Zog*'." Georgina rolled her eyes.

"It's possible we have those." Nora said, not admitting that she often read all the Julia Donaldson and Axel Scheffler books that came in for stock.

"Lots of people are still scared to come out into society like Miss Raven, so it's touch and go as to whether you will be busy or not next week." Georgina decided.

"I had that same thought, earlier." Nora confessed.

"Well, it can't be helped. We'll do the best we can by being open and safe. I'm not going to spoffle." Georgina sighed.

Nora giggled.

"Spoffle?"

"To fuss over trifles." Humphrey said, emerging from the kitchen where he had finished setting up the book cleaning station in the yard.

"Oh. Ha."

Like Nora, it appeared Georgina had been amusing herself by discovering unusual words during the Lockdown.

Georgina placed her handbag on the swivel chair.

"I'll use the ladies and then look for these silly books." She announced, picking up the loo keys from their hook under the alarm, next to the new hand sanitiser dispenser. "I'll also take a look at all the units you've put up, Humphrey."

"Right you are, sis. I'm all finished so I'm heading off in a bit." He nodded.

"Lovely. You can deal with that wretched American when you get home. He's decided to oil all the door handles around my house with his 'Tin Man' oil can." Georgina glowered. "It's such a silly squeaky thing. It sends all the dogs into bouts of howling as he travels around oiling every darn handle or hinge he can see. Silly man."

"Oh dear." Nora tried not to laugh.

"Huh. I know, I know, he probably means well. But I think I might break up with him once Lockdown is well and truly over and chuck him out. Oh! I shall probably become an old maid and end up like Miss Raven. My mother is already living with me in her annex!" Georgina snarled and marched off upstairs.

Nora and Humphrey looked at one another as they heard Georgina's loud, stamping footsteps heading off into the distance.

"It's been like this for weeks." He smirked.

"They probably need to have a bit of space from one another." Nora decided.

"You and His Grace seem to have coped quite well." Humphrey pointed out, gathering his tools.

"Yes, we have." Nora agreed, dreamily.

Humphrey glanced at her and chuckled.

The bookshop door opened. Nora turned to see a man wearing both a blue surgical mask and a plastic face visor, his grey hair up in a bizarre top knot.

"Do you have any…" He began to say but his phone pinged loudly.

Suddenly the man threw his arms in the air, turned around and ran off screaming loudly, across the cobbles, up the other side of the road and down Market Street. Nora and Humphrey watched the whole thing in mute silence.

Humphrey then laughed.

"That must have been the NHS alert. Someone nearby must have tested positive for *Polar-Bear 9.*" He realised.

"Ugh. I hope they don't come near us. I don't want that again." Nora grimaced.

"I was fortunate not to catch it. I credit the guns." Humphrey decided and flexed his bulging biceps again.

Nora snorted with laughter.

Georgina came back with a small pile of books and the loo key.

"Apparently there is no longer a shortage of toilet paper." Georgina said.

"We needn't have feared. Mrs Booth told me that coastal people used mussel shells and coconut husks for toilet paper. As well as leaves, grass, ferns and fruit skins." Nora shared.

Humphrey laughed.

Georgina screwed up her nose.

"Silly old woman." She said, unhooking a blue plastic carrier-bag for Miss Raven's books.

"Hemmy-hem-hem." A familiar voice joined in from the opened shop doorway.

Georgina turned as Humphrey and Nora recognised Dora Magic standing on the threshold.

"We're currently closed to the general public!" Georgina pointed out loudly.

Dora Magic blinked.

"Ahem. *I* am not just any member of the public, I can assure you, Georgina Pickering." Dora pointed out.

"Do I know you?" Georgina screwed up her nose even more.

"Erm…this is Dora Magic. Our local independently published author." Nora said, warily.

Georgina's eyes narrowed.

"Oh, yes." She recalled, drily.

"And Miss Nora Jolly's greatest admirer, recognising her for the wonderful bookseller she truly is! Deserving of her own shop, her own enterprise, the rightful owner of The Sec..."

"Can I help you with anything?" Georgina interrupted impatiently.

Nora and Humphrey watched as Dora Magic bristled, like a porcupine, and gave Georgina the evil eye.

"No. No, I don't believe *you* can, Ms Pickering." Dora said, aloofly. "I wished to just convey to Nora Jolly that I now have a new series of novels available. I…"

"I'm afraid we don't stock self-published books at The Secondhand Bookworm. It's a policy. And we're currently closed. So, good day to you, Miss Tragic."

Georgina sang, walking towards Dora and then closing the door firmly.

Dora Magic blinked several times in stunned astonishment through the window, until Georgina reached up and pulled down a blind that Humphrey had fitted for Nora's Book Club last year.

Nora gulped.

"Ridiculous woman." Georgina said slipping on her sunglasses and gesturing for Humphrey to pass her handbag. "I don't know how you put up with the maddos, Nora. I can never last more than five minutes in this town."

"You get used to it." Nora decided with a grimace.

"I don't know why your Duke of Cole chose to live here when he has all those marvellous properties in less eccentric parts of the nation."

"Well. James is rather eccentric, too." Nora reminded her, fondly.

Georgina chuckled.

"I suppose he is a little." She allowed, just as fondly.

Humphrey rolled his eyes.

"Close up now, Nora and enjoy a nice weekend break before it all returns to chaos back at The Secondhand Bookworm." Georgina instructed, opening the door again to leave.

She turned and yelped. Dora Magic was still standing there.

"Excuse me. We're *closed*." Georgina told her firmly.

"Yes. Yes you are." Dora said with narrowed eyes, stuck her nose in the air, turned around and stomped off, clutching her Mary Poppins carpet bag with a menacing look.

Georgina looked back at Nora and shook her head.

"Good luck!" She said and set off, eager to put as much distance between herself and Castletown as quickly as she could.

"I'm not sure it was wise of Georgina to make an enemy of Miss Dora Nora Magic." Nora told Humphrey nervously.

"I agree." He nodded, watching the latter stomp across the cobbles, shaking her head of bouncing brown curls. "Oh well."

Once Georgina and Humphrey had left, Nora checked the shop, turned off the lights, locked up the yard and the kitchen, hung up the keys and gathered her things, satisfied everything was ready for her return to work on Monday.

She set the alarm, turned off the downstairs lights and stepped through the front doorway only to collide with a small man who was helping himself to hand sanitiser.

"Erm…that's for customers coming into The Secondhand Bookworm." Nora pointed out as she locked the shop door.

The man quickly pressed out four more dollops.

"Keep your wig on. I'm just doing my civic duty." He retorted rudely and ran off.

Nora shook her head.

"Several people have done that to our doorway dispenser, too." Alice called across the small road between the delicatessen and the bookshop.

"Really? I can't believe the audacity."

"Hmm." Alice agreed, cleaning the outside of her bay window. "It's going to be great fun next week."

"Looking forward to it." Nora laughed, waved and set off up the hill to the castle gates and a long awaited lunch with the Duke of Cole.

During sandwiches and tea back up at the castle, James told Nora he had booked to go to Myanmar for about a month to help the poor and neglected, especially the Rohingya Muslims, in the aftermath of *Polar-Bear 9*.

He would be leaving mid-September and would be back at the end of October. Nora was proud of him but also wondered how she would feel being apart from James for about five weeks after having spent six months solid together.

The Duke had also organised the return of his staff for Monday morning, so was making the most of being able to kiss Nora about the grounds and castle corridors without being noticed by a maid, footman or housekeeper.

After they had eaten lunch they made their way to the stables to wave off the donkeys, taking five times longer than normal because of James 'making the most of' his staff absences (much to Nora's delight). When they arrived, Jonathon was already there with Mrs Booth, Jeeves and two volunteers, organising the exodus.

"I shall miss having them around. They've been so entertaining." Nora sighed, leaning on the paddock fence as they were herded along.

"I'll get you your own donkeys, Nora." James promised, leaning on the fence next to her.

She looked at him.

"You're teasing me."

"Not at all." He promised. "The estate won't ever be complete without donkeys."

"That would be amazing, James!" Nora beamed. "We can keep the live feed going too."

"Hmm, I don't know." The Duke mused. "It's been incredibly hard to keep from hugging you without the locals watching."

Nora grinned.

"We'll have to discover the dead zones." She proposed.

James liked that idea.

As they sat in the library that evening, listening to the jackdaws heading for their nests in the trees around the estate, reading and drinking *The Jib-Jab*, a new quarantini Nora had invented, a text message arrived on Nora's phone.

"It's from Heather." Nora said, picking it up from the coffee table.

James turned a page in his book, watching Nora open the message.

'Hello! All packed up and ready to go. We'll stay another two nights (watching movies and playing your Jupiter Cube games console, lol), and we'll give the flat a big clean and hoover and tidy on Saturday. We'll be gone Sunday morning. Xxx' Heather had written.

Nora smiled.

'Thanks so much! Hope you enjoyed your stay! Speak soon xx' She sent back.

James closed his book.

"Is everything alright?" He smiled.

"Yes." Nora nodded, pondering him thoughtfully. "Heather and Milton are going back to our parents' house this weekend because college is opening up again in September and they've finished their work with The Secondhand Bookworm. I shall have to start thinking about returning to my flat. I was thinking I would go on Sunday night since I start back to work at the bookshop on Monday." Nora said.

James was putting his book on the coffee table and held still. He then put his head in his hands and ran his fingers back through his hair to the back of his neck, eyes closed, before turning and looking at Nora who was watching him.

"I would like you to stay, Nora." The Duke said seriously.

Nora took an unladylike gulp of her quarantini.

"Are you asking me to be your tenant here at the castle, Your Grace?" She asked with a smile, watching him take her glass from her hand and place it on the coffee table next to his book.

James smiled, too.

"Oh no. I have something more in mind for you than just being my tenant." He replied, seriously.

Nora's eyes widened, searching his gaze as he turned more fully to face her.

"Your Grace, we can't cause a scandal by *living together* and I would certainly be dismayed at people getting the wrong idea about our setup here. Not many people would believe I have my own quarters and stick to them…"

"Except when we both have *Polar-Bear 9*." He corrected her, biting his lip.

"Yes, well that was different, those were extenuating circumstances…but …well, the point is, you're the only Catholic Royal and you remain under scrutiny regarding Catholic morals and practices and..."

James moved aside Nora's fringe, smiling as she rambled on worriedly about the value of good example and good reputations and how important it was to her that people thought well of him, seeing as he was a practicing Catholic often in the public eye, and that it would make tongues wag if the Catholic Duke of Cole was living with his girlfriend. He leaned forward and pressed a kiss to her lips so that Nora blinked and stopped talking.

"Nora. You know how I feel about you?" He asked seriously.

Nora gulped.

"Yes." She squeaked.

"And that I intend to propose marriage to you." He said, just as seriously, easing a little back.

Nora felt her knees weaken.

"I had a feeling." She admitted, feeling the tips of her cheeks redden.

James grinned but cleared his throat, holding both her hands.

"But I won't propose to you in Lockdown. And I want a large, public wedding. I want it all to be done properly once everything is back to normal."

"Me too." Nora nodded.

"I would marry you here and now, Nora. Believe me, I've thought about asking Canon Gerry to come and do it in the castle chapel since the first day of Lockdown, the day you arrived, but I want it to be magnificent. I want to marry you in front of the whole world, Nora."

Nora grinned idiotically.

"Wow. James…"

"But I also want you to remain a part of my daily life now." He said, looking down at her hands with a furrowed brow.

"I'd like that too." She smiled happily. "Okay, well, I think I should move back to my flat on Sunday…"

"What?" James looked up at her, eyebrows raised.

Nora laughed and touched his jaw, tenderly.

"But," she continued, "I can come through to the castle as often as possible after work and on weekends. I can use the front door of my flat each evening and come through the back gate once I've freshened up and spend the evenings with you and stay in my quarters on weekends. And then, when you're away on your trips, such as the one you're going on soon, I can stay in my flat instead of alone here. That way we will still continue to be with one another as much as possible."

James pondered the idea.

Nora had never before seen him so anxious and deliberating. But finally, the Duke of Cole nodded and broke into a happy smile.

"That sounds like a very good plan." He agreed and wrapped his arms around her, kissing her lips, her cheeks and the tip of her nose.

Nora laughed.

"And that way there should be no *scandal*." She winked.

"I don't cause scandals." James reminded her. "I'm the boring Royal, only interested in rewilding projects, wading lakes, restoring properties, attending meetings and being obsessed with a certain bookworm."

Nora grinned.

"To me you're not boring. You're perfect."

James' arms tightened.

"I do intend to propose to you, Nora." He reminded her tenderly.

Nora smiled.

"And I would accept, Your Grace."

"James." He reminded her with a small chuckle.

"James." She corrected and sighed happily.

They went back to their reading and conversation and Quarantinis, sitting close together in the enormous red sofa, and, as they did so, Nora was sure she saw the ghost of a little white owl, fluttering by the windows.

Nora remembered the handwritten volume by the Duke of Cole's relative about 'The Ghosts of Castletown Fortress' and the entry that read: '*The ghost of a small white owl is often seen in the windows of the keep and the gatehouse. It is thought to be a sign of romance or good fortune.*'

She lifted her quarantini in a secret toast and smiled.

.

13 THE END OF LOCKDOWN

On Monday morning Nora's alarm woke her up at seven o'clock, making her jump. She looked around in momentary confusion as to where on earth she was, finally remembering she had returned to her flat the night before and was now in her jolly little bedroom above The Fudge Pantry. She smiled and inhaled deeply.

"Butterscotch Surprise." She deduced aloud. "Ah, it's nice to be home."

Her cute little flat perpetually smelt of many different sweet and delicious fudge smells. It was the perfect place to live (if you didn't count a magnificent castle of course)!

She jumped out of bed, stretched and set off for a shower, thinking of James and how much she would miss him today. As she was blow drying her hair, having pulled on her jeans and buttoned up her The Secondhand Bookworm blouse (black shirt, blue logo) she noticed her iPhone flash up a message on her dressing table. It was from James.

'Have a good day, Nora. I miss you so much. See you tonight xx' The Duke of Cole had sent.

Nora smiled.

'Thank you, James. Missing you, too. See you soon xx' she sent back.

"Come on, woman." She told her reflection in the mirror as she finished off drying her hair. "You're practically engaged to him." She said and squealed happily.

Castletown was silent and empty as Nora locked up her flat, slipped on her mask, dropped her keys in her bag, turned and then screamed. Scratch that: Castletown was silent and empty *except* for Harry.

"Hiiiiiii, Nora!" Harry greeted, jogging on the spot before her.

"Argh. Morning, Harry. Thanks for the heart attack." Nora replied.

"Do you require CPR?" He hoped.

Nora pushed him aside.

"Bye, Harry."

"Nice to see you back home after Lockdown, neighbour." He said and winked and flexed his muscles, watching her start walking down the hill before turning away and continuing with his morning jog.

"Annoying man." She sighed; glad to see Corrine wasn't with him to look at her with daggers.

Oliver and Gertrude, who ran The Fudge Pantry, waved at Nora from the shop window where they were displaying fresh blocks of fudge.

"So nice to have you back, Nora. That brother and sister of yours almost ate us out of our entire supply of fudge while staying at your flat." Oliver said from behind a brown, fudge coloured mask, opening a small window to speak to her. "At least they kept us in business during the Lockdown!"

Nora chuckled.

"They certainly love your shop."

"That they do." Oliver agreed. "And thank you for promoting us on your Livestream with His Grace over Lockdown. We had lots of orders!"

"Well, I have to keep you in business too for my own ends." Nora laughed.

Oliver laughed as well, although he knew she wasn't actually joking!

Nora continued down the hill, noticing that there were adverts and posters in several art gallery windows now advertising a Lockdown photography competition to take place at the town hall as well as many featured Lockdown art pieces on display and now for sale in the galleries by local artists.

The town was still empty of people when Nora made it down to the bottom of the hill where Betty had just arrived, too.

"Nora! How lovely to see you again at last and in the flesh! Although mine is a lot more shrivelled since we were last together! How pretty you look!" Betty greeted through a plain peach-coloured mask, holding out both elbows in greeting.

Nora giggled and they touched elbows in front of the bookshop door.

"It's so wonderful to see you again, Betty."

"Can you believe it's been six months since we were all here?" Betty shook her head in amazement. "That's me six months nearer the grave. I'm amazed I survived the whole ordeal, but I'm still breathing. As I've always said, only the good die young. Oh how wonderful. We have a sanitiser dispenser here!" She noticed and promptly pumped two blobs onto her hands.

"Humphrey fitted twelve throughout the shop at the weekend." Nora explained, unlocking the door.

"Very wise. He's such a good boy. And what an *Atlas* he is now. Those biceps of his! If only I was fifty years younger." Betty drooled, following Nora into The Secondhand Bookworm.

Nora ran and turned off the alarm and then turned on the lights.

"Will he be dropping in at all today?" Betty asked with a lecherous wink and a playful lick of her lips behind her mask.

Nora laughed.

"If he knows you want to ogle his muscles I'm sure he will." She said. "But I think he may be heading up to London to his former business firm. He was working back up there are a lot before Lockdown."

"Hmm. I have his number." Betty teased.

They filled up the till with the float, turned on the computer, Betty admired the plexiglass and then turned on the rest of the shop lights, opened the kitchen door and the door to the yard, put the kettle on to boil for tea and saw that the fridge was empty of milk.

"I'll go and buy a bottle from the Co-Op." She suggested.

"Ok. I'll check the emails." Nora nodded, having wheeled out the postcard spinners, clipped the four boxes of cheap paperback holders either side of the door and placed the free maps box against the bay window.

Betty set off, pausing to squirt two blobs of hand sanitiser onto her palms in the doorway.

There were five messages, each of them asking when The Secondhand Bookworm was reopening, so Nora replied to them all.

A message came through from The Secondhand Bookworm in Seatown where Cara and Roger were working.

'Hallo! Hooray! Here we are again! Xx' Cara had sent through the Skype chat.

Nora smiled.

'Helllloooo! It's weird to be back! Here's hoping we have a good day xx.' She replied.

Georgina had left them instructions that there must only be three people allowed in the shop at a time and that they had to wipe down the books in the gazebo regularly and place them back on the shelves.

Nora shared this with Betty once she had returned and made them both a nice hot cup of tea. Betty gave her a look.

"There are also masks there by the door for people to wear. It's a personal choice but it would be better if they did." Nora added with an equal look.

"At least people don't have to pay for them. It normally costs me thirty pounds to have a haircut but it cost me thirty one pounds because I had to buy a face mask!" Betty shared. "I didn't have mine with me when I went but it was compulsory so I had no choice."

"Oh dear." Nora sympathised.

"Oh Nora, the water in the river was so clear when I walked past this morning. Have you seen it? It's because of Lockdown. There was a lot less pollution while we were all imprisoned in our houses."

"Yes, I did see that. James was really pleased about the benefits on the climate." Nora nodded.

"And how is that magnificent Duke of yours? With his magnificent legs?" Betty asked, pulling down her mask to sip her tea.

"He's wonderful." Nora smiled, happily.

"I bet he is." Betty winked.

The door knocked, announcing the arrival of their first post-Lockdown customer. He was a beefy man in a red mask and an additional face visor.

"Are you open?" He asked.

"Yes, hello." Nora stood up to greet him behind the safety of the plexiglass.

After helping himself to three squirts of hand sanitiser in the doorway, the beefy man stepped down into The Secondhand Bookworm. Betty stood too, watching him over the top of her spectacles.

"I'm looking for some books." Beefy said.

"One normally does in a bookshop." Betty pointed out in a low voice.

"Which ones?" Nora asked, smiling behind her mask.

"Air Fryer Cookbooks." The man replied.

"Hmm. I'm not sure if we have any."

"Can't you check your computer?" Beefy asked, coming so close to the plexiglass that if he hadn't been wearing two face coverings his nose might have flattened.

"We don't list our titles on the computer." Nora explained, having not missed saying that one hundred times a day.

"Oh. Still in the stone age, eh." He concluded rudely.

"We can check our shelves for you. Or you can look for yourself." Betty said tartly.

Beefy looked at Betty but decided to ignore her.

"Where's your cookery section then?" He asked.

"On the next floor landing. Up the stairs through there." Nora indicated.

Beefy set off.

"Horrid old boil." Betty said once he was creaking up the first staircase.

They didn't have time to insult him because another customer arrived, pausing to squirt sanitiser on his hands from the doorway dispenser.

"I can see that running out in no time." Nora pointed out to Betty.

The customer was a woman.

"Books about parapsychology?" She asked dreamily from behind a white sparkly mask. "In particular, crystals, lunar living and oracles."

Betty gave Nora a look.

"We have a self-help and spiritual section on the top floor, front room." Nora explained.

"Do I have to look for myself?"

"It's up to you. We probably have a whole case full."

"I'll go and look for myself then." The woman said and glided off in the direction Nora pointed.

A man stood in the doorway.

"Is it true this used to be where Sweeny Todd cut peoples hair, followed by their throats?" He asked after lowering his mask.

Nora grimaced.

"There is a local legend about it," she said, thinking of Humphrey's theory having made it into Castletown folklore. "But Sweeney Todd is a fictional character from 19th century penny dreadfuls."

"Oooooh." He said, peering inside and then squirting ample amounts of hand sanitiser on his palms. "Mind if I have a browse?

"If you like. We sell books." Nora said, hoping to take some money to cover the amount of hand sanitiser they were going through.

"Thanks. HEY, SANDY! BOBBY! KEN! ADRIAN! COME IN HERE. IT'S TRUE ABOUT SWEENY TODD!" He hollered over his shoulder.

"I'm afraid we can only allow three people in the shop at a time." Nora said hastily. "And there are already two people upstairs."

The man slapped his forehead.

"That's a shame. FORGET IT, GUYS! THERE ARE LIMITS ON HOW MANY PEOPLE THEY ALLOW IN HERE. I'LL ONLY BE A MINUTE." He shrieked and hurried inside, through the walkway and up the stairs. Nora was sure she spotted an iPhone and a pair of scissors in his hands.

"Blooming Humphrey." She said to Betty.

"Back to normal then." Betty smirked.

By the time noon had arrived, Nora and Betty had dealt with only a handful of customers. The town remained empty due to people still avoiding the public or avoiding entering confined spaces such as pokey old shops and stores. Several locals popped in to say they were pleased The Secondhand Bookworm was open again, but they weren't pleased enough to buy any books. They just seemed to want to stare at Nora and gush over the Duke of Cole (Nora joined in the latter).

The cleaning station in the yard had only accumulated ten books by lunchtime so Betty cleaned them with the special spray and put them back on the shelves while Nora added up their sales, which amounted to twenty-five pounds.

When Betty came down from returning the books to the shelves she looked horrified.

"Oh Nora! Some flippin' pig must have emptied the whole contents of the dispenser on the next floor landing. It's a big sopping blue puddle at the top of the stairs!" She revealed with a wail. "Either that or it has a ruddy great leak!"

"You're joking." Nora's mouth dropped open at the same time she dropped her pen. "Ugh, how awful. I'll go and check it out."

"Oh Nora. I hope it's not going to be a regular thing. I bet it was that horrid old boil with the red mask and face visor earlier. He looked like a villain." Betty glowered.

"I wouldn't be surprised." Nora said and stomped off up the stairs.

On the next floor landing she stopped dead. A very large, dangerous puddle had formed beneath and around the humour section dispenser and was dripping down the steps like blue slime. Nora grimaced, turned around and headed back down to grab the mop and a bucket of hot water from the kitchen.

"Maybe don't let any customers up until I've cleaned this." Nora told Betty.

"Right you are, Nora. I could have cleaned it up instead of you having to do it, Nora." Betty said.

"It's fine. It shouldn't take me long." Nora assured her, hoisting up the mop and bucket.

She was wrong. The big blue puddle was so bubbly that foams and froths spilled out of the bucket as she mopped up, with some floating down the staircase like cloud babies. It took Nora half an hour with four bucket changes. She was worn out and sweating when she finally finished.

"The other ones seemed okay but we should keep an eye on them, Nora." Betty said as Nora flopped into the swivel seat, exhausted. "You poor thing! Go and have your lunch break, Nora! I can manage here. I haven't seen a single person the whole time you were up there salvaging the landing. I've been messaging Roger and Cara about it all. They're having a heck of a time with several mad customers and some confrontations."

"Really?" That cheered Nora up. She leaned forward to read the Skype chat, chuckling and snorting with amusement as she scanned down the conversation.

Apparently Mr Hill had arrived to sell his books while wearing a white plastic hooded chemical protection suit that he obviously didn't realise was partly see-through. Cara had been put off her lunch when she had spotted his red underwear and bony limbs through the material. Five people had tried to enter the shop at once and when Roger had attempted to deter them they had all almost come to blows, with Roger being pummelled with postcards from the spinner, which he then had to disinfect for half an hour. A man touched almost every book in the front room, so Cara and Roger had had to empty all the shelves and spend most of the morning spray cleaning them all and putting them back. And after all that they had only sold five books.

"It's not just here, then." Nora said once she had finished reading it.

"I think everyone's having a bit of a ball." Betty decided.

The telephone started to ring.

"Why don't you have a lunch break first while I sit and recover and deal with this phone call?" Nora suggested.

"Oh if you don't mind, Nora. That would be lovely. My stomach has been making the most terrible sounds. I'll go and get some fresh air and have a sandwich by the lovely clear river." Betty agreed, gratefully.

Nora smiled and lowered her mask to answer the telephone call.

"Good afternoon, The Secondhand Bookworm."

"Hi Nora. It's me!" Georgina's sing-song voice greeted.

"Oh hello!" Nora waved Betty off, who paused to sanitise her hands in the doorway.

"How's it going?"

"Do you really want to know?" Nora asked.

"The usual rubbish then." Georgina deduced. "Well, it'll take some time to get our bearings again. I doubt many people are about."

"Not really."

"Hmm, maybe we should have kept up the mobile bookshop buggies for a while, until the general public has their confidence back." Georgina pondered.

"I'm sure James would be more than happy to keep lending us his refurbished golf buggies." Nora knew.

"Perhaps I'll have a word with His Grace about maybe using one for a while. I think Roger would be happy to do it every day. Apparently he's already almost had several fights in Seatown."

Nora and Georgina giggled.

"It might be a good idea." Nora agreed.

"Okay, I've made a note. There, that's done-did. Now, the reason I'm calling is that I've arranged for you to give an interview to the county newspaper about reopening the bookshop after Lockdown and our bookselling experience during the pandemic." Georgina revealed.

Nora blinked.

"Is that a good idea? It won't come across as positive." She decided, grimly.

"Don't be daft." Georgina laughed. "You can talk about the bookmobiles and the email and phone orders and the book delivery service we offered during the Lockdown. And you can say all about the wonderful safety measures we have in place to encourage customers back, such as the hand sanitiser dispensers."

"About those." Nora grimaced and told Georgina the blue puddle episode.

"Rats. I did worry about that happening. Rats, rats, rats! Fiddle-di-de!" Georgina moaned. "Well, you'll just have to keep an eye on them and salvage the shop if it happens again. We have to have them by law. I'll get Humphrey to check them out tomorrow."

"Okay." Nora nodded, watching Betty heading for the bench by the war memorial in the town square instead of going down to the river.

"Okay, well good luck with the interview. He will be with you at about three o'clock. Make it all sound good and safe and we might get some customers! Fluffy! Those are mother's biscuits!" She rebuked her cat.

They said their goodbyes and Nora pressed end, returning the phone to its cradle. In the town square, Betty had been joined by a familiar figure who was bent over with her head and shoulders buried in her Mary Poppins bag.

"Erk." Nora grimaced, watching Dora Magic hand Betty a book and then start walking towards The Secondhand Bookworm.

Deciding it wasn't worth diving under the counter, and that there was now at least a plexiglass wall of protection between her and customers, Nora waited and watched as Dora arrived, stepped down into the shop and greeted Nora exuberantly.

"So glad to see that it's you, Miss Jolly; you are wonderful, you are loved, you are important, you are better than that terrible old sock, Georgina Pickering!" Dora gushed.

"Hello, Dora." Nora replied warily.

"As I wished to say on Friday, before that wicked deflated balloon, Georgina Pickering chased me away, I have written fifty more books which are currently being printed. I think you will enjoy them immensely."

"I have been enjoying the zombie saga." Nora admitted to her.

Dora shrieked with happiness, making Nora wince.

"Oh I am soooooo pleased to hear that, Miss Nora Jolly! Wonderful, wonderful, wonderful indeed! But of course, you do have superlative taste in literature. If *you* were the owner of The Secondhand Bookworm, not that soggy slipper Ms Georgina Pickering, then what a magnificent franchise we would have together."

"Erm…"

"I would be your most sought-after author and you would achieve global fame and adulation. You are special, you are adored, you are magnificent!" Dora rambled madly.

Nora found herself wishing Mr Hill would telephone.

"Erm…thank you."

"Mark my words, Miss Nora Jolly. Your time will come! Soon, mind you. Your time will come when you will indeed rule the literary world."

"Brrrring, brrrrring. Brrrrring, brrrrring." Nora said out of the side of her mouth behind her mask, attempting the best imitation of the sound of a telephone ringing that she could. "Oh I'm so sorry, I'd better answer that. Nice to see you again, Dora."

Dora blinked.

"Hello, The Secondhand Bookworm, how can I help?" Nora said into the telephone receiver.

"Goodbye, Miss Nora Jolly!" Dora waved, walking backwards. "You are loved, you are magnificent, you are…gaaaaaah!"

Nora watched Dora almost walk backwards into Betty, who had seen her coming and moved aside so that the back of Dora's legs knocked against the step up into the street and she went down like a domino.

"Oh my. Are you okay down there?" Betty asked as Dora scrambled hastily up.

"Ahem. Yes, yes. No problem at all." Dora assured her, picking up the carpet bag and straightening her flowery skirt. "Goodbye, Miss Nora Jolly. Goooooooodbyyyeeeeeeee."

Betty gawped and Nora stared as Dora legged it across the cobbles.

"That woman belongs in a crazy house." Betty said, walking around to the counter.

Nora placed the telephone receiver back in its cradle.

"Tell me about it." Nora concurred.

Once Betty had settled in ready to deal with non-existent customers, and flick through a copy of book one of The Caterpillar Wars that Dora Magic had given her at the war memorial, Nora went for lunch.

She made herself a sandwich back up at her flat, watered her house plants, put some laundry on, sat and ate her sandwich, washed and dried up the dishes and cutlery and headed back down to The Secondhand Bookworm.

The afternoon passed easily, with Nora and Betty serving a handful of customers, selling two Penguin book jacket mugs, some book design wrapping paper, some postcards, a run of Dickens, several new Wordsworth paperbacks, three art books, a handful of poetry books, a new ordnance survey map and a showbiz biography. One of the hand soap dispensers on the top floor exploded so Nora spent half an hour cleaning it up with her mop and several bucket loads of water, finally returning down to the front room in time for the reporter for the county newspaper to stroll in.

"Gah." Nora was hot and sweaty again but fanned herself with a David Bone book (the Rocks of Littlesea) and answered the reporter's questions from behind the plexiglass.

"How damaging did you find Lockdown to the bookselling trade?" The reporter asked.

He had a very thin moustache, green rimmed glasses and very thick lips, with a head of thin blond hair that had been greased back.

"Oh, well, it was difficult at first because we don't have our books listed online."

"Why not? Isn't that a bit backwards?" The reporter asked, poised with his pencil, keenly.

"No." Nora said defensively. "We just happen to have about 27,000 books in this branch. It wouldn't be worth the time spent listing them all and having to keep up with the database. Most of our books don't have barcodes."

The man scribbled on his notepad.

"What did you do to counteract the premises being closed because books are so dirty?" The reporter next asked.

"What do you mean?"

"Rumour has it that *Polar-Bear 9* was spread through books. Are you planning to burn your stock? Tell all!" He poised once more with his pencil.

"Erm, no we don't plan to burn our books. We actually had a very successful plan for keeping people supplied with books during the Lockdown. The Duke of Cole kindly let us refurbish three golf buggies with shelving so that we could operate a mobile bookselling service. We also…"

"Rumour has it that you yourself are dating the Duke of Cole. Is it true he's the most boring man on the planet?" The reporter interrupted, keenly. "Do tell!"

Nora stared.

"Actually, I don't find him boring at all."

"In what way? Does he have a secret temper? What about the rumour he's related to Count Vlad Dracula? Any coffins in the castle?"

Nora pursed her lips.

"How did you find living with the Duke during Lockdown? Does he snore?" The report next asked, pencil at the ready.

"I wouldn't know." Nora said flatly. "I had my own quarters while I stayed at the Duke of Cole's castle."

The reporter scribbled frantically. Nora leaned forward and saw him write '*Duke kept me up all night snoring his head off*'.

"I think you've gone off topic!" Nora pointed out.

"So you're due to close this bookshop because people no longer read books. Is that true? The Kindle has taken over?" The reporter next asked, eagerly.

"No, we're not closing and we haven't really noticed a drop in printed book sales with the arrival of the Kindle..."

"Rumour is the Duke of Cole is breeding killer rhinos on his rewilding land throughout his estate here in Castletown. At any point of your stay with him, did you find yourself in danger?"

"What the what?"

"How do you feel that you're engaged to marry the most boring Duke in the country? Is it true that his first language is Elvish?"

"Who told you that?!" Nora suspected the reporter was a journalist for one of Spencer's periodicals.

"So you and the Duke of Cole are planning to get married next year! What a scoop!" The reporter concluded, scribbling frantically before turning around and running off. "Thanks for the scoop!"

Nora stared mutely, finally looking at Betty who had been standing behind the reporter while she examined the folio society books on the shelves next to the bay window.

"Did that just happen?" Nora blinked.

"Oh Nora, what a stupid pig he was!" Betty sympathised. "He must have written for The Daily Idiot!"

Nora's lips twitched.

"Well, I don't think that went the way Georgina was hoping. Who knows how that will turn out?"

"As for him calling your magnificent Duke a dreary old bore! He might have that reputation but we all know how wonderful he is!" Betty defended.

Nora chuckled.

"James doesn't mind being thought of as boring. But I'm not sure he'd embrace a reputation for breeding killer rhinos." Nora decided and burst out laughing.

"Oh Nora, that grimy old reporter reminded me of my dentist. I went to the dentist last Thursday and when I arrived I had to put my handbag into a box and carry it up onto the second floor. The receptionist, a silly old cabbage, asked if I had a mask, so I said no, so she gave me one and practically wrestled it onto my face. She said, go and sit on a chair called Catherine. When I got there, there was no chair called Catherine, so I just stood there. I was only having my gums checked, Nora, but when I went in the room they treated me like I was infected with syphilis. They put masks on and aprons, gloves and a huge plastic shield each, it was like I was going into surgery. Then the flippin' man said, you need a small filling, Bettina, so they geared up and it took them ten minutes to get all their kit on, then when it was done they said, we have to suck all the air out of the room so they handed me my box with my handbag and told me to get out. I had such an effing headache." Betty relayed.

Nora was laughing so that tears rolled down her cheeks.

"Oh Nora, what the heck is that?" Betty then pointed, noticing the old people from the retirement home passing by the shop window singing the conga while sporting their facemasks. "Flippin' greyheads! Someone should lock them up."

Fortunately Nora had composed herself when two locals arrived.

"Hello, Nora!" Merrie and Pip chorused from the doorway. "How's it going? Glad to see you're open at last."

"Hello, we're doing fine thank you. How are things with the prosecco shop and warehouses opening?"

"We're planning to do our Prosecco Festival at the winter carnival this year." Pip replied, keenly.

"We've just been speaking with the Duke of Cole. We would like him to officially open the warehouses and the new shop on the first day of the winter carnival." Merrie explained.

"He told us that the town is already planning a magical winter land for December with a carnival and fair in the Duke's grounds." Pip added. "So we'll get launched then!"

"That sounds wonderful." Nora enthused.

"It's just what the town needs." Merrie said. "We expect everything should be back to normal by about November so a whole festivity over December will be just what everyone will want."

"The Duke of Cole is so supportive. He spoke about you for ages, Nora. He's definitely smitten." Pip then added with a wink.

Nora blushed red.

"He is a wonderful man." She agreed, dreamily.

Once Merrie and Pip had said goodbye, a customer replaced them. He was a small, rotund man, like a beer keg, and he stood on the doorstep and sneezed against his plastic face visor. Nora felt faint.

Fortunately, Betty dealt with him, so Nora ran off to the kitchen to make a round of tea before they closed up for the day.

At ten minutes to five, Nora brought the free maps and their holder back into the shop, sprayed it liberally, did the same with the two postcard spinners and paperback boxes and locked the door behind her.

"Well that was about as mad as I expected it to be!" She declared to Betty who was counting out the float from the till.

"Oh Nora, people seem to have gone bonkers over Lockdown. We only took one hundred and four pounds today, too. I did enjoy working with you again though.

It's nice to be away from the house and Danny and his groping." Betty decided.

Nora choked.

While Betty cashed up, Nora went upstairs to make sure all the customers had left. She spoke with Georgina on her iPhone as she did the rounds, telling her about her interview. Georgina found it more amusing than disappointing and thanked Nora for enduring the day.

There were splats all around the shop under the hand sanitiser dispensers, as well as small puddles and a strong smell. Nora decided she wasn't going to spoffle about it. She would deal with it all tomorrow. So she turned off the lights and skipped down the stairs.

Betty had cleaned the few books that had been left on the table under the gazebo, locked up and placed them on the floor behind the counter so they could be put away the next day.

"I'm in Seatown on Thursday." Betty explained, unlocking the door.

Nora set the alarm.

"I'd be interested to know how that goes." She said, running around the desk and across the floor. "It sounds like Cara and Roger had a zany day."

"Yes, we shall see! It's been lovely working with you, Nora!" Betty blew kisses and they touched elbows again as a goodbye.

"You too!"

"Have a nice evening. With you-know-who." Betty winked, referring to the Duke of Cole.

"Thanks. Speak to you soon!" Nora grinned.

They parted ways and Nora hiked up the hill, finding it strange to be going to her flat instead of to the castle. She had told James she would freshen up and phone him once she was back from work to decide what their plan was for the evening. She wondered if he had missed her as much as she had missed him.

Once she reached the door next to the Fudge Pantry, Nora unlocked it, stepped into the little hall, kicked off her boots, hung up her coat, locked the door behind her and hiked up the staircase to her flat.

When Nora opened the door at the top of the stairs to the right she stopped dead and stared. The entire lounge had been filled with the most spectacular purple, pink and white heliotrope flowers. They were in vases of various sizes standing on her mantelpiece, kitchen counter, coffee table, windowsills, and the floor and side units.

As she gawped in delighted amazement, she heard a movement at her side.

Before she could turn, a pair of strong arms snaked around her waist. She turned and found herself wrapped in a warm embrace. James, Duke of Cole, pressed a kiss on her lips, chuckling softly.

"James!" Nora laughed, still amazed. "How did you do this?"

"I used my master key. I'm your landlord, remember?" He grinned and kissed her again.

"Of course you are." Nora chuckled.

"I wanted to be here when you returned from your first day back at The Secondhand Bookworm and do something significant and special for you. Truth be told, I couldn't stay away. I do have *basorexia* remember." He said and proved it by peppering her mouth, cheeks and eyelids with kisses.

Nora laughed.

"James. The flowers are beautiful. And I'm so glad you're here. I missed you so much."

"I missed you, too."

Holding his hands, Nora eased away to admire the flowers. She bit the side of her bottom lip.

"James. You do remember what the heliotrope symbolises in the language of flowers, don't you?" She asked him, curious.

James nodded.

"I do. They are traditionally symbolic of eternal love and devotion."

Nora looked at him and gulped.

"Which is why I chose them." He added, seriously.

"I see." Nora squeaked.

"Nora. When I return from my trip, there's something important I want to ask you." He told her, meaningfully.

"Hmm. I wonder what that could be." Nora said, ignoring her somersaulting stomach.

"We shall see." James smiled back.

"This truly is beautiful, James." Nora surveyed her flat again, enchanted.

"I remembered as well that the heliotrope doesn't affect your hay fever."

"Only roses and lilies do." Nora nodded. "And only a little bit even then."

"I wasn't sure what you wanted to do this evening; if you wanted some space or if you wanted to come to the castle." James then said, dropping her hands to head into the kitchen. "So I thought I would decide for you. I brought dinner."

Nora watched him pick up a silver covered tray, regarding her hopefully.

"That sounds perfect." Nora agreed. "We can eat here and spend the evening together, My Lord."

James arched an eyebrow, smiling.

"My Lord?"

"You are my landlord, after all." She pointed out.

"I think I could get used to that." The Duke of Cole decided on a grin and set about organising plates and dishes for their meal.

As Nora left him so as to change out of her bookshop blouse in her bedroom, she smiled happily at her reflection in her dressing table mirror.

"Well, Miss Jolly. It seems as though things might work out perfectly well after Lockdown. In fact, *more* than perfectly well." She told herself with an excited squeal and set about choosing something special to wear in the company of the magnificent, and totally un-boring, Duke of Cole.

Later that night, as Nora and James snuggled on Nora's sofa, watching a movie with a big bowl of popcorn, surrounded by bouquets of flowers, down the hill at The Secondhand Bookworm, in the silence of the deserted town, someone stepped up to the bookshop door.

A key was placed into the lock, turned easily, and the door squeaked gently open. The darkly clad figure hurried inside, closed the door, walked around the counter and punched in the code to the alarm. As the shop fell silent once more, the figure turned, looked around and rubbed their hands together.

"And so it begins, Nora Jolly." The voice said determinedly. "So it begins."

EMILY JANE BEVANS

THE END

EMILY JANE BEVANS

ALSO IN THE SERIES

'The Secondhand Bookworm'
'Nora and The Secondhand Bookworm'
'Christmas at The Secondhand Bookworm'
'Summer at The Secondhand Bookworm'
'Halloween at The Secondhand Bookworm'
'Black Friday at The Secondhand Bookworm'
'Book Club at The Secondhand Bookworm'
'Valentine's Day at The Secondhand Bookworm'

Available in paperback and Kindle

Coming next:
'Strange Things at The Secondhand Bookworm'

Watch for more novels in the Bookworm series

Also by the author

'House of Villains'
Available now from Amazon

ABOUT THE AUTHOR

Emily Jane Bevans lives on the south coast of England. For ten years she worked in, and helped to manage, a family chain of antiquarian bookshops in Sussex. She is the co-founder and co-director of a UK based Catholic film production apostolate 'Mary's Dowry Productions'. She writes, edits, produces, directs, narrates and sometimes acts for the company's numerous historical and religious films on the lives of the Saints and English Martyrs. She also likes to write contemporary and historical fiction.

MARY'S DOWRY PRODUCTIONS

Mary's Dowry Productions is a Catholic Film
Production Apostolate founded in 2007 to bring the lives
of the Saints and English Martyrs, English Catholic
heritage and history to film and DVD. Mary's Dowry
Productions' unique film production style has been
internationally praised for not only presenting facts,
biographical information and historical details but a
prayerful and spiritual film experience. Many of the
films of Mary's Dowry Productions have been broadcast
on EWTN, BBC and SKY.
For a full listing of films and more information visit:

www.marysdowryproductions.org

EMILY JANE BEVANS

Printed in Great Britain
by Amazon